Village of Satan

Margaret Bingley

GUILD PUBLISHING
LONDON · NEW YORK · SYDNEY · TORONTO

This edition published 1990 by
Guild Publishing
by arrangement with
Judy Piatkus (Publishers) Ltd

CN 3267

Printed and bound in Great Britain by
Mackays of Chatham PLC, Chatham, Kent

For Sam and Tom Baumber and Alex.
Their enthusiastic help in the graveyards
was much appreciated

Author's Note

Although there is a Scott Willoughby, a West Willoughby and a Silk Willoughby in Lincolnshire there is no South Willoughby. The village of South Willoughby is a product of my imagination and all characters in this book are fictitious. Any resemblance to any living person is entirely coincidental.

Prologue

It was a lovely dream. Everything about it was perfect. The sun was shining, there were other children for her to play with and – best of all – no one asked her about her father. All the adults were smiling but there was one lady who seemed to Jasmine to be especially kind. Her beautiful green eyes followed the little girl wherever she went, and she sensed that no harm would be allowed to come to her while the lady was there.

Just as she was wondering where her mother was, the lady came across to her, leading a small boy by the hand. He was older than Jasmine and his eyes were not particularly kind, yet she was convinced that he also would look after her.

When the woman reached Jasmine she crouched down in the grass until her face was level with the child's. She was wearing a long flowing dress and smelt faintly of lemons and honeysuckle. Her hair was as dark as Jasmine's but long and straight where the child's was short and curly.

'Hello, Jasmine,' she whispered and as she spoke she smiled, showing small white teeth that gleamed in the sunlight.

'Hello,' responded the little girl.

'Do you like it here?' she continued.

'Yes, but I can't see my mummy.'

'She'll be here soon. You're a very pretty little girl,' she added.

Jasmine didn't reply because she couldn't think what she was supposed to say. Instead she hung her head, noticing that the daisies beneath her feet were very large and the grass extraordinarily green.

'This is Luke,' continued the lady. 'I'm sure you and Luke are going to be great friends. You have a lot in common.'

Jasmine stared at the boy, who flicked his eyes over her then stared off into the distance, still holding his mother's hand. 'I don't like boys,' murmured Jasmine. 'They shout all the time and keep playing shooting games. My mummy doesn't like me to play shooting games.'

'How silly!' said the beautiful lady, and for a moment she didn't look beautiful at all but rather sharp and cross.

'I haven't got a mother,' volunteered Luke, glancing back at Jasmine with a slightly warmer expression in his eyes.

'I haven't got a daddy,' responded Jasmine.

'I know. That's why we belong together.'

'I thought this was your mummy,' said Jasmine.

'It is.'

'You just said you didn't have one!'

'She's dead,' said Luke casually. 'Can't you tell? Touch her face. Go on, touch it.'

She put out a hesitant hand and encountered ice-cold flesh that made her fingers burn. With a startled exclamation she jumped away, feeling the tears prickling behind her eyes.

'Cry-baby.' The comment was half-hearted, a token jeer from the boy that he didn't seem to mean.

'If she's dead,' continued Jasmine, 'how can she be here with us?'

'Because this is a dream, silly! She can only be with us in dreams.'

The woman glanced around her at a suddenly darkening sky. 'I have to go,' she informed them. 'I'll see you again, Jasmine. Kiss me goodbye now.' It was an order, not a request. Jasmine's bottom lip quivered but she leant forward and her lips brushed a cold cheek. 'That's right. You see, there wasn't anything to be afraid of, was there?'

Before she could answer, the sun disappeared behind a dark cloud, a strong cool wind swept across the field where she stood and there was a crash of thunder that made her clap her hands over her ears. Now the other children who'd been laughing and playing near her were screaming, running frantically away towards a small stone building on the far side of the field, and only Jasmine and Luke were left.

'Do you know how to get home safely?' the boy asked her. She frowned, realising that she didn't know where she was but certain it didn't matter because it was only a dream.

'Well, do you?' he sounded impatient now.

'Not really. I suppose I'll just wake up.'

His eyes widened. 'That's dangerous. You've got to get back first, otherwise you might die too. I'll show you. Take my hand.'

She obeyed him, and suddenly they were flying through the air and she felt dizzy and sick, as though she were on a ride at a funfair. They rushed madly through the dark sky and she closed her eyes tightly, hoping that she'd soon wake up in her own bed again.

'We're here!' he shouted triumphantly. 'See you soon.'

'But . . .'

It was too late. She felt herself falling down a deep hole, falling faster and faster until with a terrible crash she landed on something hard that hurt her back and made her cry out. Once she'd begun to cry she couldn't stop and it was only the sound of her mother's voice that finally calmed her.

'Jasmine, wake up!' urged Kathryn. 'You've had a bad dream and fallen out of bed. Wake up, darling.'

She opened her eyes and saw her mother looking anxiously down at her. 'Was it really a dream, Mummy?' she asked, unable to believe that Luke and his dead mother hadn't existed.

'Of course it was. Come along, back into bed with you. Would you like a drink of water?'

Jasmine shook her head. 'It was a strange dream, Mummy. There was this boy and – '

'Just forget all about it. Would you like the landing light left on?'

'No, thank you. It wasn't a nasty dream, it was just . . . strange.'

'You ate too much supper!' Kathryn laughed as she left her daughter's room.

Jasmine snuggled down under her duvet and quickly drifted off to sleep again, her small fist gradually unclenching until the fingers finally relaxed and one unusually large daisy fell gently to the soft pink carpet.

Chapter 1

'Wake up, sleepy head!' said Kathryn with a laugh, tugging gently at her daughter's duvet. 'It's a lovely morning.'

Jasmine opened her eyes and blinked in surprise. Strangely she hadn't expected to see her mother. She'd felt certain that her new friend, Luke, would be waiting eagerly for her to play with him again and for a fleeting second her bottom lip trembled with disappointment.

'You had a bad dream last night,' continued Kathryn, drawing back the curtains and letting the sun stream in on the pine furniture and gleaming white walls. 'That's what happens to little girls who stay up late in the evenings.'

Normally Jasmine was a placid child with a merry smile for everyone but suddenly she felt grumpy and her mother's relentless chatter irritated her. 'Didn't!' she muttered, swinging her sturdy brown legs out of bed. 'Keely *always* watches *Disney Time*.'

'That explains why Keely's such a moody miss! Come on, Jasmine. I've got a lot to do today. June's a busy month for weddings.'

'Can I help stir the mixture?' All at once Jasmine's good humour returned and the strange darkness of spirit that had been lurking like a black cloud disappeared.

'Of course you can. I've got a letter from Grandma downstairs. I expect she's back in her own home by now.'

Jasmine ran into the tiny bathroom, splashed some water on her rosy cheeks and dabbed herself dry with her mother's towel. 'Is Grandma better?' she asked.

'Not quite. It takes a long time to get over things when you're old.'

'Can I catch a stroke?'

Kathryn smiled. 'No, sweetheart; it's something that happens to people when they get older. Mind what you're doing!' she cautioned as her daughter jumped down the last three steps, landing lightly at the foot of the narrow stairs.

'Is it eggs for breakfast, Mummy?'

'No, it's cereal and toast this morning. I'll cook spaghetti for lunch,' she promised as consolation.

'OK. Has Daddy written to me yet?' Jasmine added casually.

Kathryn thought of her ex-husband. She remembered the classical Greek features, inherited from his mother, and his quick, volatile temper. How could she explain to their daughter, so like him in looks, that now he was living abroad with a new wife and two small children he'd forgotten his first family. No doubt Effingham was dull in comparison with Rome; certainly she was very dull in comparison with the beautiful Pia. Dark, sultry Pia, who'd worked as an au pair for Kathryn's closest friend.

'Not yet, Jasmine. He's very busy,' she added in an attempt to explain his neglect.

'I'm busy, busy, busy, said the bee!' Jasmine laughed, filling her bowl to the top with chocolate Weetoes.

'Right, let's see what Grandma has to say.' Kathryn was relieved that Jasmine was so easily satisfied. She never seemed to suffer the overwhelming sense of rejection that caused her so much misery.

Jasmine pulled a soggy ring out of the pool of milk and fed it to Tammy, the overweight and temperamental cocker spaniel that had been her father's pride and joy before Pia arrived on the scene. 'It's good for you!' she assured the tawny animal as it coughed and spluttered its way through the treat.

'Don't feed the dog,' said Kathryn automatically, but she was frowning at the contents of the letter and her reprimand was half-hearted. Jasmine took her bowl to the sink, emptied the remaining Weetoes into the bin and picked up a piece of granary loaf. Tammy eyed it hopefully but Jasmine still had the butter and Marmite to spread before she was going to give any away. She loved spreading things on bread.

Unaware of the mess accumulating on the table, Kathryn reached the end of the letter, sighed and wondered if it would make better reading second time through. She rather doubted it. It was written by a friend of her mother's, making it plain that she was needed urgently. 'She's doing remarkably well but there's a long way to go' were her closing words, and Kathryn wondered why people assumed that women could always drop everything to go running to a sickbed.

'It looks as though we may have to stay with Grandma for a time, Jasmine,' she said with a sigh.

'Where is her new house?'

'In a little village called South Willoughby. It's in Lincolnshire.'

'Good, I wanted to see it. Grandma says there are plants all over the walls.'

'As long as they're not full of spiders and beetles! I can't imagine what I'm meant to do about the cakes,' she continued, talking to herself. 'She doesn't seem to have considered the possibility that I might work. I suppose she assumes your father keeps us in food and clothes. If I sat around waiting for his money to arrive we'd be naked and starving.'

'Rude! Rude!' crowed Jasmine, delighted by the thought of the pair of them without clothes on.

'Don't be silly, *and what have you done with the butter?*' she screamed in horror.

Jasmine looked at the lumpy mess that was left in the butter dish and then at her bread, totally invisible beneath its golden covering. 'Spread it!' she said triumphantly. 'I spreaded my own bread.'

The ensuing argument drove the letter out of Kathryn's head, but it returned as soon as she was weighing out the cake mixture. Deep down she knew she'd have to go. Her father had been dead for over ten years and since she was an only child there was no one else for her mother to call on. Sometimes she wondered how liberated women coped with demands like this. Presumably they just hardened their hearts and refused. Some day, she promised herself as she picked up the phone to call Lucy, some day I'll learn to be like that.

Lucy was quite chatty, but she didn't invite Kathryn round as she would have done before Philip ran off with her au pair.

6

His passion for Pia had deprived her of both her husband and her best friend. 'I suppose I'll have to go,' she told Lucy in annoyance. 'I don't seem to have any choice.'

'You are feeble sometimes,' said Lucy unsympathetically. 'Of course you've got a choice. If your mother's not well enough to look after herself she'll just have to go into a nursing home for a few weeks. That's what my mother did after her hysterectomy.'

'It seems rather unkind. She hasn't seen us since she moved and . . .'

'Fine,' said Lucy crisply. 'If you want to go and help, that's wonderful, but don't keep bleating on about how you're trapped by circumstances. You're not. You want to go, which is quite a different matter.'

'Thank you for your help, Lucy,' retorted Kathryn and quickly hung up. The fact that there was an element of truth in Lucy's comment didn't make it any more acceptable.

Jasmine, watching from half-way up the stairs, looked at her mother's short urchin-cropped hair and remembered the lady in her dream, or what her mother insisted on calling a dream. 'Mummy, why don't you have long hair?' she demanded.

'Because it's easier to manage when it's short.'

'I like long, dark hair.'

'Do you indeed?'

'Perhaps Daddy liked long, dark hair. Do you think he did? Pia's hair's long and black. Is that why he went to Italy with her?'

Kathryn flushed, surprised by Jasmine's accusing tone. 'Of course not. I've already explained to you that Daddy – '

'. . . fell in love and didn't want to be your husband any more. I know that, it's boring! I just thought that if you'd made yourself prettier . . .'

'It may surprise you to know that I used to be quite pretty!' she laughed.

'If you died, could I still talk to you?'

The change of subject took Kathryn by surprise. 'Died? Jasmine, what are you on about? I've no intention of dying for a long time yet.'

'But if you did,' she persisted, 'could I talk to you?'

7

'No.'

'Not even at night?'

'Not ever, Jasmine. I can't imagine where you get these strange ideas from.'

Jasmine didn't reply.

In the middle of the afternoon a customer called to collect her daughter's wedding cake for the following Saturday. 'It's beautiful,' she enthused. 'My sister-in-law has her silver wedding next month. Shall I give her your name and phone number?'

'I'm afraid I'm going to be away for a while, Mrs Gregory. My mother's convalescing from a stroke and . . .'

Mrs Gregory obviously didn't hold with Kathryn's sense of duty. 'That's no way to build up a business, Mrs Talkes. You've only just started out.'

'These things happen,' said Kathryn equably, but the woman shook her head disapprovingly.

After she'd gone Jasmine came in from the garden, her mouth red from the early strawberries she'd been eating. 'May I have a drink, Mummy?'

'Please,' said Kathryn automatically.

Jasmine sighed. 'Luke doesn't have to keep saying please.'

'Doesn't he? Lucky Luke! Squash or fizzy?'

'Lemonade, *please*.'

'Who's Luke, anyway?'

Jasmine smiled happily. 'My new friend. I met him last night.'

'Last night?'

'Yes, in my dream.'

'Oh, I see. He's a pretend friend, is he?'

Jasmine frowned. 'I'm not sure. I don't think so but . . . No, I'm sure he's real.'

'Then I'd like to meet him,' replied Kathryn. She didn't mind Jasmine having invisible friends, realising that it was probably consolation for losing her father, but she was anxious that she learnt to differentiate between dreams and reality.

'You will,' announced Jasmine with a smile.

That evening Kathryn was on the phone to South Willoughby for nearly an hour. As soon as she finished she

8

went up to her daughter's room and found Jasmine sitting on the windowsill staring out into the dusk. 'It's all arranged,' she told her brightly. 'I've spoken to Grandma's friend and we're going there on Friday. You'll be able to sleep in the attic bedroom. I expect there are plenty of children for you to play with in the village.'

Jasmine chewed on her thumbnail. 'Will Daddy know where to find us if he wants to come home?'

'I'll let him know where we're going,' said Kathryn gently, 'but I don't think he's very likely to come now that he's got a new wife and babies.'

'His new babies are boys; Daddy always said he liked girls best.'

'It's a long way for him to come, Jasmine.'

'Perhaps we should stay here. Is it nearer to Italy here?'

'About the same, darling. Don't worry, I'm sure he thinks about you a lot.'

'He sent me a nice doll for my birthday.'

'Yes,' lied Kathryn, who'd bought the doll herself and got a friend to write the label.

'Does he know I call the doll Jezebel?'

'Not yet.'

'Then I'll tell him. Why does Grandma call Pia Jezebel? Is it her other name?'

'No. I think you ought to be in bed.'

Jasmine jumped down to the floor and did a quick handstand. 'Look at me, Mummy! I'm going to be in a circus when I'm big.'

'Very clever! Come on, into bed.'

'I can walk on my hands as well, watch me!'

'Get into your bed, Jasmine.'

Jasmine's legs wavered for a moment and then she sprung back on to her feet, her face even more flushed than usual. 'You made me lose my concentration, Mummy! I don't want to go to bed. It's too hot.'

'You have such wonderful dreams I'm surprised you're not anxious to get off to sleep.'

'I forgot that! I might see Luke again. Good night, Mummy. God bless Daddy,' she added hastily as she tore off her shorts and T-shirt.

Kathryn pulled the sturdy little figure towards her. 'Don't forget my kiss.' She laughed, but Jasmine turned her face away. 'No kiss?'

'No, because you don't believe in Luke.'

'I do, darling. I know he's very real to you, it's just that . . . Oh, what does it matter, forget it!'

'Then you do believe in Luke?'

'I do believe in Luke.'

Jasmine beamed and hugged her mother back. 'Good! Now we can all be friends, because Luke's mummy . . .'

'Yes?'

'Nothing.' Jasmine was frowning again. 'I thought . . . It's all right. Good night, Mummy. Sleep tight.'

Much to Jasmine's annoyance she didn't dream of Luke again, and on the carpet beneath her bed the daisy crumpled away to powder after the heat of the day.

The journey to South Willoughby took over four hours and by the time Kathryn turned the car off the A52 and along the narrow winding lane that led to the village both she and Jasmine were worn out. 'Nearly there,' she promised her daughter. 'Grandma's cottage is the second on the left.'

Jasmine stared out of the back window at the flat fields and wrinkled her nose. 'I don't like it here. It's horrid.'

'Nonsense! You're too used to crowded towns. This is the way people ought to live.'

'I can't *see* any people.'

'That's because they're busy.'

'What do they do?'

'Well, work on the farms and . . .'

'Is this field a farm?'

'It's part of a farm. Look, that must be Grandma's cottage, the one with the chickens outside the gate.'

Jasmine's eyes brightened. 'I'll be able to collect eggs for breakfast. Why isn't Grandma outside waiting for us?'

'Because she can't walk very well yet. It certainly is quiet,' added Kathryn as she got out of the car and looked about her. The entire village was strangely silent. There were no children playing on the tiny village green, no customers walking out of the small village store opposite and no cars or bicycles. In her imagination she'd peopled the village with cheerful mothers and their children and she'd always imagined that the chatter of birds provided background music in the country. Not, it appeared, in South Willoughby. Or not today. Today it was as silent as the grave.

Jasmine scrambled out of the car, hesitating at the gate to the cottage. 'Can we go in, Mummy? I'm thirsty.'

With a small shiver Kathryn took her daughter's hand and hurried up the path. Although no one was visible she had the unpleasant conviction that they were being watched and was suddenly anxious to get inside. She knocked on the door and waited. There was no reply.

'*Mummy, I'm thirsty.*'

'Perhaps Grandma's having a rest in bed. I'll see if she's left the door unlocked.' Kathryn pushed on the solid wooden door and it swung gently open. 'There, I was right. In we go.' They stepped straight into the front room and Kathryn stumbled over an imitation snake draught-excluder that had been left in the middle of the floor. 'Mother!' she called loudly. 'Mother, we're here!'

Jasmine's dark eyes widened as she stared round the overcrowded room. 'Perhaps she's died!' she whispered nervously.

'Don't be silly! Mother, where are you?'

'She's at the hospital,' said a light, clear voice from behind them. Kathryn turned quickly. A small boy was outlined in the doorway. 'She got sick again and they took her to the hospital.' He moved slowly towards them, clutching a toy bear in his right hand.

'Who are you?' asked Kathryn.

'I'm Luke.'

Kathryn felt as though she were in some strange dream. 'You can't be,' she murmured in confusion. 'Luke isn't real.'

He shrugged and held the bear more tightly.

'When did my mother go to hospital?' she continued.

'This morning. I saw the ambulance stop outside.'

'I'd better ring at once.'

He watched her gravely, his small-boned features impassive. 'There isn't a phone. It hasn't been put in yet. Everything takes a long time here.'

11

'I forgot! Where's the nearest one?' Kathryn was beginning to panic.

'I don't know, nor does my bear.' He looked away from her as Jasmine came in from the kitchen where she'd been having a drink of water. She smiled at him shyiy.

'What's your name?' she asked, but Kathryn – silent and uneasy – was convinced her daughter already knew.

'I'm Luke Hughes and I'm four. I live in the Manor House.'

'I'm Jasmine Talkes and I'm nearly five. I live in Sussex.'

Luke's features relaxed. 'I'm glad you've come, my bear likes you. We'll be best friends,' he said confidently.

'My best friend in Sussex is called Keely but I think I like you better.'

'Of course you do. I haven't got any other best friends. My bear and me have been waiting for you.'

Kathryn felt uncomfortable and glanced uneasily at his tattered, glass-eyed bear. 'Listen, Luke, I've simply got to ring the hospital. Does the shop opposite have a phone?'

'Yes.' For an obviously bright child he was annoyingly monosyllabic.

'Then I'll just run across and ask them if I can use it.'

'My bear says they won't let you,' he said solemnly.

'I'm sure your bear's wrong. This is an emergency and I'll pay for the call.'

'My bear's never wrong.'

Kathryn smiled at him. 'Lucky bear! Jasmine, you wait here with Luke. I won't be a moment.'

Quickly she dashed across the road to the small, all-purpose store. There were several women in the shop. As she entered they stopped talking and listened as impassively as Luke's bear while she explained her problem to the plump lady behind the counter.

'I'm sorry, dear,' she said flatly. 'Our phone's out of order. There's a call box at the far end of the village.'

'Out of order?'

'It happens a lot here. This isn't London, I'm afraid.'

The customers mumured in agreement among themselves as Kathryn hesitated. 'I suppose none of you know where my mother is?' she asked hopefully. They exchanged glances before shaking their heads briefly. 'Well, in that case I'd

12

better . . . I'm sorry to have bothered you,' she concluded, aware that they were anxious for her to leave. As she closed the shop door carefully behind her she heard them resuming their interrupted conversation.

She ran through the village to the phone but once inside stared furiously at the dangling receiver and a large 'Out of Order' notice stuck across the small mirror above the phone. 'Damn!' Unable to believe her bad luck she stood by the door, staring helplessly about her. It was beginning to look as though she'd have to drive to the hospital if she wanted to find out about her mother, and she was already overtired. 'Damn and blast!' she repeated aloud, and was immediately mortified by the sound of a man's laughter.

'Out of order, is it?' The voice had the faintest suggestion of a Welsh lilt. Turning she saw a tall, dark-haired man, probably in his early thirties.

'I'm sorry,' she apologised quickly. 'I don't usually swear in the street! It's just that my mother's been taken to hospital and . . .'

'I am sorry. Is she going to be all right?'

'I don't know!'

He frowned. 'You're not from round here, are you?'

'No, but my mother is. She lives opposite the village shop.'

'Mrs Laing?'

'Yes. I'm her daughter, Kathryn. I only arrived half an hour ago and a little boy told me that she'd been taken to hospital so it's important that I find a phone. She's already had one stroke, you see, and if she's had another bad one I really ought to be with her, but I can't leave Jasmine – that's my daughter – alone in a strange village.'

'Calm down!' His dark eyes smiled into hers and she felt a quick surge of relief that here at last was one helpful inhabitant. 'I live right here. You can use my phone with pleasure and if you're needed at the hospital you can leave your daughter with me. My mother's living with us and she'd be delighted to have another female in the house.'

'I'm so grateful,' said Kathryn as they walked towards a large, imposing house made of grey Ancaster stone and set well back from the road. 'I felt as though I was in the middle of a nightmare. Is there a directory? I'll need to look up the number.'

'You'll find it on the shelf above the phone. Mind how you go, it's a bit dark in the hall until your eyes adjust.'

As she waited for the hospital switchboard to answer, Kathryn's eye was caught by a frighteningly lifelike stuffed fox in a glass-fronted cabinet on the opposite wall. It was snarling ferociously, its top lip curled back to show the razor-sharp teeth. She shivered slightly and looked away to where the man was waiting by the door.

His voice had been gentle but he was built like a rugby player. Idly she wondered what he did for a living. Probably something to do with farming, although he didn't really look like a man who spent his life out of doors. His complexion was too pale.

It took some time for her to get through to the ward but finally she was relieved to discover that her mother had only suffered a slight fall and would be allowed home the following morning. When she replaced the receiver the man raised his eyebrows questioningly. 'How is she?'

'She's fine. She can come home tomorrow.'

'What a relief for you! I don't think I introduced myself outside. I'm Owen Hughes.'

Kathryn held out her hand. 'And I'm Kathryn Talkes. A very grateful Kathryn Talkes as well! Now I'd better get back to the cottage. I left Jasmine alone with a little boy. I do hope he's still there.'

'Is the little boy fair and slight and wearing a rather loud orange T-shirt?'

'Do you know him?'

'He's my son. Why don't I walk back with you and collect him? I do hope he wasn't being a nuisance. There aren't a lot of pre-school children in the village and he gets rather bored during term time.'

'He was very helpful,' she said, trying to forget the disquiet she'd felt in his presence. 'But for him I'd still be searching for my mother.'

Owen walked briskly and Kathryn didn't have enough breath for further talk until they arrived at the cottage. Both children were swinging on the already fragile gate and at the sight of her mother, Jasmine climbed over the top and broke one of the hinges.

14

'Careful!' exclaimed Kathryn. 'You're much too heavy for that gate.'

'I'm not! Luke and me have been looking round the cottage, Mummy. It's not very clean.'

'That's because Grandma's been away in hospital for several weeks. We'll have to give everything a good scrub before we leave.'

'Did they let you use their phone?' asked Luke.

'It was out of order.'

He smiled. 'My bear's never wrong.'

'Time to bring your wonderful bear home,' said Owen lightly. 'You can see your new friends another day. It's time for tea.'

Luke went to climb over the gate, thought better of it and climbed off instead. 'Why can't I come back *after* tea?'

'I'm afraid we'll be busy unpacking after tea,' apologised Kathryn. 'Perhaps tomorrow morning?'

Luke's eyes shifted away from hers and he shuffled his feet. 'I'm busy tomorrow morning.'

'Doing what?' asked Owen in obvious surprise.

'My bear thinks we should tidy the graveyard.'

There was a long silence which no one seemed anxious to break.

'OK, see you in the afternoon then,' said Jasmine agreeably, and went into the cottage without a backward glance. With a quick smile at Owen, Kathryn followed her, leaving the man alone with his son.

15

Chapter 2

The next morning it was nine before Kathryn woke, and by the time she'd roused Jasmine and found her way round the kitchen another half an hour had gone by. 'Hurry up, Jasmine!' she shouted for the third time. 'Grandma's ambulance will be here soon and I must get breakfast cleared away.'

'I'm tired, Mummy. I got tired last night.'

'We both got tired last night.'

'I meant in my dream!' said Jasmine impatiently. 'I was running around all night.'

'Well, when I looked in on you this morning you were safely in bed.'

'Was not,' muttered Jasmine as her mother rushed back into the kitchen. At the breakfast table her eyes were sullen and she picked lethargically at her toast. 'This bread's got bits in it! I wanted an egg. Mummy, why can't I have an egg?'

Kathryn sighed and picked up a pile of dirty clothes that she'd found in her mother's washing basket. 'Because I can't find where the hens are laying them! Now finish your breakfast. I can't think what's the matter with you. You're normally so helpful in the mornings.'

'*I'm tired.*'

'You can rest later.'

'Don't want a rest.'

Kathryn decided to ignore Jasmine's ill humour and started loading the clothes into the machine. Within an hour they were on the line in the tiny but secluded back garden and she was just wondering what to do about feeding the chickens when she heard the ambulance arrive.

16

'It's Grandma!' shouted Jasmine, all smiles again as she ran round the side of the cottage. 'Two men are carrying her in a funny chair.'

Once inside the cottage Kathryn's mother had great difficulty in getting out of the chair and looked to her daughter for help. With a glance of annoyance at the ambulancemen who were standing idly by, Kathryn took hold of her mother's arm.

'Aren't you allowed to help?' she asked them ironically as she struggled to get her mother to her feet. Reluctantly they moved forward.

'Lived here long?' asked the younger of the two, taking the elderly woman's other arm.

'I only arrived yesterday.'

'Planning on staying?'

'Just for a few weeks, until Mother's better. There, if we could get her to the chair in the corner that would be great.'

As the men were leaving the younger one turned back towards her. 'Best of luck!' he said dryly, and Kathryn wondered if he meant with her mother or the villagers.

'Grandma doesn't look very happy,' whispered Jasmine loudly.

'Don't whisper, darling. It's rude.'

Jasmine sighed and wandered out into the front garden again. Grateful for the peace, Kathryn sat down by her mother. 'Are you all right now?' she asked anxiously. 'How did you fall? They didn't say much when I phoned. I suppose they were busy.'

'Did you phone, Kathryn? I wasn't told. I worried all night in case you hadn't arrived.'

'I rang as soon as possible after we got here. Mind you, it wasn't easy to find a phone. The villagers didn't fall over themselves to help.'

Her mother looked surprised. 'They've always been very kind to me. Perhaps you sounded too bossy. You can, you know, and that would have upset them.'

'I imagine I sounded more panic-stricken than bossy! Never mind, tell me about your fall.'

'Did I fall, dear? You should have phoned the hospital. I worried all night . . .'

17

Kathryn wondered if the journey in the ambulance had disorientated her mother. 'I did phone, she repeated gently.

'Where's Jasmine?' asked her mother abruptly.

'In the garden.'

'On her own? Is that wise?'

'She should be safe enough here.' Kathryn smiled, but as her mother continued to look agitated she decided to humour her. She could always let Jasmine go out again later. However, once outside she discovered that the garden was empty. She glanced along the road but there was no sign of her daughter. 'Jasmine!' she called loudly. 'Jasmine, milk and biscuit time!'

On the footpath opposite, a young woman about Kathryn's age with a baby in a pram and a toddler at her skirt stopped and glanced across the road. 'I've lost my little girl,' Kathryn explained anxiously. 'We're only visitors and she doesn't know her way around. You haven't seen her by any chance, have you? She's . . .' To her astonishment the woman simply turned away and walked on without a word.

'Incredible!' exclaimed Kathryn in disbelief. She was wondering what to do next when Jasmine came running round the bend in the road, waving cheerfully at her mother.

'I've found a lovely church, Mummy. It's tiny; the tiniest church you've ever seen.'

'Come inside at once!' snapped Kathryn, her fear turning to annoyance now that she knew Jasmine was safe. 'What do you think you're doing going off on your own? I was very worried.'

Jasmine's smile vanished. 'Sorry, Mummy. Is Grandma feeling better now?'

'She's a little confused but apart from that she's not too bad.'

'I hope Luke comes to play this afternoon,' said Jasmine as she walked slowly into the house. 'He's nice. Do you like him, Mummy?'

'Of course I do!' said Kathryn brightly, but they both knew it wasn't true.

After a makeshift lunch of tinned ham and tomatoes, Kathryn settled her mother on the sofa for a rest. 'While you're asleep I'll go over to the shop and get something for tea,' she said as her mother closed her eyes.

Jasmine was sitting on the low wall at the front of the house, her feet kicking idly against the rough stones. 'Where are you going, Mummy?'

'To the shop. Do you want to come?'

'Yes, please. Do they sell ice creams?'

'I expect so.'

This time there was only one other customer in the shop, a tall, elderly man who glanced briefly at Kathryn but more carefully at her daughter. Mrs Cook waited in silence as Kathryn tried to decide what to buy for the evening. 'And what's your name?' asked the man, bending down a little so that he could pat Jasmine on the head.

She tilted her head to one side in an unconsciously flirtatious manner. 'Jasmine Talkes. I'm nearly five,' she added quickly.

'You're a big girl for nearly five.'

'Yes. How old are you?'

'I'm eighty-three,' he said with pride. 'Eighty-three and never a day's illness in my life. What do you think of that, Jasmine?'

'Haven't you ever had a cold?'

'A cold isn't an illness.'

'It isn't a wellness,' she pointed out with perfect logic.

'True enough! Have you come to live here, Jasmine?'

'No, I'm staying with my Grandma. This is my Mummy. She's got to buy something for tea. We only had ham and tomatoes for lunch.'

Kathryn waited for the man to speak to her but he didn't. Instead he looked at Mrs Cook and seemed to nod his head. 'Would you like an ice cream?' asked the shopkeeper cheerfully. 'It's a hot day. I expect you hoped Mummy would buy you one, didn't you?'

'Yes.'

'Well, we'll let Mummy save her pennies. Here you are, a strawberry cone.'

'That's my favourite!' squealed Jasmine. 'It's my favourite, isn't it, Mummy?'

'Yes. Thank you very much,' put in Kathryn. Mrs Cook glanced briefly at her and then turned back to Jasmine.

'Do you go to school yet?' asked the elderly man.

'Not until after Christmas.'

19

'Good!' He sounded genuinely pleased and suddenly Kathryn was seized with a peculiar sense of unease. It wasn't only the way both the adults were monopolising Jasmine, it was also the fact that she herself could have been invisible for all the notice they took of her.

'I'd like a pound of the Lincolnshire sausages, please.' After she'd spoken she was aware that her voice was too loud and both Mrs Cook and the old man looked at her in surprise. 'I'm sorry but I can't leave my mother alone for long,' she added by way of explanation.

'One moment, dear. Had you finished your order, Mr Bentley?'

'Not quite. I think I'll take half a pound of humbugs as well.'

Kathryn felt herself flush with annoyance. She knew that the old man was deliberately making her look ill-mannered but there was nothing she could do about it. 'I'm sorry,' she mumbled.

'You've gone red, Mummy,' said Jasmine in surprise. 'Are you hot? Would you like a lick of my cone?'

'No, thank you, Jasmine. I'll buy one of my own.'

'I'm so sorry, the strawberry cones have all gone,' said Mrs Cook with a pleasant smile.

Mr Bentley, slowly making his way out of the shop, winked at Jasmine as he passed. 'See you around, little girl.'

'See you around!' She smiled up at him, her eyes sparkling and her dark curls gleaming in the sunlight that came through the open door. He hesitated in the doorway and finally looked across at Kathryn.

'That's a lovely little girl you've got there. South Willoughby's always been a good place for children. She probably won't ever want to leave.'

Instinctively Kathryn moved closer to her daughter, putting a protective hand on her shoulder. He may have meant well but the old man's words had frightened her and for a brief moment she wished that she'd never agreed to come and help her mother.

When she finally got back to the cottage she was relieved that Jasmine was content to play in the back garden because she didn't want her out of her sight.

'I'm bored!' announced Jasmine, trailing indoors again before Kathryn had even put the groceries away. 'I wish Luke would come and play.'

'He will, it's early yet.'

'When he comes, may we go and play in the field down the road?'

'Well, the farmer might not like – '

'I'm here!' Luke didn't knock on the half-open door, instead he walked confidently into the front room and stood there, his bear under one arm. 'I've come to play with Jasmine,' he announced.

'She was just saying how bored she was.'

'My bear and me usually play in the field by the church. Can Jasmine come with us?'

'What does your mother say about it?'

'My mummy's dead.'

Kathryn felt terrible. 'I'm so sorry,' she murmured apologetically. 'I had no idea.'

'Can we play in the field?' he repeated doggedly.

'Doesn't the farmer mind?'

'It doesn't belong to the farmer; it belongs to the church. Anyone can play there if they want to.'

'All right then. But be careful, both of you; and don't talk to strangers.'

The children set off together and Kathryn went down the path to shut the gate behind them. 'My bear thinks she's a fusspot!' she heard Luke saying to Jasmine. 'There aren't any strangers here. I know everyone in the village.'

'I like your bear,' exclaimed Jasmine. Kathryn had the feeling that Luke's bear might become very tiresome to adults. He was obviously a mouthpiece for the boy's less acceptable statements but adults would feel very foolish contradicting a stuffed toy.

As soon as Nancy Laing awoke she looked anxiously round the room. 'Where's Jasmine?' she demanded.

'She's playing with a little boy called Luke. It's perfectly all right. I met his father yesterday. They seem a nice family.'

'Luke Hughes?'

'Do you know him?'

21

'I knew his mother. She was rather strange.'

'In what way?'

Mrs Laing frowned. 'I can't remember. It was something to do with . . . No, it's gone. I don't know what's wrong with me these days. I keep forgetting things.'

'It's left over from your stroke. I'm sure it's only temporary. Would you like a cup of tea?'

'Tara!' said her mother triumphantly. 'That was her name; Tara Hughes.'

'How did she die?' asked Kathryn as she filled the kettle.

'Is she dead, dear? When did that happen?'

Kathryn sighed, realising how difficult things must be for her mother. 'Tea,' she said, settling herself in a comfortable chair, aware now that she and Jasmine would be staying in South Willoughby for quite a few weeks.

'How long will you be staying here?' asked Luke as he and Jasmine crouched on top of one of the graves that were scattered in apparently random confusion in the overgrown ground that surrounded the tiny village church.

'Until my grandma's better. Who's buried here?'

Luke studied the old gravestone. 'Someone called Sarah Gillick. She was only twenty-three when she died.'

'My mummy's twenty-nine already,' said Jasmine confidentially. 'How old was your mummy when she died?'

'I don't know. Pretty old, I think. Daddy's thirty-four.'

'My daddy lives in Italy now. He's got a new wife and new children.'

Luke's eyes locked on to Jasmine's. 'Do you mind?'

She hesitated. 'I miss him quite a lot but if he likes his new children better than me there isn't much point in him coming back, is there?'

'I guess not. Does he send you presents?'

'He sent me a doll. It was a nice one. I saw it in our toy shop at home.'

Luke settled himself more firmly on his heels. 'If he lives in Italy how could he buy a doll from a shop in England?'

Jasmine frowned. 'I don't know. Perhaps he came back and bought it.'

22

'I expect your mummy paid for it and pretended it was from your daddy.'

'She did not. My mummy wouldn't tell me a lie.'

'Ask her,' challenged Luke. 'I bet I'm right. You can't trust grown-ups,' he added wearily. 'They all tell you lies.'

'I'll ask her tonight. Why can't we play with your mummy again?'

'Because she's resting. She has to rest in the daytime.'

'Why?'

'To get enough strength for the evenings. Besides, if she came here in the day and people saw her it wouldn't be our secret any more.'

'Will I see her tonight?' asked Jasmine anxiously.

'No. There's a special party tonight. You can't come.'

'Why not? I'm your friend and I like parties.'

'You're not allowed to come. You don't belong yet.'

'Then let me join.'

Luke shook his head. 'You'll be able to join when you've been here longer. It's too soon yet.'

'I'll tell!' shouted Jasmine, thoroughly annoyed.

Luke glanced at his bear and then stared at her. 'If you tell, my bear says you'll die.'

'No I won't! You're just trying to frighten me.'

'I am not! My bear told me!'

'He isn't real. It's just you pretending.'

It isn't. My bear's a special bear.' Suddenly, Luke glanced around them, making sure that they were alone in the churchyard. 'Come and see something magic,' he urged her. 'Quickly!'

Jasmine followed him to the far side of the church. 'I can't see anything.'

'Over there, by the big headstone, see?'

Jasmine stared and slowly made out a small black shadow on the grass. At first it was no bigger than her hand, but gradually it grew to the size of a football and continued growing until it was taller than her mother. Then, like a huge black cloud, it lifted in the summer air and floated towards Jasmine. As it approached it blocked out the sun and everything around her was obliterated. All at once it seemed to the petrified child that there was nothing left on earth except her and this terrible mass of darkness that was now threatening to consume her.

She thought that she heard Luke urging her to run but her legs wouldn't respond and she stayed rooted to the spot. It came nearer and nearer and then there was only a little patch of light around her body. Everything else was blackness. A terrible blackness that made her want to cry in terror and despair as images of pain and death flashed through her brain; images that meant nothing to her child's mind and yet had the ability to chill her until her bones ached with tension and fear.

At the very moment that the blackness reached the edge of her light summer skirt she opened her mouth and screamed. She screamed as loudly as she'd ever screamed in her life and kept her eyes tightly closed as she continued screaming for the one person who always saved her, her mother.

'What *are* you doing?' asked Luke in surprise.

Shaking with terror, Jasmine opened her eyes and found herself crouched on top of one of the gravestones. She looked nervously round and then blinked in surprise. There was no sign of any black cloud. No feeling of darkness and fear. It had all gone. The sun was shining again and she was perfectly safe.

'I was calling for my mummy.'

'Why?'

'Because . . . Didn't you see the blackness?'

He shook his head. 'No. Perhaps it was because you threatened to tell.'

Jasmine's eyes opened very wide as she scrambled down on to the grass. 'Is that really why?' she whispered.

'Could be.'

She chewed on her thumbnail and looked towards the spot where the darkness had begun. 'I don't think I want to play with you any more.'

'Of course you do. We'll have lots of fun. Come on, let's go and have some tea.'

Back at the cottage, Kathryn was cooking the sausages when the children arrived. Her mother seemed agitated by their chatter and kept glancing towards the pair of them. 'Play more quietly, darling, there's a good girl. Grandma isn't well yet,' said Kathryn.

'We can't get any *more* quiet, Mummy.'

'It's time for Luke to go home now. Your tea's ready.'

Jasmine pouted. 'I'm not hungry. Luke and me are playing.'

'He can come back after you've eaten.'

'My daddy might not let me,' said Luke. 'My bear thinks your grandma should go back into hospital,' he added, glancing towards Kathryn's mother.

'Why?'

'Because she's making funny noises.'

Kathryn realised her mother was indeed making strange noises. Small, whimpering sounds in the back of her throat, and she was staring fixedly at the children. 'Run along Luke,' she said quickly. 'We'll see you later if your daddy doesn't mind.'

Jasmine walked to the door with Luke. 'Ask her,' he whispered. 'Ask your mummy about the doll. I bet I'm right.'

After he'd gone, Jasmine watched her mother very carefully. She looked the same. She was cheerful and kind as always but Jasmine no longer felt quite the same about her. She didn't have the dream lady's special smile, and her clothes were just ordinary jeans and a jersey. The dream lady wore long, flowing dresses. In fact, it was hard to believe she was Luke's mother, she seemed more like a princess in a fairy story.

'Stop staring and sit up to table,' said Kathryn sharply, worried about her mother.

When they were all eating, Jasmine decided to find out the truth about the doll. 'Mummy, how did Daddy buy Jezebel for me? Did he come to Effingham to get it?'

Kathryn looked uncomfortable. 'Well, he . . .'

'Because if he did, he should have come to see me.'

'No, he didn't come to Effingham, he . . .'

'Did *you* buy it?'

Why now? thought Kathryn despairingly. She wasn't in the mood to cope with her daughter's abrupt, penetrating questions. All she wanted was a quiet meal and an early night, but Jasmine's dark eyes were fixed on her and she knew that she had to answer truthfully. 'Yes, I bought it for him,' she admitted.

'Did he ask you to buy it?'

'Jasmine, why are you asking all these questions now?'

'Because Luke says that all grown-ups tell lies.'

Kathryn sighed. 'It isn't as simple as you and Luke might think. Daddy wanted you to have something nice and . . .'

'Did he really? I don't think he did. I don't think Daddy even remembered my birthday. I think you made it all up, and *I don't like my sausages*,' she added defiantly.

'I'll explain later,' said Kathryn, realising that her mother had stopped eating. 'Please eat the beans even if you don't want the sausages.'

'He's bad.' Nancy Laing's voice was surprisingly strong.

'Do you mean Philip?' asked Kathryn.

'I mean Luke. He's a bad boy.'

'He's not!' shouted Jasmine, dropping her knife and fork in her agitation. 'He's my best friend and he's nice. *You're* bad. You're old and ill and you keep dribbling. I don't like you one bit.'

Kathryn was so stunned by her daughter's outburst that for a moment she couldn't speak. Before she could recover herself they were interrupted by the sound of someone tapping on the front door. 'If that's Luke he can go straight home again!' she announced. 'I'm ashamed of you, Jasmine. As soon as you've eaten you're going to your room.' But it wasn't Luke. It was his father.

'I hope I'm not disturbing you?' queried Owen with a smile. 'Ever since I got in, Luke's been pestering me about having Jasmine round. After a hard day fiddling my expenses I'm a bit of a pushover, which is why I'm here now, inviting Jasmine to play this evening.'

Kathryn realised that he was looking at her with undisguised admiration and flushed slightly. 'I'm sorry, she's been very rude this evening and has to go to bed early,' she apologised.

Owen's calm, friendly expression didn't waver. 'In that case, why don't you both come to dinner tomorrow night? We usually eat around seven-thirty.'

'I'd like to but my mother really can't be left. I think I'll have to ask the doctor to call. Her memory's terrible.'

'I'll give him a ring if you like. I assume it's Dr Potter?'

'I think so, but . . .'

'No trouble. As for tomorrow, my mother would be only too pleased to spend a couple of hours here. She and your mother are well acquainted.'

Kathryn hesitated. 'I don't know. She might not like seeing strangers at the moment.'

'Why don't I come in and ask her?'

'Who is it?' called the older woman anxiously. 'Is it the boy?'

'It's me, Mrs Laing.' Owen's voice was reassuring and he patted Jasmine on the head as he passed. She looked up, beaming happily at him, her sulkiness disappearing like magic in his presence. 'My mother wondered if you were well enough to have visitors,' he continued, settling himself in Kathryn's chair. 'She's very anxious to see how you are.'

Mrs Laing looked closely at him. 'Who are you? I don't remember seeing you before.'

'I'm Owen Hughes, Mary's son.'

'Mary? I thought her name was Tara.'

'Tara was my wife, Mrs Laing.'

Nancy Laing nodded to herself. 'That's right, your wife. The mother of the boy.'

'Do you mean Luke?'

'I mean the boy who came here.'

'That's right, Mother,' said Kathryn quickly. 'He was here today, playing with Jasmine.'

'Not today, I meant . . .' All at once her eyes clouded in confusion. 'He's a bad boy, a very bad boy,' she whispered starting to rock to and fro in her chair.

Owen stood up and raised his eyebrows. 'How long's she been like this?'

'Ever since she got back from hospital. It isn't all the time, but she seems to go off at tangents. Obviously she's confused and I don't know what to do for the best.'

'She definitely needs to see the doctor again. If I ring him tonight he'll call in the morning. We'll see what he has to say, but I'm sure he won't object to my mother taking a turn here tomorrow. I should think you could do with a change of scenery; this cottage is a bit claustrophobic.'

'I really am grateful,' said Kathryn warmly.

'It's nothing. Actually I'm grateful to your mother for falling ill. After all, it did bring you here.'

'He's a nice man,' said Jasmine, after he'd gone. 'I think he likes you too.'

'At least he's friendly, which is more than can be said for some of the other villagers.'

'I'm sorry I was rude to Grandma.'

'Have you apologised to her?'

'Yes.'

'When?' asked Mrs Laing, her eyes suddenly alert again. 'I didn't hear any apology.'

'Oh, Grandma, surely you can remember!'

'Would you clear the table, Jasmine?' asked Kathryn quickly.

'Are we going to Luke's house tomorrow night, Mummy?'

'We'll have to wait and see what the doctor says.'

'He'll say yes,' said Jasmine confidently. 'I know he will.'

Kathryn hoped her daughter was right. No man had looked at her as admiringly as Owen Hughes had for a long time, and she found him equally attractive. His calm self-confidence was in pleasant contrast to Philip's highly strung anxieties and she was sure that he had a good sense of humour too. It was rare to find such an attractive unmarried man and she laughingly decided he was her reward for coming to South Willoughby against her will.

Chapter 3

'What seems to be the problem?' asked Dr Potter as he swept into the cottage. He was a short, plump man in his early fifties with a bald head and eyes that peered out from behind gold-rimmed glasses. He reminded Kathryn of Dickens' Mr Pickwick, but without the good humour.

'I'm rather worried about my mother's memory. I know that she's had a stroke but I hadn't expected . . .'

'Hadn't expected what? Did you imagine she was going to be the same as before?'

'Of course not. It's just that . . . well, the way she is now I can't imagine how she coped on her own at all.'

'She didn't,' he said bluntly. 'Lots of people helped out, until you were finally persuaded to come here yourself. Heather Masters wrote to you, I believe?'

'Yes, although I haven't seen her yet.'

'Died last week. Complications after summer flu.'

Kathryn stared in astonishment at his off-hand manner. 'Does my mother know?'

'Not yet. I suppose you hoped you were only here for a week or two? Anxious to dash back home again, are you?'

'I do have a job, doctor. I can't stay here indefinitely. Shouldn't my mother be told about Miss Masters? I understood they were close friends.'

'You can tell her when she's stronger. Unless you have to dash home to your husband first.'

'I'm divorced and my ex-husband's married again. I need to work,' she added pointedly.

'In that case your mother may have to go into a nursing

29

home. Something I was anxious to avoid,' he continued. 'I find that patients convalesce better at home. How long can you stay?'

'I suppose I could manage a month,' said Kathryn doubtfully.

The doctor's frown cleared. 'Excellent! A month should be long enough. Right, I'll go and take a look at the patient. Is she in bed?'

'Yes. As she gets tired I thought . . .'

'Quite! Quite!' He hurried up the stairs and Jasmine stared after him thoughtfully. 'Don't forget to ask about tonight, Mummy.'

'Let's see what he has to say when he gets down,' responded Kathryn.

He wasn't gone long and seemed prepared to dash straight out of the cottage. 'I wondered if Mrs Hughes could come and sit with my mother tonight,' Kathryn suggested, stopping him in his tracks. 'We've been invited out.'

'Of course, of course. Any competent nurse will do.'

'So much for needing me then!' muttered Kathryn.

'In the short term, Mrs . . . ?'

'Talkes.'

'In the short term, Mrs Talkes, a friendly face will do. But long-term it's quite a different story.'

'When will you call again?'

He looked surprised, as though he hadn't intended to make another visit. 'Some time next week,' he said vaguely. 'Unless you phone, of course.'

'I was wondering when Mother's telephone was going to be installed?'

'Ask British Telecom. We doctors have quite enough to do without seeing to telephone installations. Good morning.'

'What a rude man!' exclaimed Kathryn as his car drew away. 'Never mind, at least he said we could go out tonight.'

'I liked him,' announced Jasmine with a smile. 'I thought he was neat!'

'Neat? Where did you hear that expression?'

'In my dreams.'

'It's a pity you weren't reminded about washing your face in the mornings in one of your dreams. You'd better go up to the

30

bathroom, you've marmalade all round your mouth.'

'I wish it was tonight already!' shouted Jasmine as she began to climb the stairs. Kathryn agreed, she thought that it was probably going to be a long day.

When Owen's mother arrived that evening, Nancy Laing was obviously pleased to see her. Kathryn had gone over the arrangements several times during the day but was still relieved. She'd been afraid that once again her mother would become confused, in which case she'd already decided that she'd stay with her. 'We won't be late,' she assured the older woman as she set off.

'I can't think why you're going,' replied Nancy querulously. 'I'm sure Tara won't be pleased.'

'Tara's dead, dear,' said Mary Hughes gently. 'She died six months ago.'

'Come on, Mummy!' urged Jasmine, tugging at her mother's hand. 'I don't want to be late. Luke's going to show me something exciting.'

'And what's that?' Kathryn smiled as they walked along the street.

'His mummy's bedroom. It's got lovely pictures and special wallpaper.'

'I doubt if Mr Hughes will want you in his bedroom.'

'It isn't *his* bedroom. He sleeps in the room next to Luke.'

'Does he?' Kathryn wondered whether Owen had moved after his wife's death or if they'd always had separate bedrooms. She was slightly surprised to realise that she half-hoped it was the latter.

'I'll show you round before we eat,' said Owen after he'd welcomed them. 'That way you won't get lost going to the loo!'

It would certainly be easy to get lost, thought Kathryn. All the rooms looked the same with their high ceilings, cold stone walls and shadowy corners that made her unreasoningly nervous. Only in the book-lined library were there any pictures, and they were all dark portraits of black-haired women with high cheekbones and eyes that seemed to follow Kathryn round the room.

'Tara's ancestors,' said Owen casually. 'She brought them with her when we got married.'

31

'You can see they're all related,' she said politely.

'I suppose so. Everywhere could do with a good spring clean I'm afraid. I'll get round to it one day.'

Jasmine stayed close to her mother and Kathryn could sense that she too felt uneasy in the house. As they moved towards the stairs Jasmine saw the stuffed fox and gave a cry of alarm.

'Don't worry, it's dead,' said Luke. 'There's a rabbit too, up by the front door, see. Mummy liked him best.'

Kathryn didn't. The rabbit was frozen in an attitude of terror, as though aware that death was imminent. 'Let's go upstairs,' she said brightly, hoping there weren't any more dead animals there.

Jasmine looked up the gloomy stairwell, saw that there were gleaming pistols and bright but ominously stained swords to be passed and tugged at Kathryn's skirt. 'I don't like it here,' she whispered.

'Don't let the armoury put you off!' Owen laughed. 'They're safely fixed to the wall.'

'I'll show you my room,' said Luke. 'That's got nice things in it. I chose them myself.'

'Let's eat first,' said Owen, and Kathryn felt very relieved. The house seemed cold and unwelcoming, the mullioned windows like disapproving eyes and she was surprised that Owen could be comfortable there.

'Good idea!' she said warmly, and with one final glance at the fox, Jasmine followed them into the dining-room.

After the meal the two children were able to go off on their own, leaving Kathryn and Owen lingering over their brandies. 'I take it your mother didn't mind you coming out?' asked Owen.

'She was pleased to see your mother.'

'How's Jasmine settling in?'

'Luke occupies most of her time; Mother and I are just adults who get in the way! They seem to play well together, although I'm a bit worried that they like to be away from the cottage.'

'You don't need to worry. They'll be perfectly safe round by the church. It's overlooked by quite a few houses and I'm sure no one would let any harm come to Luke.' He sounded amused.

'I suppose the villagers have rallied round to help since you lost your wife?'

He smiled. 'That's one way of putting it. I sometimes feel that they'd like to make Luke the village mascot. Everyone wants to help me with him. Unfortunately it undermines my authority because no matter what I say they buy him sweets and ices on demand. I will have to put my foot down, but somehow the time never seems quite right. As you may have gathered, I'm basically a rather lazy person. Tara had enough energy for both of us!'

'You must miss her a lot.'

He looked down into his brandy glass. 'I certainly miss her presence. It's things like coming home to an empty house or expecting to find her in the kitchen – not that she did much cooking but she used to potter around out there – that are disconcerting. But to be honest we led very separate lives. Her hobbies took her off round the villages for hours on end. We'd rather drifted apart over the last few years.'

'What sort of hobbies?' Kathryn was intrigued.

'Nature studies, flowers, animals, that sort of thing. She often went out at night looking at badgers and foxes. I think she preferred them to people!'

He certainly wasn't a conventionally grieving husband, thought Kathryn with surprise; neither did he seem to feel obliged to put on any sort of pretence for her benefit. 'Had she been very ill?' she asked.

'Tara was never ill. It was an accident.'

Kathryn waited but that seemed to be all he was willing to say on the subject. 'Is Luke coping reasonably well? Jasmine finds her father's absence very difficult to handle.'

'He has the occasional nightmare, but that's only to be expected. I'm afraid that some of his passion for hanging round the church is because his mother's buried there. I don't encourage it but he's quite determined. Probably he'll give up of his own accord once he's come to terms with her death. Then there's Edward Bear! He's only come on the scene since Tara died.'

'What does your doctor say?'

'To leave Luke alone. He'll work through his grief in his own way; he just needs time. But that's enough about Luke. Tell me about yourself.'

33

'I'm very ordinary. I went to a convent from the age of five and met Philip at evening classes when I was eighteen. We got married two years later. He was half Greek – very dashing and handsome – and I was so naive and protected that I didn't see beneath the surface charm.'

'What do you mean?'

'I found his refusal to conform very attractive but he was actually immature. Once Jasmine arrived I realised I had two children to look after and lost patience with him. I turned into a horrible, nagging wife and he found someone more understanding to take my place.'

'Did you mind?'

'Of course I did! I thought he loved us; I never expected the marriage to fail and when he left I was shattered. I kept ringing him up, asking him to come back, it was terrible. When I look back at myself I cringe!'

'Has he remarried?'

'Yes. He now has an Italian wife and two sons under two. He's even settled down to a steady job in Italy, so presumably some of his behaviour was my fault.'

'Obviously you weren't well suited. It must be hard on Jasmine.'

'She can't understand why she doesn't hear from him. He used to dote on her, you see.'

'Sounds a self-centred sort of chap. You deserve better, both of you.'

'I'm not so sure about that,' she said ruefully.

'Look, I've been asked to a party on Saturday night. Why don't you come with me? My mother can stay at the cottage.'

'What about Luke?'

'He can stay with friends for the night. He enjoys that, they let him stay up horrendously late. Please come, Kathryn. I never go anywhere these days. I feel all wrong on my own.'

Still she hesitated. Since Philip left she hadn't been out much either. Somehow the ease with which he'd discarded her had taken away all her self-confidence and she hadn't dared attempt to try and form any new relationship. But this was different, she told herself. Owen was lonely too and there was no chance of anything long-term because she wouldn't be staying. All he was offering was an evening out with people around her own age and she knew that she ought to go.

'I'd love to come,' she said at last. 'You are sure your mother won't mind?'

'Absolutely! Now we'd better go and find the children.'

Upstairs, Jasmine and Luke were sitting on top of a king-size bed covered with a heavy gold bedspread and Jasmine was staring about her in wonder. 'What's that?' she whispered, pointing to a painting on the opposite wall.

'That's a Goya,' said Luke proudly.

'It looks like a skeleton.'

'Goya painted it, stupid! It's good, isn't it? My bear likes skulls,' he added with relish.

'It's spooky. Why did your mummy paint these funny stars on her walls?'

'They're not stars, they're magic signs. See that bookcase over there?'

'Yes,' muttered Jasmine, who was beginning to feel uncomfortable.

'Well, it's locked but inside there are lots of special books about magic. One day, when Daddy's at work, I'll show them to you.'

'Is it tricks and things? I can do a card trick my daddy taught me.'

'It isn't that sort of magic! It's spells and witches and – '

'*Get out of this room at once!*' shouted Owen, throwing open the door and striding across to the bed. 'If I catch you in here again, Luke, I shall have a lock put on the door. You know perfectly well this is out of bounds.'

Startled by his sudden burst of temper, Jasmine caught her foot in the bedspread and fell, hitting her nose hard on the floor. She started to cry and immediately Owen crouched down, holding her against his shoulder. She clutched his jacket, remembering how her father used to let her snuggle up against him.

'I'm sorry, Jasmine, I didn't mean to frighten you. I was cross with Luke, not you. You didn't know this room was out of bounds. Come on, let's dry your eyes before Mummy comes. That's a good girl, now blow.'

He was leading her out of the bedroom as he talked, and closed the door carefully behind him before sitting on the top stair and settling her on his knee. 'Better? Good girl! How about looking at a video before you go home? Do you like the *Care Bears*?'

Jasmine sniffed and blinked her long, damp lashes. 'Not much, they're silly. I like *Trap Door*. Have you got any *Trap Door*?'

'Let's go and find out.'

'What happened?' asked Kathryn after the children were settled. 'I thought I heard Jasmine crying.'

'I shouted at Luke. It didn't bother him but it upset Jasmine.'

'What were they doing?'

'Nothing serious. Why don't I put on some music? Do you like Rossini?'

She did and *The Thieving Magpie* was still running through her head and she and Jasmine walked home along the poorly lit path through the main street. As they neared the bend opposite the tiny church, Jasmine caught hold of her mother's hand. 'Quickly, Mummy, let's go faster. I don't want to see the blackness.'

'What blackness?'

'It's a special sort of magic. Luke showed me it.'

'I hope he doesn't frighten you. I thought you liked playing together.'

'Not when he does bad things.'

Kathryn stopped and looked down at her daughter. 'What exactly do you mean by bad things?'

Jasmine wanted to tell her. She actually opened her mouth to explain about the blackness but all at once she heard a rustling in the privet hedge next to her, and when she turned her head she saw a dark shadow at her feet. It was no bigger than her hand but she knew that didn't mean anything. It could grow; she'd seen that for herself. Sadly she closed her mouth and turned her face away from her mother's concerned gaze. 'He just gets overexcited,' she explained lamely. 'I think he misses his mother.'

'Are you sure that's all you meant?' asked Kathryn anxiously.

'Yes. Come on, let's go and see Grandma.'

'Why don't you show me round the churchyard? I haven't seen it yet.'

Jasmine looked across the road. Everything seemed quiet. She wished that she could ask Luke about letting her mother see their special place but she supposed it would be all right. 'OK,' she agreed slowly. 'Only we mustn't stay once it's getting dark.'

'Why ever not?'

'Because that's when the spirits come back.'

'Do you mean ghosts? Come on, Jasmine, you don't believe in ghosts, do you?'

'I don't know,' murmured Jasmine, threading her way between the old headstones.

Kathryn was amazed at how tiny the church was. It couldn't have measured more than eighteen by seven metres and looked more like a very small village hall than a place of worship. Most of the inscriptions on the headstones dated back to the eighteen hundreds but there were one or two more recent ones, including Heather Masters', all in a small area of freshly cut grass a few feet from the church door. Bending down to read one of the new inscriptions she was surprised to see that it belonged to a child. A little girl, Penelope Winthrop, who'd died only twelve months earlier aged six years and two months. There was no mention of any tragic accident, nor of her parents' names, simply her name and the two dates.

'What are you looking at?' asked Jasmine, glancing across. Then she nodded. 'I saw that. Luke says her throat was cut. Shall I show you Luke's mummy's grave?'

Kathryn shuddered. 'How horrible! Why did Luke tell you that?'

'Because I asked, of course! Look, here's his mummy's grave.'

'Jasmine, did Luke tell you who . . .' She couldn't bring herself to repeat the words. '. . . who killed the little girl?' she finished weakly.

'No one knows. Her mummy and daddy have moved away and left her here all alone. I think that's very sad. Now she hasn't got anyone to talk to.'

'She doesn't need anyone to talk to.'

Jasmine's head whipped round and she frowned. 'Of course she does. She gets very lonely, she . . .'

'Yes?'

'Nothing. Do come and see Luke's mummy.' Jasmine pointed to a white marble headstone and Kathryn began to read the inscription:

Tara Hughes
Wife of Owen
and beloved mother of Luke.
Died tragically on 26th December 1987
aged 35 years.
He casteth out devils through the prince of the devils

She stared at the quotation for a long time. For some reason it disturbed her.

'She was very pretty, Mummy,' said Jasmine, slipping her hand into her mother's.

'How do you know?'

The child flushed. 'I saw a photograph in Luke's bedroom.'

'Was that where you were when you got told off?'

'No, we were in his mummy's room. It's got a lot of pictures in it and – ouch!' She put her hand to her left temple.

'What's the matter?'

'I've got a pain in my head. It's horrid, like a knife going jab! jab!'

Remembering Penelope Winthrop's fate Kathryn didn't want to think about knives if she could help it. 'Come along,' she said briskly. 'I expect you're overtired. Let's get home to Grandma.'

'But you didn't look inside the church.'

'I've seen all I want to for tonight. You really look exhausted,' she added, noticing her daughter's white face.

Jasmine blinked sleepily and her feet dragged along the last few yards. 'I might not go out tonight,' she muttered when she was drinking her glass of milk.

'You never go out at night!'

Because she was busy thanking Mary Hughes and helping her mother up the stairs, Kathryn failed to see the look of pity that Jasmine directed at her. Later on, when her daughter tossed and turned in her bed, crying out for help and searching for her mother, Kathryn was lost in her own world of dreams. A world that had suddenly acquired the new and extremely personable figure of Luke's father.

'My daddy's taking your mummy out tonight,' said Luke as he and Jasmine entered the churchyard.

'I know. She wanted to have her hair done but the shop couldn't fit her in.'

'That's because she doesn't belong. Why wouldn't you come with me last night?'

Jasmine crouched down beside Penelope Winthrop's grave. 'Because I can't play all the games and some of the people frighten me.'

'I could teach you how to play all the games,' he promised.

Jasmine ignored him. 'I wonder why Penelope keeps crying?'

'Because she doesn't want to be here. She'd like to see her parents again, but she can't.'

'Why not?'

Luke shrugged. 'I told you. They've gone away.'

'If she can see your mummy and all the people who join her at night, why can't she go off and see her own family?'

'It's the rules.'

'I don't understand the rules.'

'Let's have a special game today!' said Luke eagerly, anxious to change the subject. 'I'll show you some of the magic.'

Jasmine hesitated. Despite the sun overhead it felt cold in the churchyard and she shivered.

'You've got to be skyclad,' Luke continued. 'If you're not skyclad I can't do anything.'

'What's skyclad?'

'It means taking your clothes off.'

'I'm not going to do that!' said Jasmine indignantly. 'It's rude!'

'My bear says that in the beginning everyone was skyclad. Clothes get in the way.'

'I won't.'

'Then we'll have to play ordinary games.'

Jasmine didn't mind. 'How about hide-and-seek?'

'If you learnt some magic we could let Penelope come and play with us,' coaxed Luke cunningly.

'Would that cheer her up?' asked Jasmine eagerly.

'I expect it would. Well, will you take your clothes off?'

Jasmine glanced around and saw a face in one of the windows that overlooked the church. 'I can't, there's someone watching.'

Luke followed the direction of her gaze. 'That's Florence Reevely. She doesn't matter, she's one of us. Come on, Jasmine. I shall go home if you don't.'

Trembling from cold and excitement, Jasmine went behind the largest headstone and peeled off her summer frock and socks. When she went back to Luke he frowned. 'You've left your knickers on, that's no good.'

'But I . . .'

'I'm going!' announced Luke, starting to walk away.

'No! I'll take them off. Come back, Luke. I want to learn some magic, really I do.'

When he turned round he was scowling ferociously and Jasmine quickly scampered away to remove the pink cotton knickers that had annoyed him. When she walked naked on to the grass he closed his eyes and sat cross-legged, his back very straight and his breathing slow. She watched him for a few minutes, but felt chilly and rather bored and couldn't keep quiet for long. 'What are you doing? This isn't much of a game.'

'Sit down next to me and close your eyes. I'm going to let you see something.'

Obediently she settled down on the grass beside him. 'I can't see anything; just blackness with bright spots.'

'Wait!' ordered Luke. 'Be quiet and concentrate.'

Jasmine sighed, exhaled slowly and continued to see nothing but darkness. 'Why aren't *you* skyclad?' she demanded loudly. 'If it's . . . What's that?'

Luke didn't answer, instead his breathing slowed even more and he lifted his face to the sun.

'It's Mummy!' shouted Jasmine. 'I can see Mummy! She's trying to put the ironing board up. Look, there's Grandma by the stairs. Hello, Grandma!' For a brief moment it seemed to the little girl that her grandmother could see her as well because she turned her head towards the front door and her mouth opened as though she was going to speak.

'*Idiot*!' shouted Luke, opening his eyes and turning on Jasmine. 'You mustn't ever speak to people when you're a traveller. It's dangerous.'

'Why?' Jasmine was frightened by his anger, but Luke quickly regained his self-control and the fury faded from his eyes.

'It doesn't matter. I forgot that you didn't know any of the rules. It is fun, isn't it? I can travel around whenever I like, but I don't do it much; it takes a lot of energy.'

He'd turned very pale and there were dark circles under his eyes. However, Jasmine was too young to notice and began skipping around him, chattering with excitement. 'Is it really magic, Luke? Can anyone learn it? Who taught you?'

Luke caught hold of her hand and pulled her down beside him. 'You mustn't tell *anyone* what we did. If you do I'll never speak to you again.'

'I wasn't going to!'

'And your hair will fall out and you'll get big spots all over your face.' he continued menacingly. 'You won't be a pretty girl any more, you'll be ugly and no one will like you.'

'I won't tell!' Jasmine was very indignant. 'I promise I won't tell. How's it done, Luke?'

'You have to practise a lot, for years and years, and even then not everyone can do it.'

'But you're only four. You haven't been here for years and years.'

'I'm different.'

'Why?'

'Do you believe in God?' he asked.

She suspected that he'd laugh at her if she told him the truth. 'No. But I believe in Jesus,' she added, hoping that God wouldn't be too annoyed as long as she mentioned Jesus.

'You should believe in God. If you don't you won't believe in our magic.'

'Is your magic from God?' Jasmine was totally bewildered. 'I didn't know he could do things like that! I thought you just prayed to him.'

41

'Do you know what evil means?' he asked quietly.

'It's badness. Murder is evil.'

Luke clutched his bear very tightly by the arm. 'That's right; murder is evil. Have you ever done anything evil?'

'No!'

'Well, you can't play with Penelope until you have,' he announced dramatically.

A gentle breeze moved the branches of the sycamore trees surrounding the churchyard and the leaves rustled. The sound seemed to Jasmine like a soft murmur of approval. 'I can't,' she whispered, her eyes wide with shock.

'Poor Penelope,' said Luke sadly. 'Now she'll be lonely for ever and ever. Long after we're grown up she'll still be here, crying for her parents and trying to find her way home. And all because you wouldn't help her. My bear thinks you're mean.'

'Don't!' Jasmine clapped her hands over her ears and stamped her foot. 'I don't believe you!' she shouted. 'Penelope's not lost. She's in heaven.'

'She is not. You've seen her. She isn't anywhere. She's a lost soul. Like people who drown at sea. They're lost souls. They have to search all over the land looking for their family.'

'I've never seen a dead sailor.'

'They come back as seagulls. That's why seagulls make such a sad noise.'

Jasmine had heard enough. She ran over to her pile of clothes and began pulling them on. She didn't want to cry in front of him but if she didn't get back to the cottage quickly she knew that she would. It had been a horrid morning, and she didn't care if she never saw Luke again. All she wanted was her mother and a nice, comforting hug. She was running full tilt between the headstones when a large shape loomed up in front of her and she gave a scream of terror, pushing frantically at the figure blocking her way.

'My goodness, what a noise!' It was a very reassuring voice; calm, masculine and not in the least mocking. Jasmine risked a quick glance up and found herself looking at a young, fair-haired man with cheerful blue eyes and a sprinkling of freckles across his nose. 'Did I frighten you?'

Jasmine swallowed hard and looked back to where Luke

was slowly getting to his feet. 'Yes, I thought you were a spirit.'

'Coming back to haunt you? No wonder you screamed. Has young Luke been frightening you with his stories?'

'Not really.'

'I don't think I've seen you before,' added the man. 'Luke, aren't you going to introduce us?'

'She's Jasmine from the cottage,' said Luke proudly. 'She's my best friend.'

'Is Luke *your* best friend, Jasmine?'

'Sometimes,' she muttered.

'Well, I think you should run home to your mother. It's nearly lunchtime.'

'If I left some of my lunch, would I be evil?' asked Jasmine hopefully.

The man glanced thoughtfully at Luke. 'I think not,' he replied carefully.

'Well, that's the baddest thing I can think of.'

'Dear me, for a potential convert you seem to lack imagination!' he said with a laugh.

Jasmine frowned. 'What's a . . . what you said?'

'Never mind. Run along to lunch. Luke, I promised your grandmother I'd take you to have your hair cut.'

'My bear says I'm not to have it cut,' said Luke firmly.

'Your grandmother doesn't agree, I'm afraid.'

Jasmine looked from the man to the boy and back to the man. She had the feeling that although the man was older he wasn't going to win the argument and, as he walked towards the little boy, she noticed that his hands were trembling. 'Come on, old chap. Don't be difficult.'

'I'm not to have my hair cut in the shop.'

'Well, you can't have it cut on the village green!'

Jasmine giggled, but quickly covered her mouth at the look in Luke's eyes. 'I'm going home,' she called, 'and I don't want to play here this afternoon!'

Luke watched her run off. She wasn't proving quite as easy as his bear had said, but there was plenty of time. The bear had an astonishing amount of patience.

Chapter 4

'Andrew and Maggie have spent the past two years convert-
ing their house,' explained Owen, driving rapidly along the
winding road to Dayton. 'This is a "thank heavens we've
finished" party.'

'Do you work with Andrew?'

'Not exactly. I'm his accountant – he's a freelance architect
– and in return he casts his professional eye over any
properties that interest me.'

'What kind of properties?'

'Mostly old terraced houses. They're a kind of hobby for
me. With the aim of ultimately making money, of course. It's
a good vendor's market round here at the moment. Prices are
going through the roof.'

'That can't please the local people.'

'No, it's the wealthy commuters who are snapping up the
houses now.'

'Which probably explains a lot,' murmured Kathryn as they
arrived at what was obviously a massive barn conversion set
on the side of a slope.

'It will be a bit chaotic,' Owen warned, taking her by the
hand. 'Most of the people here grew up together. Their
conversation's usually loud and continuous.'

Kathryn was glad he'd warned her as the sound of laughter
and excited exchanges hit her the moment they walked
through the front door. She wasn't normally a shy person but
found herself moving closer to Owen's side. All around her,
young men and women were locked in animated conversation
and none of them spared her a second glance. One or two

greeted Owen briefly, but he had no chance to introduce her and suddenly she understood why he hadn't wanted to come alone.

'Do you know everyone here?' she asked.

'I imagine so, but not intimately. To be honest, most of them were more Tara's friends than mine. Would you like a drink?' Before she could answer, a slim fair-haired man disengaged himself from a nearby group and came towards them smiling politely but with no warmth.

'Owen, great to see you again! How's the exciting world of accountancy?'

'Can't grumble. The house looks marvellous.'

'Bit too open-plan for my taste but Maggie loves it. No doors for anyone to slam! Have you had a drink?'

'Not yet. Andrew, this is Kathryn Talkes. She's staying in the village for a few weeks looking after her mother.'

Andrew looked penetratingly at Kathryn. 'Are you from around here?'

'I'm afraid not; I'm one of the despised southerners!'

'Oh, well, we won't hold it against you. Have a good time,' he added casually and within seconds he was immersed in his group again.

'I feel that I'm lacking the necessary sparkle!' commented Kathryn ruefully.

Owen smiled. 'I like you the way you are. I think – '

'Darling!' A small, kittenish blonde suddenly rushed across the room and flung her arms round Owen's neck. 'How *lovely* to see you. We were wondering if you'd come, well, hoping you'd come, naturally. I meant to write after Tara . . . But it was just so terrible I couldn't think what to say. Are you coping all right? Silly question, of course you're not! But are you getting over it at all?'

Owen shifted around awkwardly. 'I'm not too bad, Chrissie. This is Kathryn, she's staying in the village at the moment.'

The blonde's light-blue eyes widened. 'How rude of me! I didn't realise you were together. That's wonderful. He's an absolute sweetie, Kathryn, but I'm sure you know that already!'

'We only met a few days ago.' Kathryn smiled.

45

'Really! I didn't realise you were such a fast worker, Owen. Only joking! And how's your little boy? He was so lucky, wasn't he? You could easily have lost him as well!'

'He's OK. Come on, Kathryn, let's find that drink. See you around, Chrissie!' He took Kathryn firmly by the arm and steered her into the next room, leaving Chrissie staring after them. 'Sorry about that. She's a very overwhelming person, is Chrissie.'

'At least she spoke to us!'

'I rather think no one's sure what to say. This is the first time I've seen most of them since my wife died. I knew it would be difficult'

'I suppose so,' said Kathryn doubtfully, 'but saying "hello" isn't difficult. We could have been invisible to most of them.'

Owen looked uncertain and his hand was clenched too tightly around his glass. 'It's always possible that I'm not too popular alone. Tara was their kind of person, very vivacious and extrovert. I'm rather an introverted plodder by their standards.'

Kathryn felt sorry for him. He looked puzzled and slightly hurt, like a child whose friends had turned against him.

'Are they important?' she asked softly.

He looked surprised by the question.

'How highly do you value their friendship? Is it important to you?'

He shook his head. 'Not really, but they're a part of my life. I'm used to them and I hadn't expected . . . I suppose I thought things would be the same.'

'I know divorce isn't like death, but once I was on my own my friends vanished. They only remembered me when they wanted help with their children's parties and that's hardly the peak of any adult's social aspirations.'

Owen relaxed slightly and smiled. 'I knew it happened to women. Being a closet chauvinist I imagined it was different for men.'

'Apparently not.'

Owen put an arm round her shoulders. 'Perhaps we should leave? There doesn't seem much point in hanging about for long.'

'Andrew said you were here!' exclaimed a tall, well-built brunette. 'How are you, Owen?'

46

'I'm fine, Maggie. We were just saying – '

'I've still got some of Tara's things,' interrupted Maggie. 'Mostly books and papers. Did you want them back?'

Kathryn felt his fingers tighten on her shoulder. 'Not particularly. I'm sure she'd have liked you to keep them.'

Maggie gave a brittle, unamused laugh. 'I'm sure she would, too, especially since you've replaced her so quickly.'

'Kathryn's just a friend,' he said flatly.

'A friend who's special enough to be shown off here tonight? I suppose you don't realise what it's like for those of us who were her friends? How can you? Still, you never really belonged, did you? You just trailed around behind her.'

Kathryn realised that the other woman was nearly in tears. 'If you'd excuse me,' she murmured, but Owen wouldn't let her go.

'We're leaving, he said firmly, and turned his back on Maggie before she could speak again. They pushed their way past entwined couples until they were finally out in the fresh air.

'Sorry about Maggie. She was Tara's closest friend.'

'That's all right. Perhaps I shouldn't have come.'

'Tara's been dead six months,' said Owen, opening the car door for Kathryn. 'I can't live like a monk for the rest of my life.'

They didn't speak again until just before South Willoughby, when he swung the car into a tree-lined lay-by. 'Let's forget them,' he said softly. 'I can think of much pleasanter things to do than worry about what Maggie has to say.'

Once he began kissing her, Kathryn quickly forgot everything and concentrated on the sensual feel of his lips on hers. He kissed her with surprising passion and great skill so that when he finally drew away her body ached for him.

'We'd better get back,' he said reluctantly. 'There's always tomorrow.'

'I'm afraid I upset Maggie,' she said apologetically.

'That wasn't your fault. You were a great support. Here we are, safely home already. I'd suggest a drink but somehow . . .' He looked troubled. 'After the party, I'm not quite in the mood. I'll be in touch tomorrow.'

Kathryn was disappointed but the party had troubled her too and she could understand his feelings. She kissed him on the cheek and slid out of the car, well aware that his eyes were on her until she shut the front door behind her.

Owen's mother quickly collected her handbag and cardigan.

'Everything all right?' asked Kathryn.

'Fine, dear. Your mother and I had a nice chat and Jasmine never made a sound. I checked her room once and she was fast asleep. You're early. Didn't you enjoy the party?'

'No one was very friendly.'

'What a shame. Of course, they all knew Tara well.'

'So Owen said.'

'Have a nice sleep, dear,' urged Owen's mother as she left. 'You mustn't get overtired, you know.' Considering the pace of life in the village, that didn't seem very likely to a wide-awake Kathryn.

To her delight, early the next morning Owen arrived and suggested a trip out. 'I thought the children might enjoy Rutland Water,' he commented. 'Your mother could come too.'

Within an hour they were ready, although Kathryn thought Luke was rather withdrawn.

'What's up with Luke?' she asked as they drove out of the village.

'He's sulking because I wouldn't let him go to church this morning. It's a new obsession with him. I wouldn't mind if he behaved, but he doesn't. He's uncontrollable once the service gets under way.'

'I am not,' shouted Luke from the back of the car. 'I can't help it if the vicar makes my bear laugh.'

'That damned bear!' muttered Owen beneath his breath.

'What's Rutland Water like?' asked Kathryn, anxious to change the subject.

'It's one of the biggest man-made lakes in the country.'

'Can you swim there?'

'No,' said Owen regretfully, 'but you can windsurf, and there's a boat trip round the perimeter if you like that kind of thing.'

It was certainly well worth a visit, thought Kathryn when

they finally left her mother in the car overlooking the water and the children ran off across the grass. The lake stretched as far as the eye could see, and there was even a hut where you could hire bikes for sightseeing. Owen took her hand and together they walked silently through the dry, discolouring grass, watching as their children chattered happily together.

'What do you mean?' asked a confused Jasmine when Luke finally stopped talking to her.

'Do you want to come and raise Penelope?' he asked in exasperation.

'Raise her where?'

'From the dead! That's what you want, isn't it?'

'I just want to make her happy again.'

'Then you've got to come to the Esbat.'

'I don't know what an Esbat is.'

'It's a business meeting.'

'Who else will be there?'

'Only us,' said Luke, his eyes dancing with excitement. 'I'm going to do this myself. My bear will help too.'

'Why can't we do it in the day?'

'Because you have to have it at midnight.'

'I can't stay awake until midnight.'

'I'll come and wake you. It will be great!' he enthused.

'What will?' asked Owen, walking towards them.

'Having a Kentucky on our way home.'

'That was meant to be a secret!' laughing, Owen rejoined Kathryn on a nearby bench.

'*Are* we having a Kentucky?' asked Jasmine.

'That's not important! Listen, you've got to say some special words tonight. Do you want to practise them now?'

'I suppose so.'

Luke clutched his bear to his chest and bent his head close to Jasmine's. 'Say, "I deny my baptism".'

'What's my baptism?'

'Just say it!'

'This is boring. OK. I deny my . . . What's the word?'

'Baptism!' he shouted, and suddenly a large crow flew straight towards them, its beak wide open. Jasmine screamed

49

and got to her feet but Luke pulled her down again. 'Say it, Jasmine. Quickly!'

She looked nervously about her. 'I deny my baptism.'

'Right, and "I deny my former worship to God".'

Jasmine frowned. 'Is it all right to say that? Won't God mind?'

'It's only magic!'

'I deny my former – '

'Hello, little girl!' said a kindly voice. Startled, Jasmine looked up at a man with a smiling face and a high white collar. He put a hand lightly on her dark curls. 'What are you and young Luke getting up to, I wonder?'

'Do you know Luke?' asked Jasmine in surprise.

'I certainly do. I'm the vicar of South Willoughby, you see.'

'We're just playing pretend,' said Luke casually.

'Then you won't mind if I join you for a little while. It makes a nice change for me to – '

'My bear wants you to go away,' said Luke abruptly. 'He doesn't want you here.'

Jasmine glanced at her mother, hoping she hadn't heard Luke. 'We're just playing magic, Mr Vicar, that's all,' she said nervously.

'Magic?' He looked sharply at Luke. 'What kind of magic?'

Luke shrugged, turning his back on them both. He tucked his bear under his arm and stared out across the water, making a whistling noise through his teeth.

'Magic can be dangerous, you know,' continued the vicar to Jasmine. 'I don't mean the kind you see on television, where a lady gets sawn in half, but there are other sorts of magic that God doesn't approve of.'

'Luke said God doesn't mind this sort. He said it would be all right to say that I . . . What did I have to say, Luke?'

'Don't know.'

'It's a secret,' she said apologetically to the vicar. He put out a hand and pulled her to her feet.

'I think it's time you went back to your mother,' he said urgently, but before they could take a single step there was a low buzzing sound and suddenly Jasmine saw a dark shape in the air, a shape that was moving rapidly towards them, bringing the noise closer and closer. She frowned, dimly aware of her mother's frantic shout of 'Jasmine!' and the cries of other people as they began to run away from where she and the vicar stood.

Looking around for Luke, Jasmine saw that he hadn't moved. He was still sitting quietly on the grass making the whistling sound between his teeth. Before she could ask him what was happening, the shape reached her and she saw that it was a collection of living, moving insects whose wings were whirring in unison. Then she noticed the familiar yellow colour and understood what the buzzing sound really was. The vicar realised too and he began beating around his head, shouting for help as he tried to protect his face.

Jasmine continued to stare upwards in frozen horror, waiting in terror for them to start settling on her as well as the vicar, but amazingly they didn't seem interested in the little girl, only in the hapless vicar who was screaming and trying to outrun them, flapping his arms in wild desperation as he lurched across the grass.

His face, neck and upper arms were now totally covered by angry bees and Jasmine could see that large areas of skin were raised in huge blotches that ran one into the other, and still the bees attacked him; more and more of them were coming out of the sky, and all apparently intent on attacking the vicar.

'Get to the water!' shouted Owen above the general confusion. 'Throw yourself in the lake, hurry!' Sobbing, the vicar stumbled on, while Jasmine remained where she was and watched him go, aware that by some miracle she'd escaped them all.

The vicar reached the water's edge, but then his strength seemed to fail him and he toppled face down into the damp mud, allowing the bees to descend on his unprotected back where they remained until his legs ceased to twitch. Then, as though at some invisible signal, the bees gathered themselves together and flew away across the water, flying high into the sky until it was no longer possible to see them. Then, and only then, did Owen start running towards the fallen man while Kathryn rushed across to Jasmine and took her in her arms.

'Jasmine! Jasmine, darling, you were so sensible! I was afraid you'd panic but you did absolutely the right thing. You were wonderfully brave! I thought . . . But you're safe, that's all that matters now.'

51

'What happened?' asked Jasmine in confusion. 'Where did the bees come from? And where have they gone?'

'They were probably looking for a place to nest.'

'My bear thinks they must have been looking for a house of God,' remarked Luke, standing up and brushing grass from his legs. Kathryn stared at him.

'Is the vicar all right, Mummy?' asked Jasmine anxiously.

Kathryn looked towards the immobile figure at the edge of the lake and saw Owen shake his head. 'I'm not sure, darling. I think I should get you two back to the car. Owen will join us when he can.'

Luke twisted away from Kathryn's outstretched hand and ran to the water's edge. Owen looked up at him and then back at the vicar's body, but he made no attempt to conceal the dead man from his son. Luke surveyed the blotched and still swelling skin, and saw the purple lips and twisted features. 'He panicked,' said the child quietly. 'If he hadn't panicked they might not have killed him.'

'I rather think his heart gave out.'

'I expect he's safe with Jesus now,' said Luke after a pause. Owen raised his eyebrows but kept silent. 'He should be, Daddy. Vicars probably go straight to Jesus.'

'I hope that's some consolation to his wife.'

Luke chewed on his bottom lip and thought for a moment. 'Why didn't he take Mummy's funeral service?'

'He was busy that day.'

'My bear said the vicar didn't like Mummy.'

'Weren't you afraid?' asked Owen after a pause. 'Didn't the bees frighten you?'

'No. I knew I was safe because my bear takes care of me. He watches over me all the time, that's why I didn't worry.'

Owen nodded to himself and slowly stood up. People were beginning to cross the grass towards them and he knew that there was nothing more he could do. Death had its own ritual, he would only be in the way. 'Come along,' he told Luke. 'Take my hand; we'll join Kathryn and Jasmine. I expect they're ready to go home now.'

'Can we still have a Kentucky Fried Chicken?'

'I think Jasmine's earned it. She was very sensible.'

She's my friend,' called Luke, running ahead of his father.

'My bear wouldn't let anything bad happen to her either.'

Everyone was very quiet on the drive back. Once in Grantham they bought Kentucky Fried Chicken from a shop on the London Road before going to the Queen Elizabeth Park where they sat by the river to eat, although Kathryn's mother chose to stay in the car.

'I'm sure I've got an aunt living round here,' murmured Kathryn, licking the grease from her fingers and wishing she'd brought some Wet Wipes with her. 'I must ask Mother.'

'I'm surprised she hasn't mentioned it already,' commented Owen, busy throwing cold chips to uninterested ducks.

'Well, although it's her sister they're not very close. By all accounts Aunt Victoria's rather weird.'

'In what way?'

'I'm not sure. She never married, which was a black mark in my mother's book, and she had some rather strange friends. I suppose she's just eccentric.'

'Probably a non-conformist born ahead of her time. Luke, don't throw your carton in the water.'

'This is nice.' Kathryn smiled lifting her face to the sun. 'I could spend a whole day here, it's so peaceful.'

'Rutland Water's usually peaceful,' said Owen ruefully.

'I don't want to think about Rutland Water,' said Kathryn sharply. 'It was horrible. Don't you think we should have stayed and told them that we knew the vicar? It seemed wrong to walk off like we did.'

Owen looked slightly guilty. 'There was nothing anyone could do for him,' he pointed out. 'Besides, we might have been held up for hours. I was worried about leaving your mother alone in the car.'

'I could have stayed with her.'

'It's too late now.' Owen was getting irritated and Kathryn let it drop.

'I still can't believe that Jasmine and Luke escaped without even a sting, Owen. It was an absolute miracle.'

'It certainly was.' He looked uncomfortable at the thought. After a pause he turned and gazed down river, his attention obviously a long way away.

Kathryn glanced about them for the children and suddenly her eyes met Luke's. He was staring at her with quite startling intensity, his eyes narrowed, either with concentration or against the sun, and although his gaze was fixed on her she felt that he wasn't really seeing her but looking straight through her, as though trying to see into her mind. She felt a brief pain behind her eyelids followed by a fleeting image of faces round a table; laughing faces whose mouths were stretched wide in mocking smiles. The faces grew larger and larger before tilting at strange angles like a scene from the Mad Hatter's tea party and she was overcome by panic. The disembodied faces pressed closer to her until she could feel their breath against her skin and she heard herself whimper with fright.

'Kathryn?'

With a tremendous effort of will, Kathryn wrenched her gaze away from Luke's and immediately the vision faded. She became aware that she was shaking and her head ached. She looked blankly at Owen. 'I'm sorry, I was miles away.'

'You certainly were! I only wondered if you'd like to come to dinner on Friday?'

She remembered the strange faces leering at her and hesitated. 'I don't know. What about Mother?'

'She won't mind! What's the matter? Don't you like my company?'

'Of course I do. I'm sorry, I feel most peculiar this afternoon. It must be delayed shock or something.'

'I'm not surprised. It was a terrible thing to see. I'll get you back home. You'll feel better after a rest.' Slipping an arm through hers, he shouted for the children, who quickly ran ahead of them.

They made an attractive pair. Jasmine with her deeply tanned skin and dark hair; Luke, so fine-boned and striking with his intelligent eyes and strawberry-blond hair. Kathryn thought that she and Owen had both been fortunate. Their children looked nice and behaved well, which made her vague sense of unease about Luke all the more unreasonable.

Once in the car she turned to her mother. 'Doesn't Aunt Victoria live round here?'

'Yes. Can we go back now? I'm tired.'

'We're on our way. Do you have her address?' persisted Kathryn wondering why she suddenly needed to know.

'Of course I do; she is my sister!'

'I know, but you've never had much contact with her.'

'Only because your father didn't like her. He thought she was unbalanced.'

'And is she?' asked Kathryn.

'No! Why don't you look her up while you're here? In some ways you're alike.'

'Perhaps I should come and see her too!' Owen laughed.

For a moment his left hand rested on Kathryn's knee, and from the back of the car there came the sound of a sharply drawn breath.

'I'll wake you up later tonight,' whispered Luke as Jasmine climbed out of the car.

'I'm a bit scared;' Jasmine whispered back.

'There's no need. See you later.'

Owen walked Kathryn to her front door and kissed her on the cheek. 'I'll be in touch,' he promised, and she smiled.

Lost in her own thoughts she failed to notice Jasmine's unusual silence. She was simply grateful that her daughter went to bed so obediently and with the minimum of noise. Tired out by the day she went upstairs early herself, and by ten o'clock the entire household was asleep.

Chapter 5

At first Jasmine thought that the stones hitting her window were part of a dream, but then she remembered that she had to get up and leave her safe bed so that she and Luke could go and help Penelope. She pulled a jersey over her head and tugged on some jeans in place of her pyjama bottoms before creeping to the top of the stairs, making her way slowly to the front door. She'd forgotten that the bolt was too high for her to reach and had to move a chair from the table in order to let herself out, and all the time she could hear Luke urging her to hurry from the other side of the door.

'Come on!' he whispered. 'We've only got two hours.'

'That's a long time.'

'Not for what we've got to do.'

Nothing looked the same at night. Jasmine was frightened of the strange shapes made by the branches of the trees, and even of the tiny church itself, which looked larger and almost menacing in the pale moonlight. She caught her bare leg on the edge of a tombstone and gave a quickly muffled cry of alarm.

'Shut up!' hissed an infuriated Luke. 'Now, you've got to do everything I say tonight, or else it could be very dangerous.'

'Why?'

'It just could. I've got to make a magic circle for us to stand in. That keeps us safe when Penelope comes.'

'She won't hurt us, will she? I thought she wanted to have some friends.'

'She might not want to go back. Sometimes spirits get cross

56

when you try to send them back. I've brought some tape and candles, it won't take me long.' His voice was tight with nervous tension.

Jasmine watched as he laid the tape in a circle and placed four candles carefully round the outside. 'Points of the compass,' he explained briefly when she questioned him. Jasmine didn't know what the points of the compass were but didn't dare ask any more questions because Luke seemed so busy.

When the circle was to his satisfaction he grabbed Jasmine by the hand and pulled her inside. 'Now say the magic words,' he ordered.

'I can't remember them.'

He groaned aloud. '*Quick*! Say, "I deny my baptism. I deny my former worship to God and I cleave to thee, Satan." Go on, say it.'

Jasmine stared at him in horror. 'Satan's bad! What does cleave mean? I don't think my mummy would – '

'Never mind your stupid mother!' retorted Luke, his face pinched in the eerie silver light from the moon. 'Just say it and then we can get on. It doesn't mean anything,' he added unconvincingly.

'I want to go home.' Jasmine's teeth were chattering and all at once it wasn't an adventure, it wasn't fun and she didn't care if she never saw Penelope's spirit again. She wanted to be home in bed and she took a step out of the circle.

'No!' Luke's voice was tinged with fright. 'Stay here. Jasmine, just say the words. It's only a game to help the magic.'

'I don't like the game, I . . .'

'You'll die if you don't say it. I won't be able to save you. You'll be torn to pieces before you get home. They'll tear your throat out.' He was rapidly becoming hysterical and Jasmine began to cry. Her chest felt tight and it was hard to breathe. She'd never been so frightened. How she wished she'd stayed in Effingham and never seen Luke or the tiny church; never met his mother on their strange night-walks, and above all never let Luke persuade her to leave her bed when she'd known all along that it was wrong.

'You really will die!' His eyes were fearful as he put his face close to hers. 'Jasmine, please say it! I don't want you to die and I can't stop it all now. It's too late. Hurry! Hurry!'

Something cold and light seemed to brush across her face and she turned her head to see what it was. Suspended above her left shoulder there was a long, thin thread that was twisting and turning in the air, and she noticed that the thread had a tiny head, and a mouth that was opening and shutting to show sharp teeth that clicked together. She felt its breath on her face, felt the tip of the tongue beginning to probe her ear and tried frantically to pull herself free of Luke's hands.

'No! Jasmine, stay inside the circle. It can't hurt you inside the circle. Say the words and it will go. I promise.'

'I can't remember them!' she whimpered, her feet and hands colder than ever in her life before. Next to her, Luke gabbled the words, his own eyes wide with terror as he realised that she could get them both killed. Almost incoherent, Jasmine finally managed to repeat them after him, her voice wobbling dangerously as she tried to hold on to her self-control. Then, at the precise moment that she uttered the final word, the snakelike creature disappeared and suddenly she felt quite different. Her legs stopped shaking and warmth began to return to her feet. It was easier to breathe as well and in place of the all-consuming fear there was only excitement at what was to come and a sense of wellbeing. She felt calm, peaceful and, above all, protected.

'All right?' asked Luke quietly.

'I'm fine now. Where's Penelope?'

'I've got to concentrate on my magic a bit more. You stay here with me, OK?' Jasmine nodded and heard him muttering words that made no sense at all, but it didn't matter. Nothing mattered any more. She was doing what she wanted to do and it felt good.

Luke stopped speaking and all at once everything began to change. The headstones around them blurred, their outlines becoming less sharp, and the grass beneath their feet began to undulate, rippling as though dozens of moles were moving beneath the surface. Jasmine giggled because it looked strange. Then, straight ahead of them and directly above Penelope's grave, a wisp of fog appeared, hovered over the ground and then spiralled downwards like a worm burrowing into the earth.

58

Jasmine watched carefully, convinced that Penelope would come out of the spot where the fog had gone, but to her surprise she saw the little girl walking along the path from the main street. She came towards them in a slow, elegant glide, moving swiftly past her own tombstone until she was standing in front of the circle. 'Hello,' she said quietly. 'Have you come to play with me?'

'Yes,' said Jasmine eagerly, but Luke's hand stopped her from moving forward.

'We can't run around with you,' he explained politely. 'We can only stay to talk.'

'Why can't you run around?' She sounded so disappointed that Jasmine felt a surge of sympathy.

'I'd like to, Luke, We've played with her before.'

'Only in dream-time. This is different. If we play with her now, she could take us back when she goes.'

Penelope shook her head. I wouldn't do that. You're my friends. Come on, Jasmine. Come and play catch with me.'

There was a gleam in her eye that disturbed Jasmine, and she shook her head. 'Where do you go when you die?' she asked anxiously. 'Is it to Jesus?'

Penelope's face twisted in an expression of contempt but her voice was still low and pleasant. 'Not exactly.'

'I called you up because I want to know something,' said Luke abruptly. Penelope stared blankly at him, her waist-length fair hair fanning out round her face. 'I want to know what's going to happen to Jasmine's mother.'

Penelope smiled sweetly. 'I don't know.'

'Yes you do, and now I've called you here you've got to tell me.'

The spirit of the dead girl seemed to shimmer briefly and she moved right to the edge of the circle. 'I will, if you let me have Jasmine,' she murmured.

Luke glanced at Jasmine and gripped her hand even tighter. 'No, you can't have her. She's very special.'

'Then I shan't tell you,' retorted Penelope, and her expression became one of boredom as she drifted around the churchyard, her hands trailing over headstones as she studied the epitaphs. When she came to Tara Hughes' headstone she stopped and her top lip curled up in a snarl of dislike. 'Why

59

don't you ask her about Kathryn Talkes? I'm sure she'd tell you anything you wanted to know.'

'She doesn't want me to know. If you tell me, you'll be getting your own back.'

Penelope looked very different from her usual timid, weeping self tonight, thought Jasmine in surprise. She seemed quite confident and suddenly not at all the sort of person that Jasmine liked to play with. 'Why are you cross?' she asked her.

Penelope smiled. 'I'm not cross with you, Jasmine. I like you. Shall we go inside the church? I'd like to go indoors.'

'I can't come anywhere with you.'

'Then let me go,' said Penelope sulkily.

'I wanted to help you find your family.'

'They don't want me. I did go back once but they wouldn't take any notice. They called in a priest!' she added bitterly.

'I think you'd better go back now,' said Luke, glancing anxiously up at the moon.

'But I haven't told you anything yet!'

'I don't think you're going to. Anyway I wanted to see if I could raise you and I did. Now you can leave.'

'Let me show you something first,' said Penelope urgently, and she glanced back down the path to the village.

Jasmine followed the direction of her eyes and her mouth dropped open in astonishment as a man stepped briskly into the churchyard. A sturdy, dark-haired man with laughing eyes, his arms held wide open in a gesture of welcome. 'It's my daddy!' she shouted, and ran straight out of the circle towards him, pulling herself free of Luke in the excitement of the moment. Luke called out in horror, but Jasmine didn't hear. She was too busy running towards her father, her heart pounding with excitement.

It was only when she reached him that she realised something was wrong. Suddenly he stopped smiling, and his hair wasn't dark at all but a horrible muddy grey and his bright teeth were broken and stained. When he put his arms round her he felt bony and peculiar, not at all the way he used to feel. Shocked, she tried to pull away, but the arms were strong and felt like cords round her body. She stared up into the rapidly disintegrating face and began to scream, but she was utterly helpless as he carried her towards Penelope who was waiting by her own headstone, a smile of pure triumph on her face as she watched Jasmine screaming and struggling in the creature's arms.

Inside the circle, Luke watched in confusion. He didn't dare move but he couldn't just stand there and watch Jasmine disappear with Penelope. In his panic he screamed aloud for his mother, forgetting that she could no longer help him. At the sound of Tara's name both Penelope and the creature who held Jasmine hesitated and glanced around them, waiting, it seemed, for some sign that she'd heard and was able to respond, but when nothing happened they quickly moved closer together and the grass rippled once more as a small hole appeared by their feet.

'*Jasmine!*' screamed Luke. 'Jasmine, I'm sorry. I didn't mean . . .' but she knew that he couldn't help her. She felt the tug of some strange force pulling at her body, pulling her down, down to the terrible place where she now understood that Penelope lived.

'No!' cried Luke, stepping as near the edge of the circle as he dared. 'Give her back. I need her. I have to have Jasmine.'

Jasmine felt her head sagging against the creature's body and as Luke's cries grew fainter she gave up, surrendering herself to whatever lay ahead because she no longer had the strength to fight. It was at that moment, when both children had given up, that Owen ran down the path towards them, his eyes flashing with temper.

'What the hell do you two think you're doing? Are you both mad, sitting in a churchyard in the middle of the night screaming at the tops of your voices? I thought you'd have more sense, Jasmine,' he added, picking her up from the now solid ground where she'd fallen as the creatures fled. Her eyes like saucers, she stared at Luke's father unable to speak, her lips trembling with terror.

'Well?' he demanded furiously. 'I'm waiting for an explanation, Luke.'

Luke looked at his father in disbelief. 'How could you do that?'

'Do what?'

'You sent them away.'

'Sent who away? You're talking rubbish. And what are you doing with your grandmother's marking tape?'

'It was for a circle.'

Owen's face darkened as he picked up the four candles and crammed them in his pocket. 'I told you this sort of thing was dangerous. You look as though you've frightened Jasmine out of her wits. God only knows what Kathryn's going to say after this. She'll probably stop you two from playing with each other ever again, and serve you damned well right too.'

Jasmine clung to his blessedly substantial arm and began to sob with fright. 'Don't tell her,' she begged him. 'Please don't tell her.'

'How do you plan to get back indoors without waking her?'

'She left the door unbolted,' said Luke. 'There's no need for anyone else to know.'

'Do you really think I'm going to let you get away with this, Luke?'

Luke's shoulders lifted in a slight shrug. 'Don't know.'

'If I don't tell your mother,' he said to Jasmine, 'it's only because I'm so ashamed of my son's behaviour. Not because I'm trying to protect you. Is that understood?'

'Yes,' she whispered, wishing she was safely in bed.

'All right. Luke, go straight home, I'll see you in the morning. I'm just going to see Jasmine back to her bed.'

Luke nodded, gathered up his grandmother's white tape and hurried home, his mind in confusion.

At the door of her grandmother's cottage, Owen lowered Jasmine to the ground and rested a hand on her shoulder. 'Don't ever do anything like that again,' he said sternly. 'It's very dangerous.'

'What happened?' she asked tearfully. 'How did you get rid of them?'

'There was no one there, Jasmine. You frightened yourselves senseless. Everything you saw existed only in your imagination, right?'

'But . . .'

'You imagined it all,' he repeated firmly.

She nodded, but she didn't believe him, and somehow she didn't think he really believed that either.

*　　　*　　　*

Jasmine woke the next morning feeling tired and cross. She could remember Luke waking her in the night, and dimly recalled Owen bringing her home, but everything in between was a blur. She thought that she'd been frightened but didn't know why, and she couldn't recall seeing Penelope once. 'What a waste of time!' she muttered to herself, and feeling thoroughly out of sorts thumped her way downstairs.

'Do you have to make so much noise?' asked Kathryn with a laugh as she pushed the cereal bowl towards her daughter.

'I'm not noisy. Your ears hear too well.'

'That's original! Mother, do you want some more toast?'

'A roast? Why should I want a roast for breakfast?'

Jasmine groaned to herself and kicked her legs against the chair rung. She wished that her grandmother was more like she used to be. Once Grandma had been fun; now she was just a strange old woman who couldn't understand anything and never played with her at all. 'I wish she was better!' she muttered fiercely to herself.

'I said did you want more *toast*?' repeated Kathryn, patiently.

'Yes, please, and don't shout. I'm not deaf.'

Kathryn went into the kitchen and stared at the old and decidedly temperamental toaster. 'Please don't burn it all again,' she prayed under her breath, but in vain. She had to scrape both slices before they were fit for eating.

'This is burnt,' complained her mother. 'I hate burnt toast.'

'I'm sorry, it's the toaster. What on earth did you do with that new Morphy Richards you got last Christmas? And what's happened to your Zanussi automatic?'

'I never had an automatic. I used to do all my washing by hand.'

'Mother, that was years ago! When you moved here you had a brand-new toaster and a Zanussi automatic that was still under guarantee. What happened to them?'

'The old ways are best here,' she murmured.

'In that case don't complain about the toast. Jasmine, stop kicking your chair.'

I don't like Mummy, thought Jasmine in surprise. I don't like her at all. She glared at her mother, but Kathryn was busy writing a shopping list and didn't notice. 'We need rather a lot,' she commented. 'I think I'd better go into Grantham and try one of the supermarkets.'

Jasmine hated shopping and was just about to say that she didn't want to go when she felt something brush her sleeve. Before she could react, small fingers pressed against her mouth and with a suppressed squeal of fright she saw Luke materialising beside her. He was very faint but she could see his breath like smoke in the air and his penetrating stare was unmistakable. Swallowing hard, she glanced at her mother, who lifted her head for a moment, smiled at Jasmine and then went back to her shopping list. Jasmine blinked, but Luke was still there. Faint, but definitely Luke. 'Let's go with her,' he whispered. 'My bear wants to go to Grantham.'

'Well, I don't!' retorted Jasmine.

'You don't what?' asked Kathryn in surprise.

Jasmine went scarlet. 'Nothing, I was thinking aloud.'

'You sounded pretty definite about it!' Jasmine pouted and with a shrug Kathryn went back to the list.

'Ask her,' he instructed, his image beginning to fade. 'Ask her if we can go as well.'

'But . . .' Before she could say any more he'd gone, leaving her staring incredulously into space.

'If you go into Grantham, can Luke and me come?' she asked.

'I doubt if Luke will want to come, darling. Boys don't like shopping.'

'He does. He really wants to come.'

'How could you know that? Ask him by all means. Shall I help you in the bathroom, Mother?'

Her mother shook her head. 'I think I feel a little stronger this morning, Kathryn. I'll call if I need you.'

Kathryn looked at her mother carefully. 'You've certainly got a better colour. Perhaps you're on the mend.'

'Or round the bend!' giggled Jasmine, quickly pressing a hand over her mouth.

Kathryn gave her daughter a sharp look. 'Hurry up with your breakfast and then go and see if Luke wants to come. I'm leaving in thirty minutes so you haven't much time.'

'Yes, Mummy,' said Jasmine with exaggerated politeness, and her smile was so outrageously sweet that Kathryn felt like

64

giving her a smack. She was vaguely aware that her daughter's behaviour was deteriorating but she felt sorry for her for being uprooted and dragged off to live with a sick and rather difficult old woman. She was certain that once they got back home Jasmine would settle down again.

Jasmine walked slowly up Luke's front path. The house disturbed her. It was cold and unfriendly and she hated the brass door-knocker, a grotesque gargoyle's face with a protruding tongue. She shut her eyes as her fingers closed round it. Only when Mrs Hughes opened the door did she feel it was safe to look again.

'We can go,' she said breathlessly. 'I asked and we can.'

'Go where?' asked his grandmother.

'Shopping in Grantham. My mummy says Luke can come too.'

'Don't tell me *you* want to go shopping, Luke!'

'It wasn't me, it was my bear,' he called as he ran down the path and his grandmother watched him go with a worried expression on her face.

'Your bear can't like shopping!' said Jasmine, trying hard to keep up with him.

'No, but it wants to see your aunt.'

'What aunt?' asked Jasmine in astonishment. 'And how did you get into our house this morning?'

'Your aunt in Grantham, stupid. And I got into your house by magic. I showed you how to do it, remember?'

'What happened last night?' she demanded, catching hold of his arm. 'I can't remember anything.'

Luke gave her a strange look. 'What do you mean?'

'When we tried to raise Penelope. What happened?'

'Oh yes, I meant to say sorry,' he said casually. 'I didn't wake up, that's why I never called. It was probably a silly idea anyway.'

'But you did wake me! We went to the churchyard and . . .'

'You dreamt it, silly. We didn't go anywhere. I never left my bed.' He was looking at her as though she were quite mad and she felt totally confused.

'Your daddy took me home,' she persisted. 'I can remember that bit. He told me it was all in my imagination and . . .'

'If my daddy had caught us in the churchyard at night he'd

65

have gone mad! Come on, race you to the cottage.'

But Jasmine refused to run and inside she felt a small, hard lump of annoyance.

'Come along, Jasmine, hurry up! Luke's already in the car,' shouted Kathryn, tapping her foot irritably on the pavement. She was surprised by the baleful look her daughter gave her and hoped that if – as she planned – they were able to call in on her aunt it might get Jasmine out of her bad mood.

After a chaotic forty-five minutes in Morrisons superstore an exhausted Kathryn dumped the shopping thankfully in the boot and drove carefully out of the car park. 'How would you like to meet my aunt Victoria, Jasmine?'

In the back of the car, Luke and Jasmine exchanged a brief glance. Luke looked complacent, Jasmine surprised and slightly resentful.

'Well?'

'Is she very old?' asked Jasmine.

'She must be about seventy-five now. I hope she remembers who I am. I haven't seen her since I was ten.'

They found Kingsley Court without any problem and Kathryn looked at the modern flats in some surprise. It was difficult to imagine an elderly eccentric in such typically suburban surroundings. 'This is the one,' she announced, parking outside despite a notice to the contrary. 'I'll go and make sure she's there.'

The children watched her walk away from the car. 'Why do you want to meet her stupid old aunt?' asked Jasmine. 'I'd rather have stayed in the village and played.'

'My bear thinks she's special,' said Luke quietly.

Jasmine frowned. 'Why are you such a baby about your bear? You're always pretending it's real!'

'You don't understand,' said Luke angrily. 'It isn't pretend. Sometimes I wish it was,' he added wistfully, but Jasmine was already looking towards the ground-floor flat.

Both children watched as the door opened to reveal a tall, sturdily built woman with a lined face and white hair drawn back in an old-fashioned bun. She spoke to Kathryn for a few minutes and then looked in the direction of the car. Jasmine, bored and hoping for a drink, waved at her cheerfully but Luke stared ahead, clutching his bear until his knuckles turned white.

66

'Come on,' said Jasmine impatiently. 'Mummy's waving for us to go in.'

Suddenly reluctant, Luke followed slowly up the path.

'This is my daughter, Jasmine.' Kathryn smiled, pushing the children in to the house ahead of her. 'And this is her friend Luke. He lives near Mother, in South Willoughby.'

Her aunt looked at both children with surprisingly alert blue eyes and as she studied Luke she stopped smiling and her hand – poised to pat his head – was withdrawn. 'Hello, Jasmine,' she said warmly. 'How nice to meet you at last. You're not very like your mother, are you?'

'She's the image of Philip,' said Kathryn with a wry grin. 'Mind you, I like to think that she gets her placid temperament from me.'

'I expect they'd both like a drink. They can take it into the grounds. Unfortunately we haven't got gardens, but you can't have everything and as you get older it's reassuring to have people close by.'

Kathryn found all the rooms depressingly small and noticed that books filled every conceivable space. In the tiny kitchen she saw shelves of cookery books, none of which were known to her, and numerous reference books for herbal remedies going back years. 'You've got a copy of *A Modern Herbal*! My mother used to talk about that.'

'It's very useful.'

'Do you make your own medicines?'

'A few; not as many as I used to, of course. You have to be careful. It takes years and years of practice.'

'I'm sure it does. Jasmine, Luke, come and get your drinks.'

Luke studied his glass carefully for a moment. 'My bear wants to know what it is,' he said rudely.

Victoria looked calmly at him. 'Lemon barley water. I made it myself.'

He took a mouthful, pulled a face and spat it out over the cushion tiles. 'Ugh! That's disgusting. Don't drink it, Jasmine. My bear says it's poisonous.' To Kathryn's embarrassment he dashed the glass from her daughter's hand.

'Luke!'

He jumped nervously 'Yes?'

'That's very rude. Your father would be ashamed of you. Jasmine, help Luke wipe up that mess.'

Luke's cheeks were scarlet and he looked close to tears. 'I'm sorry,' he whispered. 'It was my bear.'

Kathryn's aunt studied the small boy carefully, her eyes lingering on the dark-brown bear tucked under his arm. She watched him look up at a beautifully stitched sampler that was balanced in a frame on the top of her Welsh dresser.

'*An it harm none, do what you will,*' he read aloud and frowned for a moment before moving his bear so that its face was by his ear. 'My bear says that's stupid. Who did it?'

'I did,' said the old woman, never taking her gaze off him.

'Is it stupid?' His eyes were suddenly confused.

'It's very wise,' she said gently. He looked at her and she saw the momentary anguish in his eyes but when he spoke again his voice was defiant.

'If you're so good at medicines, my bear wonders why you don't cure your bad breath?'

Kathryn gasped and Jasmine moved to her mother's side, but the old woman simply looked at Luke, and there was a strange kind of pity in her eyes.

Luke stared back until it became obvious that she wasn't going to look away. Once he realised that, he grew red in the face and started to race round the room, knocking against the table and chairs and crashing his arms against the row of copper saucepans suspended on one wall.

'Luke, stop it!' shouted Kathryn.

'This house smells!' he retorted, running round and round the circular table. 'It smells of spells! It smells of spells!' He was yelling now and going so fast that it made Kathryn dizzy to watch him. 'Chase me, Jasmine,' he called as he hurtled past her. 'Come on, play chase. *Whee!*' And with a shriek of triumph he cannoned against the dresser. All the plates and mugs shook, a small vase of freesias tilted and spilled, and finally, after a short pause, the embroidered sampler fell face down on the floor with a startlingly loud crash.

Suddenly it was very quiet. Luke stopped running and stared defiantly at the elderly woman; Jasmine sat down on a chair and gazed at the broken glass, and Kathryn wished that she'd never decided to come. 'Gone!' said Luke triumphantly, and then his entire body relaxed as the nervous energy drained out of him.

'I think you'd better go,' said Victoria quietly. 'He isn't happy here.'

'I'm so sorry,' said Kathryn in confusion. 'This really isn't like him. He's always very polite, otherwise I wouldn't have brought him. What must you think of us?' she added despairingly.

'You mustn't blame him; he's very disturbed,' replied her aunt. 'Perhaps you should mention it to his mother.'

'He has no mother. She died last year.'

'What was her name?'

'Tara Hughes.'

Luke suddenly stood up and walked past them towards the front door, his bear held loosely by one arm.

'I must see you again,' said Victoria urgently. 'Come alone next time and we'll have a long talk. There are things that I'm beginning to think you need to know.'

'Shall I bring Mother out with me next time? I'm sure she'd love to see you again.'

'That would be nice, Kathryn, but do be careful. There's something worrying about your aura. I feel . . . I can't explain it but the little boy's involved. Come as soon as you can. Perhaps when you're alone things will be clearer.'

'All right!' agreed Kathryn, remembering her aunt's reputation for eccentricity. 'Are you on the phone?'

'Yes. Now please don't leave it too long,' reiterated Victoria as she kissed her niece's cheek.

After her visitors had gone she sat staring out of the window for a long time, aware that her self-imposed retirement could be about to come to an end.

'That's the last time I take Luke anywhere without his father,' announced Kathryn furiously after they'd dropped the boy off at the Manor House. 'I've never been so embarrassed in my life. He behaved abominably!'

'I think he was showing off,' said Jasmine miserably.

'That's no excuse at all. I hope he doesn't behave like that when you're alone together.'

'He's nice,' protested Jasmine. 'He's my very best friend.'

'The sooner we go home the better. I'm beginning to think

there's something wrong with this village,' muttered Kathryn to herself. 'Nothing's gone right since we came here. Even Mother isn't herself.'

Jasmine kept silent. She liked the village but knew that now was not the time to say so.

'I gather Luke was a nuisance the other day,' remarked Owen as he opened the door to Kathryn the following Friday evening.

'He was rather. My aunt's very old and it was a bit too much for her. I suppose I shouldn't have taken the children, there wasn't anything for them to do there.'

'Naturally he blamed his bear! I think I made my feelings clear and it shouldn't happen again. I suppose there are bound to be some problems with him for a time. I've been lucky so far.'

'Has he always been strongly attached to the bear?'

'Good Lord, no! He was never interested in stuffed toys before Tara died, and even now it's only the bear. According to Dr Potter it's not only normal, it's a positively good thing. He called it a "transitional object". Something to help Luke learn to cope without his mother. A sort of mother substitute.'

'But surely he shouldn't be allowed to blame the bear for his bad behaviour?'

'It isn't a question of "allowing" him to use it; he does it automatically. That way he can distance himself from his own negative emotions that probably scare the hell out of him, poor chap.'

Kathryn sighed. 'I can see the sense of it but it seemed to me that Luke *believed* it was the bear being bad.'

'He probably did, but as long as we don't push him he'll sort himself out in time. If you don't mind me changing the subject, you look beautiful in that dress, blue suits you. In the last year or so, Tara was addicted to black; very gloomy. How about a drink before the others get here? You already know Andrew and Maggie from their party. Then there's Clive – a junior partner in our firm – and his wife Emily. He's a nice chap, should go a long way. My senior partner's coming as well, but without his wife because she's visiting their first grandchild.'

'What's his name?'

'Douglas Randolph; he's quite a bit older than the rest of us but I think you'll like him. Most people do.'

She wasn't sure she was going to like anyone if they weren't a great deal more friendly than at the party, and felt relieved when the first to arrive, Emily and Clive, both greeted her with warm smiles.

'Sorry we missed you at the party,' said Clive, his blue eyes twinkling in what seemed to be perpetual amusement. 'Poor Emily's asthma was dreadful that night and as nothing stops Andrew smoking we didn't dare come.'

'Are you feeling better now?' Kathryn asked the slender, fair-haired young woman in front of her.

Emily pulled a face. 'At the moment, yes, but I can't promise to last the whole evening. Andrew's cigars are the kiss of death to me!'

'How long have you been living here?'

'Only six months. I'm a southerner myself. Clive's local, and nothing on earth would drag him away from his roots, would it, Clive?'

'Not likely!' Let me get you girls some wine,' he added, strolling away into another room.

'Do you like it here?' asked Kathryn with interest.

'Not much. They're a very insular lot; I don't seem to have made even an acquaintance, never mind a friend. Clive's convinced my asthma's psychosomatic; it's much worse since we married. Actually it's probably the damp but I tell him it's the people!'

'I don't think I could live here,' said Kathryn emphatically. 'I was beginning to think it was my fault, but obviously they don't like any outsider.'

'I could understand it if it was just the villagers,' said Emily. 'What defeats me is that none of Clive's friends have made me welcome either. I feel I'm intruding on something, but the trouble is I don't know what.'

'Perhaps it takes them a long time to let their guard down.'

'How long? I reckon I'll be drawing my old-age pension before they accept that Clive's got a wife. Sometimes I think

71

he's sorry he married me himself. You should hear him apologising for my feeble health!'

When Andrew and Maggie arrived Kathryn noticed that Andrew's smile was no more genuine than the first time they met. Feeling uncomfortable, she glanced around her for some wine and her eye was caught by a tall, heavily built man in his late forties who was standing in the doorway watching her closely. His light-brown hair was curly, his face tanned by the sun, and his dark eyes were sharp and intelligent. He met her glance with calm interest and she found herself unable to look away.

'You're staring at my partner!' whispered Owen, guiding her across the room to meet the now smiling man. As she shook hands and murmured a greeting, Kathryn was taken aback by the unexpected warmth of his smile and his lingering handshake. She'd almost forgotten what it was to meet someone friendly.

'So you're the lovely Kathryn. I see that Owen didn't exaggerate when he was describing you.'

She felt faintly ridiculous, aware that while she was reasonably attractive she certainly wasn't outstanding. 'I think you're both being extraordinarily flattering', she said, laughing. 'All the beauty in our family has gone to my daughter.'

'And how old is she?'

'Four and three quarters.'

'In that case I'll confine my interest to the mother. Seriously, I've heard a lot about you. Owen's really cheered up since you arrived; it's a great relief to us all.'

'He seemed perfectly cheerful when I first met him.'

'On the surface, yes; but to those of us who'd known him before his wife died, he was obviously struggling. A terrible tragedy, Tara's death.'

Kathryn saw that Owen was busy talking to Maggie and decided to take a chance. 'How did she die?' she asked softly.

'Hasn't he told you? Too painful, I suppose.' For a moment his eyes lost their warmth. 'She burnt to death, you see. A terrible way to die.'

'How dreadful! Where did it happen?'

'She had a place of her own on the outskirts of the village, a converted cowshed really. She used to spend a lot of time

72

there cataloguing her nature work, that sort of thing. She was a very careless person at the best of times, and a heavy smoker. On this particular night she'd been drinking as well, which presumably made her even more careless, and she must have set light to her papers. The whole place went up in smoke. Gutted the building. It was a miracle anyone got out.'

'You mean she wasn't alone?'

'Unfortunately she'd taken little Luke with her.'

Kathryn stared at him, wondering why Owen had never mentioned that when discussing his son's emotional problems with the bear.

'How horrible! Was he hurt?'

'Not a mark on him. He was unconscious because of the smoke but that was all. It was amazing. Made all the papers. The doctors couldn't understand why he hadn't suffocated.'

'Poor Luke! I had no idea.'

'He's coped very well, or so Owen says. The villagers make quite a fuss of him, which probably helps. Mind you, he was always a self-sufficient child.'

'Was he very close to his mother?'

'Hard to say. "Was anyone close to Tara?" would be a more pertinent question. She was a strange girl. Very striking and lively but definitely strange. I take it you hadn't heard any of this before?'

'No, I just knew she'd died in an accident. Did *you* like her?'

He looked at her almost as though assessing her reaction before he spoke. 'Tara? Not a lot,' he said at last. 'She was fascinating but not particularly likeable. A rather destructive kind of person, in my opinion.'

'In what way destructive?'

'Who's destructive?' asked Owen, putting his arm round Kathryn's waist in a rare gesture of possession that surprised her.

'We were talking about children,' lied Douglas smoothly. 'I was saying that they can be very destructive to a relationship.'

'Luke certainly can! Come on, food's ready.'

To Kathryn's disappointment she wasn't sitting near Douglas Randolph at dinner. Instead she found herself next to Douglas' daughter, younger than all the other guests and

73

understandably somewhat silent. With an uncommunicative Andrew on her other side, Kathryn found that she'd eaten her main course – delicious poached salmon – long before anyone else, and she looked round the table.

'Eventually, of course, you come to the end,' Douglas was saying to a wide-eyed Emily. 'Once that happens you qualify for perpetual bliss, unless you're one of those worthy souls like Mother Theresa.'

'Where does she fit in?' asked Emily as Kathryn struggled to make sense of the conversation.

'She's reincarnated simply to help the human race. The Hindus have a word for people like that, it's bodhisattva.'

'I don't believe in reincarnation,' said Emily. 'I think the entire theory is based on a misconception.'

Douglas smiled. 'Indeed?'

'I believe that when people feel they've been here before they're really experiencing a kind of race memory. We probably all inherit memories from our ancestors but we're not aware of it until a certain set of circumstances triggers one off. Then – because we don't understand – we think that we must have been here before.'

'Perhaps you're not sufficiently sophisticated to accept the theory of reincarnation,' said Andrew.

Kathryn would have been offended but Emily merely laughed. 'Nonsense! It's been around for centuries. Why, some religions are based entirely on reincarnation and religion's primitive. It's a very basic desire to believe there's something more powerful than us looking after our needs. A kind of father figure even for the elderly!'

'You're not a religious person?'

'I went to your lovely little church last Sunday but I don't really believe.'

'A pity. However, we must accept that there are always a few people whose minds are closed.'

Kathryn noticed that Clive made no attempt to come to his wife's assistance but Owen looked uncomfortable. 'Some people choose to give up religion in their forties or fifties,' he pointed out to the still scowling Andrew. 'That's the result of an enquiring rather than a closed mind.'

'Are we all talking about the same religion?' asked Douglas

softly and as Owen's head jerked up, Kathryn noticed a fine sheen of perspiration on his top lip.

'Surely they're all founded on the same basic belief in a god of some kind or other,' she said lightly.

It was her first contribution to any conversation since they sat down and to her horror they all looked towards her, opened their mouths and began to laugh. Their faces became disembodied and enlarged, pressing in on her from all sides, just as she'd imagined them a few days earlier by the river, and Douglas' face grew huge and ugly, thrusting itself towards her. With a horrified exclamation she shut her eyes and clapped her hands over her ears. Immediately the laughter stopped.

When she opened her eyes again everyone was staring at her in astonishment. No one was smiling. No one even looked as though they'd been smiling. In fact, Emily's eyes were full of surprised pity and Kathryn swallowed nervously.

'Whatever's the matter, Kathryn?' asked Owen, his face concerned.

'I don't know. I suddenly felt . . . I'm terribly sorry, please excuse me,' muttered Kathryn as she hurried from the room. Without any hesitation, Owen followed her into the kitchen.

'What's wrong?' As he put his hands on her shoulders he could feel her shaking beneath his touch.

'Nothing.'

'Are you ill? Would you like to lie down for a few minutes? Please tell me what happened.'

She knew that he was worried and couldn't think how to explain her bizarre behaviour to him when she didn't understand it herself. 'I don't know!' she exclaimed. In her nervous confusion she started to cry. Owen rested his chin in her hair as he held her against him. 'I'm really sorry,' she hiccuped. 'They didn't like me before this, now I've made it worse.'

'I'm sure you're imagining it,' he said unconvincingly. 'Besides, do they really matter? Surely we're the ones who count?'

'Yes, of course. Anyway, it wasn't anything anyone said. I just felt rather strange for a moment.'

'But you're all right now?'

Kathryn nodded and he smiled in relief. When they

returned to the dining-room the men had changed places and she sat next to Owen for the rest of the meal. When they went back to the drawing-room he stayed by her side and apart from Emily – who twice asked her if she felt quite well – no one mentioned the earlier part of the evening. Finally, at eleven o'clock the last car drove away, leaving Kathryn and Owen alone in the house.

'I'll pour us another brandy,' said Owen, closing the front door behind him with obvious relief. 'I'm so sorry about this evening,' he continued apologetically.

'I enjoyed it,' replied Kathryn, not altogether truthfully. 'If anyone should be apologising it's me. I ruined your dinner. I only wish I could explain what happened, but I can't.'

'Don't worry.' Owen smiled, but Kathryn thought that he looked tired and strained despite the smile. 'It got very hot in there,' he added.

'It was still unforgivable.'

'It doesn't worry me. In fact, I'm beginning to realise that I'm not too keen on my so-called friends any more. Douglas is all right, but then we work together; the others were all Tara's friends.'

'Where were you born?' asked Kathryn, sitting down in the green Parker-Knoll chair that she'd been eyeing enviously all evening.

'Here, of course. We lived in the house on the corner as you come in from Grantham.'

'The small grey cottage?'

'That's right.'

'And Tara?'

'She was from Cornwall. We met while I was on holiday in Polperro.'

'How strange!' exclaimed Kathryn. 'Since you're local and she wasn't, how come people round here preferred her company to yours? I thought even a Lincoln man was regarded as a foreigner!'

Owen looked uneasy. 'I can't really explain it,' he murmured. 'I suppose she fitted in better than I did. She had a village mentality.'

Kathryn laughed. 'What's a village mentality?'

'Well, she enjoyed local gossip, got involved in local

76

events, generally went out of her way to be part of the community.'

'I thought she spent a lot of her time wandering round the countryside alone. Surely that didn't endear her to the natives?'

'Apparently it did, and you'll just have to take my word for it.' He looked annoyed and she was surprised at how sharp his voice sounded.

'I'm sorry, Owen. I wasn't doubting you but it is odd.'

'Perhaps we should stop talking about Tara?' he suggested more quietly. 'I'd far rather talk about you.'

'We've talked about me before. I'd like to know more about you. When did you move in here, for example?'

Owen sighed and shifted uncomfortably in his chair. 'Just before we got married. Tara inherited a lot of money from her parents and used it to buy this house. I think she fancied being Mrs Hughes of the Manor House.'

'So it belonged to her?'

'Theoretically, yes.'

'Did she choose the trophies and weapons or did you inherit them along with the house?' she asked, remembering the snarling fox in the hall.

'She won the trophies in the dining-room when she was in Cornwall. They're mostly for rifle-shooting. The pistols and swords were an idea she got from some stately home we visited.'

'For someone who liked wildlife she had a strange obsession with death.'

'Why are we back to Tara again?' he asked irritably.

'Sorry. Tell me about your work. Do you enjoy it?'

'I suppose I do. It's quite interesting, especially now that more and more people are setting up their own business with redundancy money. I try to spot the high-fliers from the start but it isn't easy. I remember telling one chap that he'd be a fool to set up a haulage business at a time when whole fleets were going bankrupt. Fortunately he didn't listen, and now he could buy me out ten times over. I'm not quite that wrong very often!'

'What about these houses you buy up?'

'That's not really work, more a hobby, but there's a lot

77

of money to be made if you've got a steady nerve and a reasonable amount of spare cash. I enjoy it. It's the next best thing to gambling. I haven't the nerve for big-time gambling and there's no point in having a flutter with the odd fiver. This is my substitute.'

'Doesn't it take up a lot of time?'

'I've never been short of time.' He sounded as though the memory depressed him.

'I suppose you're busier now you've got to look after Luke?'

'Yes, although he's very little trouble.'

'But children take up such a lot of time. I'm forever feeling guilty over neglecting Jasmine. Somehow just the physical caring takes ages; you know, washing, feeding, cleaning. By the time I've done all that I haven't much energy left for the necessary emotional output. I'm sure it must be worse for a man.'

'What kind of emotional output?'

'Mainly listening to them. Taking an interest in what they're doing, giving them plenty of time to talk.'

'Luke isn't a great one for talking.'

'So he does take after you a little bit!'

'Not really,' he said curtly. 'He's all Tara's.'

'Genetically he's fifty per cent yours. That's a sobering thought, isn't it? Jasmine takes after Philip's side of the family and I'm always blaming them when she's difficult. I have to remind myself about that fifty per cent quite often!'

'I didn't expect it to be like this,' said Owen softly.

'What?'

'I hadn't realised how much everything would change after Tara died. I suppose I expected life to go on the same; they always say it does, don't they? But it isn't the same at all. It's rather sobering to realise that she was the one everyone liked, especially since . . .'

'Yes?'

He sighed. 'Well, she could be difficult. She was very extrovert – which carried me along with her – and attractive in a slightly eccentric way, but so volatile. I never knew where I was with her, and neither did her friends. Apparently that didn't matter to them.'

'I'm sure it isn't as bad as you think,' said Kathryn sympathetically. 'Probably they all feel a bit awkward. Most people don't know how to face friends who've lost their partners. I'm sure they're not rejecting you; it's the situation they find difficult.'

'I think not.'

'Perhaps you should consider moving away,' she suggested.

Owen shook his head. 'Out of the question.'

'Why? Luke hasn't started school yet, your work isn't local, a move now would be the sensible thing to do. Make a fresh start.'

'It wouldn't be fair on Luke.'

'But . . .'

'He knows everyone here, and they make a fuss of him. He's looking forward to going to school, and most important of all, his mother's buried in the churchyard. He needs to be near her right now.'

'Talking of being near people, I must go. Your poor mother will be asleep in her chair and I shouldn't leave Jasmine any longer.'

'I'll walk you back.'

'Jasmine thinks there are ghosts in the graveyard!' said Kathryn with a laugh as they passed the small church.

'That's Luke's fault. He's always on about spirits and ghosts. You know, Kathryn, I'm very glad you came here. You've made a tremendous difference to my life.'

'You've made quite a difference to mine!' she confessed 'Until I met you I never seemed to speak to another adult. I shall miss you when we go back.'

'You're not going yet, are you?'

'Not for another two or three weeks.'

'Good. Well, I'll say good night. Tell my mother I'm waiting out here, will you?'

'Of course. Good night, Owen, and thank you for dinner.'

He bent to kiss her lightly on the cheek and then changed his mind. Suddenly his arms went tightly round her and he was kissing her passionately. Once again she was shaken by the intensity of his emotion and automatically resisted for a moment before giving in and kissing him back with equal fervour. When they drew apart she gave a nervous laugh. 'I hope no one was looking out of the cottage window!'

He smiled. 'Does it matter?'

'I suppose not,' she murmured, but she still felt uneasy until she was safely inside.

Chapter 6

'. . . as bold as brass outside the cottage! My mother said, it isn't what we're used to here. Still, that's what you get when people come in from . . . Yes? Can I help you?'

Kathryn looked at the young woman behind the chemist counter and felt herself blushing. The three women she'd been talking to moved to one side, their eyes fixed on Kathryn, and she fumbled with her purse. 'A bottle of paracetamol, please.'

'Large or small?'

'How many do I get?'

'Twelve in a small, fifty in a large. Good morning, Mrs Mitchell. Lovely day again!'

'I'll have a large,' mumbled Kathryn.

'Small, did you say?'

One of the women giggled and Kathryn lifted her chin in annoyance. 'I said a large, please.'

'Sorry! That's one pound.'

Kathryn had only a ten-pound note. The assistant looked at it with suspicion and then disappeared into the back of the shop where she could be seen showing it to the pharmacist, who held it up to the light, examined it from various angles and then reluctantly nodded. In total silence, Kathryn took her bottle of painkillers and her change and then walked as briskly as possible out of the shop, hearing the wave of laughter beginning as she closed the door behind her.

Feeling both embarrassed and angry, she didn't look where she was going and promptly collided with another woman. Busy apologising, she suddenly realised that she knew the young woman, who looked equally surprised to see Kathryn.

'I'm sorry, I didn't look where I was going,' she confessed. 'It's Chrissie, isn't it? We met last weekend at a party. I was with – '

'Owen. Yes, I remember you. I thought you'd be gone by now.'

'Not yet!' Kathryn smiled. 'My mother still needs help and . . .'

'I thought you must be here to help Owen. We were amazed to see him at the party. He hasn't been anywhere since the accident. Have a safe journey home, when you do go, that is,' she concluded frostily and then walked away, leaving Kathryn glaring after her.

'I've never met such unfriendly people!' she exploded as she put the paracetamol down on the kitchen table. 'I don't know how you can live here, Mother.'

'They've always been pleasant enough to me, dear.'

'I'll certainly never consider retiring to a quiet village after meeting the inhabitants of this one! Where's Jasmine?'

'Out with Luke.'

'I was thinking of visiting Aunt Victoria this afternoon. Would you like to come with me?'

Nancy Laing shook her head. 'I don't think so, Kathryn. I still get very tired and easily upset. It's a long time since I saw my sister, I think I should wait until I'm feeling stronger. But you go, dear. It will do you good.'

'I wonder if Jasmine could stay at Luke's house while I'm there?'

'Don't you want to take her?'

'No,' said Kathryn thoughtfully. 'I rather think I should go alone.'

She arrived at her aunt's at two-thirty and found her waiting at the front door. 'Sorry I'm later than I said. The traffic was bad through the middle of the town.'

'That's all right. Come on in, I've already made us some tea. It should be ready to pour by now.'

'This is gorgeous,' said Kathryn as she drained her cup.

'It's a blend that I mix myself. There's camomile in it, very soothing, and lemon and one or two other things as well. My secret recipe!'

'Well, it's delicious. Mother sent her apologies but she really isn't up to any emotional meetings yet.'

'It certainly will be an emotional reunion. I haven't seen Nancy for years. Such a pity your father was so narrow-minded. He was the one who kept her away, you see. He thought I lived an unsuitable life!'

'In what way?'

'Just different from the way he liked to live; but that's how he was about everything. His way was right. No question of compromise.'

'I suppose not. He told me you were a witch! I was most impressed, picturing you in a big black hat with a cat for your familiar. If he'd known what a romantic picture I'd built up he'd have had a fit.'

Her aunt nodded. 'I suspected that was what he thought. In a way he was right, of course, but in other ways he was totally wrong. I was a witch, you see, a white witch. Not nearly as exciting as the kind you imagined, but still a follower of a religion he didn't understand. A religion very few people understand, I may say.'

'I didn't know it was a religion!' exclaimed Kathryn.

'Originally, it was. It's all based on nature, being at one with the earth.'

'That's coming back into fashion today, isn't it? I mean, there's a definite swing against sophisticated drugs and pro-cessed foods. To believe in natural remedies is definitely modern.'

'I suppose it is, but for a lot of people it's always been the best way. Of course I'm old now, and really I've lost touch with most of my colleagues. These days I don't do very much apart from making herbal brews for my rheumatism.'

'I wish you knew a spell to make people more friendly!' laughed Kathryn. 'It's quite unpleasant in the village. I know I'm only there for a few weeks but it wouldn't hurt them to be reasonably polite. I'm amazed anyone ever moves in from outside if they get the kind of treatment I'm receiving.'

'Perhaps they're afraid you *won't* leave,' suggested her aunt softly. 'Have you thought of that?'

'Not leave? That's ridiculous! As soon as Mother's stronger I shall be gone like a bat out of hell.'

'Well, perhaps it's just their way.'

'No,' admitted Kathryn reluctantly. 'I get the feeling it's me. I really don't think they like me, and yet they don't know enough about me to dislike.'

'Bring your cup into the front room,' suggested the old woman. 'I want to have a chat about the boy you brought with you last time.'

As they left the kitchen, Kathryn glanced up and saw that her aunt's sampler was once more hanging above the dresser, and that it was now in a new frame. 'What does that sampler mean?' she asked, sitting down by the front window.

'Just what it says. You must do what you think right as long as it doesn't hurt anyone else. It's a kind of creed for all people who believe in white magic.'

'Really? How fascinating.'

'There's more to it than that. Some more lines that I can't remember now. That's the most important part, and of course it's the complete opposite to the creed for black witches. *Do what thou wilt shall be the whole of the law.* That their basic philosophy. Such a terrible way to live. It's frightening when you think about it.'

'Are you saying that there really are people involved in black magic? Not just the kind where you dance round a fire and have . . .'

'An orgy? My dear, I may be old but I'm perfectly broad-minded and I do read the more sensational papers from time to time. The most dangerous thing about their silly articles is that they mislead people, detract from the true horror of black magic. Oh yes, I believe in devil worship, and I know that it's gaining popularity all the time, but at my age there's very little I can do but pray.'

Kathryn felt uncomfortable. 'I didn't realise how important all this was to you. I shouldn't have started talking about it but . . .'

'I'm glad you did, Kathryn, because it brings me rather neatly to what I wanted to talk about. The little boy – Luke, was it? – how much do you know about him?'

'Not a lot. I'm dreadfully sorry about the way he behaved here, but it wasn't at all in character. Normally he's a very quiet, well-behaved child. To be honest I'm not very keen on

84

him, but I don't know why because he's far more intelligent and sensible than most children his age. Perhaps that's it. Perhaps I find him too mature. He's got a very unsettling way of looking at adults.'

'He's a very troubled child.'

'That's not surprising. His mother was killed in a fire and he was there at the time. There seems to be general amazement that he even survived, so obviously it's affected him. Owen, that's his father, says that Luke's coping well but I'm not so sure. For one thing there's that bear of his. I know children use toys as a kind of mouthpiece, but I don't believe that's what Luke does. I think he believes the bear has a mind of its own. When he was here he was so obviously upset by what "the bear" was saying. As though it was in conflict with what he felt. That's positively schizophrenic and not at all the normal "transitional object" relationship that Owen mentioned.'

'That explains his aura,' murmured her aunt.

'What is an aura?'

'My dear Kathryn, it would take me hours to explain properly! Let's just say it's a person's energy field; a visible sign of one's life force. The colours vary from person to person according to character. Luke's is unusual for a child because it's a very strong shade of grey. Now grey's usually a sign of sadness, and obviously he's sad because he's lost his mother, but when it's as dark as his is it usually indicates fear. I wonder what he's afraid of. Death itself, possibly. And then he has quite a clear patch of jet-black smoke in his aura. That's normally an indication of great anger, and rare in a child so young.'

'You mean that by studying this aura you can tell that he's sad, afraid and angry, all at the same time?'

'Yes. It takes years of training and even then one can make mistakes, but not, I think, in the case of Luke. No, he's definitely frightened and angry, as well as understandably sad at his loss.'

'Poor Luke. Perhaps I should try and get to know him better. He must miss his mother terribly.'

'Kathryn, I wouldn't tell you this if it weren't for the fact that it was so very clear to me that I can't keep silent. His anger, his "black smoke" area, was at its strongest whenever he was near you. I had the distinct impression that most of it was directed against you. That you were the cause. When he was walking away from the house it faded rapidly but as you walked towards him it increased again. I'm afraid he feels strong antipathy towards you.'

Kathryn felt very hurt. 'But why?' she asked. 'I don't have that much to do with him and I've never been anything but friendly. I don't understand how you could be right.'

'Perhaps he's afraid that you're going to try and replace his mother?'

'He couldn't possibly think that! It's true that I know his father but it's only a casual holiday friendship. Luke knows we're going back south again.'

'Children sometimes see things differently from adults. It could be that he's worried you're going to take his father's love away. I don't know, dear. Perhaps it doesn't matter. What matters is that you're aware of how he feels.'

'What should I do about it?'

'Why, nothing. The reason I felt you should know is so that you're . . . prepared.'

'Prepared for what?'

'It's possible he might try and harm you.'

Kathryn couldn't stop herself from smiling. 'Now that's really ridiculous. He might resent me or, as you say, dislike me, but he's only a little boy and I honestly can't imagine him grappling with me physically, can you?'

'There are many ways of harming people, Kathryn.'

She was beginning to understand why her father had kept them away from Victoria. She was so convincing when she talked that it was easy to forget she'd always been strange. Dabbling in magic – black or white – wasn't really normal. Add to that the natural eccentricity of old age and you had quite a strong combination, she thought ruefully. A combination that had nearly convinced her that her aunt was right.

'I'll be careful,' she promised, but her amusement showed and the old woman gave an inward sigh, realising that she wasn't believed.

'What was his mother like?' she asked carefully.

'Very outgoing and friendly, or so it appears. Personally I

think she was a bit strange. Owen says she was keen on nature study and used to go wandering round the villages at night. She even had an old barn where she kept her things. Sounds very dubious to me. Probably she had a boyfriend. That seems more likely!'

'Possibly,' conceded her aunt, but she made a mental note to ask around her friends and see what, if anything, they knew about the late Tara Hughes.

'I ought to be going,' said Kathryn with a quick glance at her watch. 'I'll come again soon, I promise.'

'I'd like that. I know you didn't believe all the things I said, dear, but you will be careful, won't you? There's something not right about that boy and – '

'Don't worry, I'll make sure I'm never alone with him! Honestly, Aunty, I'll be fine. Look after yourself now,' and with a quick wave she was off, leaving the old woman standing alone on the doorstep, her eyes shadowed.

'I don't like my grandma any more,' complained Jasmine as she sat on the floor of Luke's tree house drinking a glass of the dandelion and burdock that Luke's grandmother had assured them was witches' brew.

'Why not?' asked Luke, busy drawing strange shapes on a sketch pad.

'Because she isn't the same now. She's cross and doesn't play with me.'

There was a short pause as Luke turned his head towards the stuffed bear that was sitting propped against the wall. 'My bear says you could use her for your evil deed,' he said slowly.

'How?' demanded Jasmine.

Luke shrugged. 'I don't know.'

'Doesn't your clever bear know either?' she challenged.

Luke bit on his bottom lip. 'He thinks you should kill her. Then you'd really belong to the club.'

'I couldn't kill her!' gasped Jasmine. 'I can't even kill spiders. I don't like feeling them go squishy.' The bear's eyes stared glassily at Luke, who began chewing his thumbnail. 'Your bear's stupid,' continued Jasmine. 'I think you should leave him in your bedroom all day.'

'I can't,' said Luke quickly.

'Why not? He isn't real, you know. It's all pretend.'

'It is not! He *does* talk to me. He tells me lots of things.'

'It's time you grew up!' jeered Jasmine, turning her back on her friend.

After a moment, Luke touched her on the shoulder. 'If you don't do your evil soon, you won't be allowed to come dream-walking with us.'

'How did *you* join?' she demanded. 'What was your evil deed?'

'I'm special. I didn't have to do anything.'

'That's not fair!'

'If you did manage to kill her, you'd be allowed a special present,' he whispered.

'Anything at all?'

'Yes.'

Her eyes shone. 'I'd want my daddy back.'

'Are you sure? You can't change your mind once you've chosen.'

'I'm quite sure.'

'Then you know what you have to do.'

Jasmine took a deep breath. 'Will your bear help me?' she asked nervously. Luke nodded. Suddenly Jasmine's nerve broke and she began to climb out of the tree house. 'I don't want talk about this any more!' she shouted. 'I want to go home to my mummy.'

Luke let her go without a word. His bear didn't seem worried, and the bear always knew best about everything.

Chapter 7

Owen had only been in the cottage ten minutes when Kathryn's mother decided to go to bed. 'I feel rather tired,' she explained, but in fact she was looking stronger every day and Kathryn knew she was trying to be tactful.

'Actually she's much better now,' she told Owen as he went into the kitchen to collect the tins of lager he'd brought with him. 'I don't think we'll have to stay much longer.'

'Won't you miss us?'

'Of course I'll miss *you*, but the rest of the villagers haven't exactly made me welcome.'

'I could always come down to visit you.'

'That would be nice.'

Owen hesitated. 'Kathryn, I really would like to see more of you. I enjoy your company and . . .'

Kathryn gave a small sigh. 'It's been wonderful but I have to be realistic. Once I get home I'll be working again; then, after Christmas, Jasmine starts school. That means I'll have to fit in school runs and PTA meetings, all the usual commitments that come with a five-year-old, only I haven't got anyone to share them with me. I'll be busy, Owen. It won't be like this any more.'

'I thought men were the unromantic ones!'

'Be honest,' she teased. 'If I'd moved here permanently you wouldn't have got involved with me.'

'Why ever not?'

'Most men avoid encumbered divorcees like the plague.'

'I'm not most men.'

Kathryn wished that he wasn't such a nice man. It made

going home far more difficult than she'd anticipated. 'I wasn't a good wife,' she confessed abruptly. 'I used to nag Philip when he didn't come up to my expectations. I couldn't accept that he simply wasn't the kind of man I wanted him to be, and I made things worse by constantly putting pressure on him. Philip needed his life to be easy and fun. I ended up such a kill-joy he could only be happy away from me.'

'It sounds as though he was thoroughly spoilt,' said Owen shortly.

Kathryn was anxious to be fair to her ex-husband. 'I think his mother did spoil him. She was Greek and they do make a fuss of their sons, but it wasn't only that. He was one of the Peter Pans of this world. I was attracted by his casual, carefree approach to life but once we were married I expected him to be different. It's a classic mistake.'

'Do you still miss him very badly?'

'I miss having someone to talk to in the evenings. I miss his laughter as well, but there are compensations.'

'Such as?'

'I can read all night if I like, and no one criticises my cooking!'

Owen refilled his glass and settled himself more comfortably in his chair. 'I feel guilty because I don't miss Tara more,' he said slowly. 'The trouble is, we weren't getting on and I honestly doubt if we'd have stayed together anyway.'

'I'm sorry.'

'We didn't quarrel a lot or throw things at each other, we just drifted apart. We were badly matched. She was so full of life. If you could have bottled Tara's energy and sold it you'd have made a fortune. I'm quite lazy when I'm not at work. Almost a slipper and pipe man.'

Kathryn wanted to know more but sensed that this was the first time he'd talked about his marriage in such detail and that to interrupt him now would be a mistake.

'We were in separate rooms before she died,' he continued. 'Perhaps she'd found someone else. I really don't know. Whatever the reason, she'd certainly lost interest in me.'

Kathryn thought that what he was saying was the truth, but not the whole truth. 'Did *you* have anyone else?' she asked.

Owen shook his head. 'Heavens, no! I'm far too lazy for all

the intrigue and emotional energy of an affair. I buried myself in my work and pretended everything was normal. After she died I continued to shut myself off from women, until you came along. You're so different from Tara. She was flamboyant and terribly in control, it was totally demoralising. You're very restful and you make me feel that I'm helping you. I like that.'

'You make me sound weak and feeble!'

'I didn't mean to. It's just that you're far more feminine than Tara. Does that sound better?' he asked with a smile.

'It's certainly more tactful!'

From upstairs there came the sound of Jasmine going to the bathroom and Owen looked at his watch. 'I'd better go,' he said reluctantly. 'It's nearly two o'clock.' He kissed her on the end of her nose. 'Look, it's Sunday tomorrow. Why don't we take a trip over to Lincoln? I'll show you some of the houses I'm renovating there. The children can come too.'

'That sounds nice. Call for us about eleven. I'm sure Mother can be left for a couple of hours now that she's stronger.'

The following day they all had lunch at the Castle Hotel in Lincoln and walked up Steep Hill to look at the cathedral before driving to the outskirts of the town where Owen had recently started to have a row of terraced houses refurbished. While he and Kathryn walked round the ground floor of one, the children went upstairs to explore.

In the small third bedroom, Luke suddenly went pale and stood still in the middle of the floor with his eyes shut.

'What is it?' asked Jasmine nervously.

'This is a good house,' he crooned, his voice high and light. 'I can tell that good things happened here.'

'Talk properly, Luke! What sort of things?'

'Someone was very miserable in this room.' His voice was still strange and he sounded extremely pleased.

'That's not a good thing!'

'It is for us. I really think,' he continued excitedly, 'that they died here. Yes, they definitely did.' His right arm dropped to his side and his bear swung to and fro above the dusty floorboards.

Jasmine shivered, wrapping her arms round her body. 'Let's go,' she pleaded. 'It might be haunted.'

'No, it isn't, but I can feel the sadness. Wait, I want to feel it some more.' There was so much nervous excitement in his voice that it was barely recognisable.

'You're lying,' Jasmine said fiercely. 'You're just trying to frighten me.'

'It isn't frightening at all. When people kill themselves they belong to us!' The bear swung faster and faster, one paw brushing against the floor with an insistent rustling sound.

'How do you know someone killed themself?'

'Because I can see them!' His whole body was trembling with delight. 'I can see their feet moving backwards and forwards in front of the window here, and I can see a face. It's a boy's face. He's got red hair and his tongue's hanging out of his mouth. It's all purple and his eyes are nearly popping out of their sockets. Do you want to see? I can let you if you like. Close your eyes, Jasmine. Quickly, close them now.'

The voice was no longer Luke's; it was a woman's, and shrill with emotion. The air had turned icy cold and although it had been light when they came in, the sun had suddenly vanished, leaving the room in shadow. Jasmine shook her head nervously. 'I don't think . . .'

'There you are!' exclaimed the voice. 'Now you can see him.'

And she could. He was only a foot away from her. She could see his grey and blue trainers with a panther motif on the side; could easily have reached out and touched his blue denims with their patched knees, and above her head a hand hung limp and white. With a whimper of fear she tried to back away, but Luke was behind her, holding her tightly by the shoulders and pushing her towards the gently swaying figure.

'Look at his face, Jasmine,' urged the voice. 'Look up; see what they look like when they lose all hope. That's what happened to him, you see. He stopped hoping, stopped believing, and gave us his soul. It seemed so easy to him then, because he didn't understand what would happen to him afterwards. He thought he'd go to heaven and be happy, but he couldn't because when you give up you're throwing God's present of life back at him, and he doesn't like it. That's why he lets us have suicides. That's why suicide is a sin.'

'Where is he now?' Jasmine was staring in horrified fascination at the body of the dead teenager.

'He's one of the lost ones, Jasmine. You remember the lost ones. We see them when we go dream-walking. They're the shapes that try to touch us, try and trick us so that we can't get back to our bodies. Do you know why they do that?' Jasmine shook her head. 'Because if they succeed they go into our bodies instead of us and *no one ever knows*,' the voice concluded.

Jasmine recognised the speaker, knew that it was Luke's mother, and she shook with fear. 'What would happen to me if someone else took my body?' she whispered.

'Then *you'd* be lost. Imagine that, Jasmine. Lost for eternity!' And suddenly, terrifyingly, the voice began to laugh. The laughter grew and grew until it was out of control and totally hysterical. Downstairs Owen heard and the blood drained from his face.

'That sounds like Tara laughing!' he exclaimed. 'What the hell's going on?' He raced up the uncarpeted stairs, his footsteps echoing round the house as he ran into the small back room. He saw Jasmine standing white-faced, her clenched fist held to her mouth and her eyes wide open in shock. His son was in the middle of the room, his head thrown back as peal after peal of terrible laughter shook his slight frame.

'Stop it!' shouted Owen, grabbing the boy in his arms and lifting him up until their faces were level. 'Pull yourself together, Luke. Be quiet now, it's all over. Come on, steady down, there's a good boy.'

The bear fell to the floor with a soft thud and Luke's eyes snapped open. He stared blankly into his father's anxious face. 'What's the matter?' he asked in bewilderment. 'Why have you picked me up?'

'You were screaming your head off.'

Luke's expression was one of total disbelief. He glanced at Jasmine. 'Was I really screaming?'

Jasmine nodded. 'It was a sort of laugh as well.'

He frowned. 'I don't remember laughing.'

'What's happening up here?' asked Kathryn, walking across the boarded floor to her daughter. 'Did either of you hurt yourselves?'

93

'We saw a boy,' murmured Jasmine, glancing fearfully round the empty room. 'He was up there.' She pointed at the ceiling.

'You and your silly games! If you haven't got anything better to do than frighten yourselves out of your wits, the sooner you're at school the better. Come on downstairs. We thought we'd call in at McDonald's for a milkshake before going home. Would you like that?'

'I don't want a milkshake,' said Jasmine. 'I don't want anything at all. I'd be sick.'

'My bear says he wants a big beefburger with onions and lots of ketchup,' said Luke. 'I don't. I don't want anything either.'

'I think we should all go home,' said Owen quietly and they went back to the car.

'What did happen in that room?' asked Owen when he was alone with his son.

Luke shrugged. 'I don't know.'

'Something must have frightened you.'

'My bear's still hungry. I hope Grandma's cooked us some tea.'

'What did you see?' pressed his father.

'I can't remember anything about it. My bear says I've had a severe emotional trauma.'

'Your bear has an amazing vocabulary,' commented Owen, but he decided to let the matter drop. He was beginning to suspect that he might find the truth decidedly unacceptable.

'So now I've seen Sherwood Forest!' remarked Kathryn, laughing, as Owen brought the car to a stop outside his front door. 'Every small boy for miles around will want to hear all about it, once I'm home.'

'What about the big boys?' asked Owen softly.

'I don't mix with big boys!'

'I find that hard to believe,' he protested as she followed him into the house. 'There must be some intelligent men in Sussex. How come none of them have met you?'

'I've never encouraged anyone. Since Philip left I've been

94

wary of new men. Partly because I've lost confidence and partly because of Jasmine. She still wants her father to come back. I don't think she could cope with any boyfriends.'

'She seems to like me.'

'I don't think she considers you my boyfriend. You're just Luke's father.'

'What about you, Kathryn? Do you think of me simply as Luke's father?'

Kathryn sat down on her favourite reclining chair and looked up at him. 'Of course not. Where is everyone?'

'We're home early. Mother won't be bringing the children back for another couple of hours; she was planning to take them to the cinema at Newark.'

'I hadn't realised,' replied Kathryn. But she had. She'd known they'd be alone in the house ever since they left Clumber Park. She'd been pleased, but suddenly she felt nervous.

'Come and sit on the sofa by me,' suggested Owen with a smile. Kathryn moved across the room and settled herself next to him. He put his arm along the back of the sofa. 'You're very special to me, you know,' he murmured, bending his head to kiss the side of her neck. And she did know. What she wasn't sure of was how she felt about him.

When his arms went round her she found that she responded urgently to his kisses, her body taking over from her mind and pushing all the questions into the background. Owen was less gentle than she'd expected. His mouth was hard against her skin and his hands demanded responses from her, searching her body insistently as he deftly removed her clothes. If she was surprised by him she was astonished by her own response. His touch set her nerve ends alight and she writhed beneath his fingers, hearing her own ragged breathing in the silence of the house.

She didn't know when she actually became naked. The first time she realised that her clothes were gone was when she felt his lips travelling the length of her body, leaving a silken trail on her skin, and when he moved between her thighs she was as desperate as he was, urging him on until at last she felt him enter her.

He seemed far bigger than Philip, filling her as her husband never had, and she moaned with pleasure, knowing that this was right. This was the way a woman should feel, totally abandoned to the pleasure of the moment, and as he balanced himself above her, she looked up at his face, tight with concentration, and hoped that somehow he could tell how right this was, and how perfect her pleasure.

When the climax finally swamped her, washing over her body and leaving her limp with exhaustion, she heard herself moaning with delight before collapsing limply, her body relaxed from its spasm of fulfilment. Then she lay on the bed, exhausted, sated and very, very happy.

Owen lay across her, his mouth resting against her breasts, and she could feel his heart thudding against her. Suddenly, cutting across the silence, there came the sound of soft, hastily suppressed laughter. Kathryn jerked upright, as Owen stared at her in surprise. 'What is it?'

'Someone laughed,' she exclaimed, almost in tears at the thought of someone having intruded on what had been such a private moment. 'Didn't you hear anyone laughing?'

'I didn't hear anything. I was half asleep. You imagined it, darling. There's no one here.'

'There is!' she insisted. 'Go and look. Your mother must have come home early.'

'My mother wouldn't creep up the stairs and spy on us! Be sensible, Kathryn.'

'But I heard it,' she repeated, swallowing hard to keep away the tears.

Inwardly furious at having the moment ruined, Owen reluctantly opened the bedroom door. He stood listening for several minutes but the house was in total silence. 'There's no one laughing anywhere,' he told a wide-eyed Kathryn.

'I'm sorry, I was sure . . . I did hear something, I know I did.'

'Then it must have been next door. We might as well get dressed now.'

She knew he was annoyed, but it was too late to try and undo the damage. The moment had gone, spoilt by her overactive imagination.

'I'm sorry, Owen. I was certain I heard someone.'

He was rapidly regaining his normal good humour and

smiled at her. 'That's all right. If I'd gone off to sleep you'd have had a terrible job waking me. Let's have a cup of tea and something to eat. I'm starving.'

Kathryn wished that she could tell him how special it had been for her, but now that he was talking about food the moment had passed.

'No regrets?' he asked as they sat in the drawing-room eating his mother's home-made chocolate cake.

Kathryn shook her head. 'None at all. It was wonderful.'

His eyes were gentle as he tilted her chin to look directly into her eyes.

'It was wonderful for me too. You're a very special person, Kathryn. I want you to know that – '

'My bear says there's a horrible smell in the house!' shouted Luke, careering into the drawing-room and rushing straight up to his father. 'Ugh! It's all over you as well. What is it?'

'I suspect it's my perfume.' Kathryn laughed.

Luke turned to look at her and his eyes were cold. 'My bear says you should wash more often.'

'Luke!' Owen was on his feet immediately, his face flushed. 'How dare you be so rude? Go upstairs at once, and don't come down until I call.'

Luke's features crumpled. 'It wasn't me!' he wailed, his mouth trembling. 'It was my bear. My bear's rude and nasty. I hate him.'

'I rather think it's up to you to control your bear,' commented Owen, still tight-lipped with temper.

'But I can't!'

'Oh, don't be so damned stupid. You know perfectly well the bear can't speak. Now get upstairs before I slap you.'

'He does speak, he does! He makes me say horrid things!' shouted Luke, and ran sobbing from the room.

'Good, here's Jasmine,' said Kathryn with relief as her daughter put her head round the door. 'Come on, darling. Time to get back to Grandma.'

'Where's Luke?'

'He's been sent to bed for being rude,' said Owen shortly.

Kathryn took her daughter by the hand. 'Thank you for a lovely time, Owen,' she said warmly. 'I expect we'll see you again soon. Did you thank Mrs Hughes for taking you to Newark, Jasmine?'

'Yes, Mummy.'

As Kathryn and Jasmine left, Luke watched from his bedroom window. Tears were streaming down his cheeks and when they were finally out of sight he turned to look at his bear, lying sprawled across his bed.

'You're a bad bear!' he shouted, banging it on its chest. 'A really bad bear, and I hate you!'

And he did hate it. But he also knew that it wouldn't make any difference. The bear had only just begun.

Kathryn came out of the newsagent's and said good morning to an elderly man walking his dog. He didn't answer but immediately increased his pace. A group of young girls, all under ten, also ran past her without a word, and she longed for Effingham and the people she knew.

'What's the date, Mother?' she asked, putting a pile of magazines down by her mother's chair.

'The twenty-third of July.'

'That explains why so many children are about. When we go back I must make sure Jasmine can start school after Christmas. I put her name down soon after she was born but the rules are changing all the time.'

'She needs school.'

'She certainly gets lonely at home, but she's enjoyed playing with Luke while we've been here.'

'Don't you think she's changed?' asked the older woman. 'She isn't as cheerful as she used to be.'

Kathryn saw that the bread was thick-sliced instead of medium and clicked her tongue in irritation. It was yet another so-called mistake by Mrs Cook. 'She seems all right to me,' she replied vaguely. 'I hardly get to speak to her, she's so busy.'

'She doesn't like talking to us any more. When we're all together she doesn't open her mouth.'

'Before we came she didn't know how to keep it closed. She was always chattering!'

'You know, I'm a great deal better now, Kathryn. I really think you could both go home soon.'

Kathryn looked up. 'Anxious to get rid of us?'

'Darling, it isn't that. I love having you here but you've got your own life to lead and I mustn't be selfish.'

'You still tire easily.' Kathryn was surprised at how reluctant she was to accept that it was time to leave. The thought of leaving Owen was suddenly extremely painful.

'I can always have a sleep in the afternoons. I ought to be doing more. It isn't good for me to sit around and be waited on.'

'Well, perhaps we'll go next week,' she said vaguely.

'On Monday?'

'You really are in a hurry to get rid of us!'

Although her mother shook her head, Kathryn was right. Nancy Laing was growing more and more worried about her granddaughter's friendship with Luke and felt that she had to send the little girl away soon for her own sake. 'I suppose you'll miss Owen,' she said to Kathryn.

'I certainly will. He's a very nice man.'

'He seems pleasant enough,' she agreed.

'If I leave now the villagers will think they've won,' said Kathryn.

'It isn't a competition.'

'No, more like a war! Seriously, I'd hate them to think they'd succeeded in driving me away.'

'We're not going home, are we, Mummy?' asked Jasmine, coming in through the back door with Luke.

'Yes, next week. Grandma's feeling better now and I have to get back to work. People will soon be placing orders for their Christmas cakes.'

'I don't want to go!' said Jasmine mutinously. 'I like it here. I can't leave Luke; he's my best friend.'

'You've got a best friend at home.'

'Stupid old Keely? She's wet. I want to stay here, Mummy. Please, please can we stay here?'

'I'm afraid not. Now stop whining and help me put away the groceries. You're far too big to hang round my legs like that. I'll trip up if you don't stop.'

Jasmine's mouth tightened and she wrapped her arms closely round her mother's knees so that Kathryn lost her balance and ended up full-length on the living-room floor.

The bag of sugar she'd been carrying split open and the grains shot everywhere. 'You stupid girl!' she shouted angrily. 'I told you to be careful. That was very naughty, I could have been badly hurt.'

'Say sorry to your mummy,' said Nancy Laing quietly.

'No, I won't. I'm not sorry. I wish you'd broken your neck!' In front of the two women's startled gaze she stamped her foot on the floor and then raced outside again, grabbing Luke by the hand as she went.

'Come back here!' called Kathryn furiously but she was too late, they were already out of ear-shot.

'You see what I mean?' asked her mother as Kathryn tried to sweep up the crunchy grains. 'She wouldn't have behaved like that before.'

'Before what?'

'Before she met Luke Hughes.'

'I'm afraid it's probably my fault. I know I've neglected her, but I thought she was happy with Luke's company. She's obviously trying to get my attention. She'll be fine once we're home.'

'I hope you're right,' responded her mother doubtfully.

'You're leaving on Monday?' said Owen in astonishment. 'But . . .'

'I know it's rather quick but Mother's much better now and I think she wants to be on her own again.'

'You can't just leave like that. What about us?'

She looked at him sitting in the garden swing seat, his long legs bent at an uncomfortable angle. He looked so calm and reliable that she wanted nothing more than to sit beside him, feel his arms go round her, and then tell him the truth. That she hated the thought of going back; that she didn't want to be on her own again, denying her own sexuality as she buried herself in her work and her daughter. Only pride and the suspicion that Owen wasn't quite as self-confident as he appeared kept her silent.

'What about us?'

'For God's sake, Kathryn! Surely I mean something to you?'

100

She bent down and began to pick some stray weeds out of one of the borders. 'It's always been like a holiday romance. We both knew it was going to come to an end, and if we tried to keep it going it probably wouldn't be the same at all.'

'I'm not some Spanish waiter with whom you've had a quick fling!'

'Owen, I have to do what I think's best for Jasmine.'

'I don't believe that's your reason for going. I think you're afraid of an emotional commitment.'

'I am not.'

'Is it because you haven't been welcomed by everyone with open arms? If so, I feel bound to point out that – '

'As a matter of fact,' retorted Kathryn furiously, 'this lack of welcome that you mention is the main reason I regret leaving here. I really hate the thought of your friends' satisfaction when they find I've gone; if it weren't for Jasmine I'd stay, just to spite them!'

'Steady on!' He laughed. 'I believe you, but if you must go, please let me take you out on Saturday evening for a farewell dinner. Agreed?'

She nodded reluctantly and then turned away, anxious to get back to the cottage where she could put Owen and all he meant to her out of her mind.

At the entrance to the tiny churchyard she hesitated then walked slowly along the path, her eyes scanning the headstones. She thought that there were some missing and suddenly noticed two grey slabs sticking up from the long grass near the back of the church. As her eyes registered the two raised mounds by the perimeter fence, neither of which had a headstone, she realised that someone had torn them out of the ground and then flung them into the uncut grass. Frowning she picked her way through the huge nettles until she could peer at the inscriptions.

'*The Reverend Octavius Walker. Rector of South Willoughby 1890–1910,*' she read aloud. '*Peace after pain.*' Moving the grass aside she was able to make out the second inscription. '*Miranda Walker, beloved wife of Octavius. Died 1909 aged 23 years. Not dead, only sleeping.*'

She spared a fleeting thought for the young rector's wife, who'd led such a brief and presumably uneventful life and ended up having her headstone discarded as of no importance. Shivering she turned away, unable to understand the children's fascination with the churchyard. It seemed to her to be a cold and sinister place.

'Go away!' whispered a voice urgently in her ear. 'You must leave.'

Kathryn spun round. 'Who on earth . . . ?' There was no one in sight. Annoyed, she hurried round to the side of the church, expecting to find one of Owen's so-called friends laughing at her, but everything around her was still; there was no sign of anyone. 'Who the hell is that?' she demanded angrily.

'Go home,' persisted the voice softly. 'For Jasmine's sake, go home.'

Kathryn clapped her hands over her ears to shut out the voice. As she stood there she suddenly felt totally certain that it was Miranda Walker talking to her and an image of the dead woman began to form in her brain, as clear as any photograph. She was small and plain with a sprinkling of freckles across her nose.

'Miranda?' whispered Kathryn, and immediately the picture became even clearer. The girl's hair was scraped up into an untidy bun and she was very pale. She was also clutching a sturdy, fair-haired toddler to her breast, and the hands that held him were red and work-soiled.

I'm going mad! thought Kathryn, her legs weak with fright. Suddenly she wanted to leave. Turning quickly, she caught her heel on a concealed stone and cried out as her ankle twisted beneath her. She lowered herself to the ground, hoping that it was only a sprain, and pushed at the grass to see what had caused her fall. It was a tiny piece of stone set in the soil, its inscription so inlaid with mud that it took her several minutes to clear it. She persisted, her fingers scrabbling frantically at the stone. Finally it was done and she traced the letters carefully.

Joseph Walker
Died 1909 aged 11 months.
Beloved son of Octavius and Miranda Walker.
Safe in the arms of Jesus.

She realised that he must be the child clasped in Miranda's arms and for a moment shock seemed to close her throat as a sense of the inevitability of death and suffering pressed down on her, darkening her mood until she felt she was experiencing the sorrows of the whole world. She felt a surge of grief for the dead child, grief such as his mother must have endured, and close behind that came a sensation of terror. She knew it was Miranda's fear and wondered what had caused it. Intrigued, she attempted to probe further, but was blocked by a darkness so final that she knew it wasn't to be. Weighed down by this heart-stopping and ancient terror, she whimpered to herself, wishing that she had never come to the churchyard.

'Are you hurt?' demanded a man's voice curtly. Startled, Kathryn looked up and was surprised and relieved to find Andrew looking down at her. He might not be friendly but he was definitely human.

'I twisted my ankle,' she explained shakily, still trying to come to terms with her strange experience.

'Why were you here? Are you keen on old churches?'

'No. I just wanted to look round before I leave. We're going home on Monday. Come to that, why are you here?'

'I've brought some flowers for Tara's grave. Owen never seems to bother. You're actually leaving then, are you? And what does Owen have to say about that?'

'He isn't pleased, but you are, aren't you? Since I am going, perhaps you wouldn't mind explaining what you and all your friends have against me?'

'Why, nothing. It's only that Tara was the kind of woman it's difficult to replace.'

'I wasn't trying to replace her.'

'I think Owen thought differently.'

'Do you expect him to remain single for the rest of his life?'

Andrew shrugged. 'Let's just say that it might be better if he moved away before remarrying.'

'I think you're all totally mad!' said Kathryn angrily. 'Tara's dead, nothing can change that. It was Owen who was her husband. Why should other people dictate what he does?'

'You don't understand,' he said rudely. 'How could you? After all, you're a southerner.'

'Exactly, and none of this has anything to do with me! I

103

came here to look after my mother and Owen was kind enough to take me out. He's just a friend, nothing more.'

'Do you mean to say that you sleep with all your "friends"? My goodness, and I had you marked down as a nice girl!'

'Do you know something?' said Kathryn furiously. 'When I listen to you I get an overwhelming urge to marry Owen and spend the rest of my life here, just to annoy you.'

Andrew raised his eyebrows. 'Somehow I think you mean that!' he said sardonically.

'I certainly do. If it weren't for Jasmine things might have been very different. She's the only reason I'm going, and I'd be grateful if you'd pass that on to all your friends when you next see them.'

'I certainly will. Goodbye, Kathryn. It was interesting meeting you.'

'Patronising chauvinist!' muttered Kathryn as she left the cold graveyard behind her. 'I hope his new home's full of draughts!' But she was pleased to have had the chance to tell him the reason she was leaving.

Chapter 8

Kathryn was struggling with the zip of her pink silk shift when Jasmine came into the bedroom, swinging the doll, Jezebel, by one hand. 'Will you be gone long, Mummy?'

'I should be back by twelve, but you'll be fast asleep long before then. Don't drag Jezebel along the ground, please.'

'She's been bad. I'm punishing her.'

'She's a very nice doll. If you can't take proper care of her then she'll go to a little girl who can.'

'I don't care. I don't like her any more. Where are you going tonight?'

'To a restaurant. Look, I know you're unhappy because we're going home but you'll soon settle down again. Owen and Luke can visit us before the winter.'

'Who's looking after me tonight?'

'Grandma says she can manage on her own. You will be good, darling, won't you?'

'Yes,' said Jasmine listlessly and Kathryn paused. She realised that her mother was right. Jasmine's face was no longer cheerful. Her expression at this moment was shuttered and sullen and there were no longer the displays of affection that she used to shower on her mother.

'Things will get back to normal once we're home!' promised Kathryn, hugging her daughter against her.

'Don't do that, Mummy. You're hurting me.'

'You're turning into a proper little crosspatch, Jasmine. I hope Keely still wants to be your friend when we're home,' remarked Kathryn, hurrying downstairs with the unpleasant certainty that Jasmine was glaring at her back.

'Don't care!' shouted the child from the top step, and Kathryn believed her.

Her mother was sitting at the kitchen table sorting through her crochet patterns for something uncomplicated. She smiled at the sight of Kathryn. 'You look beautiful, dear. At least your stay here has accomplished something. I'd begun to wonder if you were ever going to recover after Philip left.'

'I'm sorry it took something like this to put me back on the right track. I do hope Jasmine won't be difficult tonight.'

'She's never been difficult before.'

'I know,' said Kathryn thoughtfully. 'But she's in a funny mood tonight.'

Upstairs, Jasmine pressed her face against the bedroom window and watched her mother hurrying towards Owen's car. She saw how Owen took hold of her arm and noticed her mother's hand lingering on his a moment too long. She thought briefly of her father and was consumed by a longing for him that made her eyes fill with tears, but then she remembered what she'd asked for in return for joining Luke's club and the tears vanished. After tonight her father would be returned to her; her heart raced in excited anticipation.

It was hard, but she must persevere. Everything would be so wonderful once she'd killed her grandma.

'This is very nice,' commented Kathryn, glancing down the menu. 'When you live in the south you do rather think it's the only civilised place in the country. A restaurant like this would make a fortune in Sussex.'

'Don't tell the proprietor. He might be tempted to move away and see if you're right.'

'I can't make up my mind what to have. It all looks delicious. Perhaps you'd help me choose?'

'I wish you'd let me help you choose when to go back south,' he said sadly.

'Owen, this is meant to be a cheerful evening out!'

'Sorry! Well, the watercress soup is very good, and so is the soufflé.'

'I'll go for the soup. Mother would enjoy it here; she used to be a great one for eating out. It must be terrible when your husband dies. Single women over fifty never get asked anywhere. Except Sophia Loren look-alikes, I suppose!'

'I'll bring her here with my mother if you like. We usually come before Christmas, your mother could join us. It used to be a peace gesture because Tara would never have her for Christmas Day and I always felt horrendously guilty. This year she'll be cooking our meal herself, so she'll deserve a treat even more.'

'Didn't Tara like your mother?'

'They didn't get on. Mother found Tara difficult and didn't hesitate to show it, which antagonised Tara even more.'

'In what way difficult?'

'Tara would insist on reminding us that Christmas was originally a pagan festival. She refused to play carols or have any nativity scene in the house. Although Mother isn't particularly religious she thought this was all wrong once we had Luke. She used to bring some pretty tacky mangers and plastic oxen for Luke's room. In the end there was no way the pair of them could spend Christmas Day in the same house.'

'Didn't you mind?'

'About the religion? Not really. She made sure Luke believed in Father Christmas, and that's the most important part for small children. I thought I'd deal with the religious side when he was a bit older. Have you decided on the next course yet?'

'I think so. I do hope Mother and Jasmine are all right.'

'Jasmine never wakes, does she?'

'No, but she was in a funny mood tonight.'

'The worst thing that can happen is that she'll wake up and go downstairs, but then they'll keep each other company, won't they?'

'I hadn't thought of it like that,' she agreed happily, and promptly forgot about them both.

Nancy Laing was dozing quietly in her chair when she heard a faint tapping sound at her back door. She jerked awake, her heart pounding rapidly, and waited nervously to see if it happened again. A few minutes later the sound was repeated, but louder this time, as though the visitor was getting impatient.

107

Getting out of her chair she walked unsteadily into the kitchen. 'Who is it?' she called, her voice quavery. There was no reply but she could see a small shape outlined against the glass top of the door. 'I'll call the police if you don't go away,' she said angrily, wishing that she'd had the telephone installed. Then she watched an outlined fist raised in the air again, followed by the sound of a slow, steady knocking. Nancy's heart was racing and there was a slight tightness in her chest as she edged up to the door. 'Who is it?' she repeated querulously.

'It's all right, Grandma,' called Jasmine from the living-room. 'It's only Luke. He's brought me a present.'

'Why are you out of bed? You should be asleep.'

'I heard you calling. Shall I let him in?'

Nancy Laing wondered why she was feeling so uncomfortable. It was only a child on the other side of the door, but she couldn't get rid of a deep sense of unease. 'I'll let him in, Jasmine. You stay in the front room. It's far too late for . . .' She hesitated.

'For what, Grandma?'

She shook her head, pressing a hand to her eyes. 'I seem to have lost the thread of what I was saying. I . . .'

'You're old!' said Jasmine rudely, pushing her way to the back door and turning the heavy key with surprising ease. 'Come in Luke. I've been waiting for you.'

'What's this present you were on about?' queried her grandmother, suddenly remembering why the boy had come. 'Give it to her at once, Luke, then you can go straight back home again.'

Luke walked past her and laid something gently on the dining table. 'There you are, Jasmine. Your doll.'

The old woman peered across the room. 'It's a very small doll,' she said doubtfully.

'We made it,' said Luke proudly. 'Me and my bear made it as a present for her.'

'Made it?' She moved towards the table, wishing that she felt more secure on her feet and aware that her granddaughter was just behind her. 'Let me look. How odd, I seem to recognise the dress,' she finished in surprise.

'Of course you do!' Jasmine laughed, jumping up and down

and clapping her hands. 'It's made from your old pinafore. The one you lost yesterday.'

Her grandmother felt the constriction round her chest increase as she looked down nervously at Luke's gift. It was a small wooden doll with short legs and arms and an oversize head covered with thin grey hair. Its features were just blobs of paint but even so it was obvious who the doll resembled. With a sharp stab of fear she recalled the tales about Luke's mother.

'It's you, Mrs Laing!' Luke's voice was proud as he smiled up at her. 'Can you see that it's you?'

'Why would Jasmine want an old Granny doll? That's not much of a present.' The old woman laughed nervously.

'The hair's yours, Grandma,' explained Jasmine. 'I kept some when Mummy cut it for you.'

'It's a good likeness,' commented Luke, withdrawing his hand from his right pocket. His intended victim stared in hypnotised fascination at the long hatpin that was now visible. 'Come on, Jasmine. You've got to actually do it.' He extended the pin to the little girl.

For a moment, Jasmine hesitated. She looked from the already greying face of her grandmother back to the grotesque little doll and wondered if she could make herself stick the pin in while the old woman was standing right next to her. Her hand shook and Luke realised what was happening. 'You do want your daddy back, don't you?' he reminded her. 'This is the only way to get him. Go on. My bear says do it now.'

Jasmine blinked nervously. Everything was hurtling out of control and she didn't know what she wanted. Sometimes she longed to belong to Luke's special club, but there were other times – such as when they were in the haunted house at Lincoln – when she wished that she'd never met him and his dead mother. She knew that once the hatpin had been pushed through the doll there would be no turning back. Then she remembered her father and how he used to sing to her, his pride in her obvious even when she was little, and with a sigh she grasped the pin firmly in her hand and stabbed it through the doll's large head.

Mrs Laing was rooted to the spot as the full implications of what was happening rushed through her stroke-damaged brain. *This* was what she'd been trying to remember about the boy ever since Kathryn arrived in the village. He was evil. His mother had been a witch and he'd inherited her power. Her friend Heather Masters, now dead, had told her all about it just after she'd written asking Kathryn to come to the cottage.

Heather had also been certain that Kathryn was walking into danger and Nancy had resolved to send her daughter straight back south, but then her fall had set her back and wiped her memory blank. Now, suddenly, it all came flooding back.

'You pushed me!' she gasped, catching hold of the arms of her chair. 'I remember now, you came in here and – '

'It wasn't me!' he protested. 'It was my bear.' He held his stuffed toy protectively in front of him, as though afraid of her anger.

Her brain was racing, but everything was beautifully clear and long-forgotten childhood memories – such as the lavender scent of her mother when she bent over her at night – came rushing back, almost overpowering her with the sharpness of her vision. She gasped as the images whirred faster and faster through her brain. The pictures were rushing by so quickly that she couldn't absorb them and there was a dull pain in the back of her head that seemed to be pressing in on her. She felt her forehead would explode if it didn't stop.

'She's dying,' said Luke sadly, watching her stagger towards her chair by the empty hearth. 'It won't be long now.'

'What's happening to her?' asked Jasmine, astonished by the assortment of expressions crossing her grandmother's face.

'She's going out of her body, like we do at night. That's the way it often happens with killing spells.'

Nancy knew that the boy was talking but she couldn't hear the words, and neither could she control her body any longer as it collapsed in a heap on the edge of her chair. All she could do was try to remain conscious as a strange light filled her head. Then she felt herself floating up in the air, almost like a balloon, she thought with a smile, and as her mouth opened her false teeth slipped forward but she didn't realise because now she was looking down at the front room of the cottage, watching the two children move nearer to what she assumed to be her discarded body.

110

She felt wonderful; totally free and unafraid. If this was death, she thought, then it wasn't so terrible, and she moved gently through the kitchen wall until she was looking down on the sink and the crockery from their evening meal. Intrigued by what was happening to her, she continued her journey, entranced to discover that she was now out of the cottage, travelling high in the air, floating over the tiny church and looking down at people sitting in their back gardens in the welcome cool of the late summer evening. She wanted to shout to them about her magical journey.

Then the sky darkened and within seconds it was pitch black as she began to move higher, away from the houses and gardens, up into a strange void that she sensed held nothing of beauty or light.

As the darkness increased, so too did her fear. She tried to turn around, to return to the cottage and her waiting body, but she was thrown off course by a sudden movement of air that spun her round in a tight circle. When she was still again she found herself confronted by a vision so terrible that she instinctively tried to close her eyes, only to discover that this was no longer possible. She had no choice but to stare directly at what hovered in front of her.

It was a pulsating, glutinous mass of grey and silver that shifted constantly, revealing smaller visceral substances beneath its outer skin. It seemed to pulse with life and yet it smelt of decay and death; an odour so terrible that it took her breath away, overpowering her with its clinging sharpness and making her long for a cool breeze. It had no eyes, no obvious way of seeing her, but she knew that it did, and was aware that it was assessing her, trying to discover something that it needed to know.

Trapped by its rapidly spreading boundaries, kept in place by some power that held her faster than a magnetic field, she understood that the longer she stayed in front of it the more she was filled with a dreadful sense of despair. Not ordinary despair, such as she'd experienced in her life, but a total annihilation of hope that seemed to suck all positive emotions from her, leaving nothing but the hideous sense that life was pointless, leading only to death; death as the final, appalling conclusion.

111

This amalgamation of negative emotions was far worse than any physical pain, causing a deadly despair and anguish of the spirit. This absence of all hope and beauty was – she understood – what finally awaited humanity and her soul cried out in trepidation as her brain absorbed the awful revelation that what she was confronting was death itself. A final, primeval cry was torn from her as she faced up to her fate.

The sound reverberated round the cottage and made Jasmine cover her ears in shock. She couldn't believe it had been made by her grandmother, but one glance at the body in the chair, one glimpse of the wide-open eyes still glazed with horror and the twisted open mouth with its false teeth slipping grotesquely downwards, confirmed that it had. Whimpering, Jasmine moved nearer to Luke. 'Is she dead?' she whispered.

'Almost. Quickly, ask for your reward.'

Her mind went blank for a moment, tears falling from her eyes as she continued staring at her grandmother. Luke nudged her arm and she sniffed noisily. 'Please let me have a daddy again!' she sobbed. 'That's all I want. To have a daddy again.'

The two children crouched, waiting, over the dead woman's body and eyed each other fearfully. 'That's funny,' said Luke apprehensively. 'My bear's laughing. I've never heard him laugh before.'

'Thank you for a wonderful evening.' Kathryn smiled as Owen's car came to rest outside the cottage. 'I'll always remember it.'

'You sound as though we won't see each other again. I'm coming to visit you, remember?'

'Once I'm gone you might decide I'm not worth the journey.'

'I hope you know me better than that!' he protested, following her up the front path. 'I still can't believe you're going. Isn't there any chance of you changing your mind?'

'No, and I don't want to talk about it again. Goodness, look at that!' she said, laughing, as they tiptoed into the front room. 'Mother's fallen asleep downstairs. She doesn't look very comfortable.'

'Wait!' said Owen sharply, putting out a restraining hand. 'What's the matter?'

'I'm not sure, but . . .'

Kathryn looked more carefully at the figure slumped on the chair and gave a sudden anguished cry. 'Oh no! Mother! Mother, what is the matter?' But when she touched her mother's cold hand she knew that there was no point in asking questions; her mother was dead.

For a moment she couldn't move, but then she remembered Jasmine and ran upstairs, leaving Owen alone with the body. Carefully he lifted the dead woman further on to the chair and as her head fell back he saw her panic-stricken eyes staring at him and noticed that her whole face was twisted with blind terror.

'Jasmine's all right,' gasped Kathryn, hurrying back to him. Then she looked more carefully at her mother and made a sharp sound of distress. 'What's happened to her? She looks petrified. You don't think someone broke in, do you?'

'Of course not.'

'It looks as though something terrified her. I shouldn't have left her here. If I'd been in I could have called a doctor. She probably knew what was happening to her, that's why she looks so dreadful.'

Kathryn was becoming hysterical and Owen led her to the sofa. 'Sit there for a moment. I'm going to fetch Dr Potter.'

'Don't leave me, Owen! I don't want to be left with her.'

'She won't hurt you,' he said gently. 'And you can't leave Jasmine alone upstairs. I'll be very quick.'

Miserably, Kathryn twisted her handkerchief between her fingers. 'All right, but please hurry.' She heard the door close behind him and tried not to look in the direction of her mother. Instead she thought back over the evening, concentrating on recalling the colour of the restaurant walls and the pattern on the plates, anything to keep her mind occupied, but it was no good. Eventually she had to look across the room and the expression on her mother's face drew her to her feet. She went across to the body and laid a hand on the fragile frame. 'What happened?' she whispered, but as a door slammed upstairs she jerked her hand away.

'You're home!' called Jasmine excitedly.

113

Kathryn glanced up to see her daughter standing at the top of the stairs. She looked different. Her back was very straight, her head high, and there was a new air of self-assurance about her. She isn't a baby any more, thought Kathryn in surprise. 'I'm afraid something very sad has happened,' she said quietly.

Jasmine came half-way down the stairs and her eyes widened as she saw the figure in the chair. 'Is Grandma ill?' All at once there was a look of panic on her face.

'Not exactly ill, Jasmine.'

The panic faded and she regained her former confidence. 'She's dead, isn't she?'

'I'm afraid so.'

'Will she be buried in the churchyard, beside Luke's mummy?'

'No!' The rejection was automatic. Kathryn didn't want her mother left in South Willoughby. She wanted her buried safely near their Sussex home.

'I've never seen a dead person. Can I look?' asked Jasmine, creeping further down the stairs.

'Get back to bed!' ordered Kathryn sharply. 'I'll talk to you later.'

'You shouldn't be sad, Mummy. It wasn't nice for her after her stroke. I expect she's happier now.'

She doesn't understand, Kathryn told herself; she's too little to grasp the implications of death. It's good that she isn't frightened. But try as she might to convince herself, Kathryn still found her daughter's response disturbing.

'He won't be long,' called Owen, hurrying into the room. 'He wasn't surprised but . . . What are you doing there, Jasmine? This is no place for you. Go back to bed.'

Jasmine scowled angrily.

'Go on,' he said more gently. 'Your mother will come and see you very soon.' For a moment he thought that she was going to argue but then with a brief shrug she did as he'd asked.

'See how she's changed,' said Kathryn sadly. 'The real reason mother wanted us to leave here was because she thought Jasmine was changing.'

'She's growing up, that's all,' he said reassuringly.

'A nasty shock for you, my dear,' said Dr Potter, walking heavily into the room. 'Go and have a cup of hot, sweet tea while I write out the certificate.'

'But you don't know what happened yet!' protested Kathryn.

'I've been expecting this for some time. No doubt she had another stroke. No one could have prevented it, young lady. Owen, take Mrs Talkes out of here. She's upset.'

'He doesn't care!' protested Kathryn through her tears. 'He's pleased that she's finally died.'

'Darling, doctors see a lot of death. They can't let it affect them personally or they'd go mad. I know it must seem callous to you but think of it from his point of view.'

'I'm not asking him to cry, just to show some kind of compassion.'

'This has come as a terrible shock. You must get some rest.'

'How can I possibly rest? I shouldn't have left her, Owen.'

'Drink this,' he said gently. 'Then you'd better go upstairs to bed.'

'I can't ever sleep here again.'

'Of course you can. I'll sleep on the sofa if you like, then you'll know you're not alone.'

'I wish she hadn't looked so frightened. I keep wondering what she went through at the end. It must have been dreadful.'

'She probably went quite peacefully. She hadn't even left her chair.'

'She didn't look very peaceful to me.'

Owen put his arms round her and eventually she slumped against him, crying until she was exhausted and numb with grief. When she'd reach the hiccuping stage he made some more tea before going out to see the doctor and when he returned she seemed a little less distraught.

'Mother always kept a photo of me with Jasmine in her kitchen,' she murmured. 'I haven't seen it since we came here. I was wondering where it could be.'

'I'm sure it's somewhere around. Shouldn't you have a word with Jasmine?'

'Not until the doctor's finished. I'll have to . . .'

'She's gone, Kathryn. The undertakers have taken her away.'

Kathryn stared at him. 'You had no right to let them do that! How could you, Owen? Now she's gone and I didn't even say goodbye.'

'You can go and see her in the chapel of rest. I thought you were too upset to cope with them tonight.'

'I wanted to speak to them before they left. She was *my* mother, Owen. It wasn't anything to do with you!' she added furiously.

'I'm sorry. I only wanted to help.'

Kathryn shivered and wrapped her arms round herself. 'Just go away,' she said at last. 'I want to be alone with Jasmine.'

'I'll come round in the morning and take you into Grantham to register the death.'

'Must I?'

'I'm afraid there are lots of arrangements to be made. I'll take some time off, Douglas won't mind. That way I can keep you company.'

Kathryn drained her tea. She felt exhausted, her limbs were heavy and she had difficulty in thinking properly. 'But I was going home tomorrow,' she said stupidly.

'You'll have to stay a few days longer, until you've straightened things out here. It won't take too long.'

She felt a ridiculous urge to cry because she couldn't do as she'd planned. 'I suppose so,' she agreed, watching Owen's features blur in front of her eyes. 'I am tired,' she confessed, trying to suppress a yawn. 'I think I'd better get to bed.'

He helped her out of the chair and half carried her up the stairs. Once in her room, Kathryn slumped on the bed, too weary to take off her clothes. Owen removed her high-heeled sandals and put her legs under the duvet. 'You'll feel better in the morning,' he promised, kissing her on the forehead. She was asleep before he'd left the room.

On the landing Owen found Jasmine waiting for him. She looked anxious and cross. 'Is Mummy all right?' she demanded.

'She's very tired.'

'Why did Grandma die?'

'Because she was old and worn out.'

'Will she be buried here?' she asked.

116

'That's up to your mother.'

'She should be buried here. She belongs to this village now. Do you belong?'

'I suppose I do. I live here, remember?'

'Will you always live here?'

'I hope not. I'd like to see some other places before I die.'

'Then you don't belong,' she said firmly.

'What about you, Jasmine?' he asked curiously.

'Oh, I belong. The trouble is, Mummy doesn't. I want us to stay, but it's a bit difficult because how can my daddy come if we're here?'

'What makes you think your daddy's coming back?'

'Luke promised.'

'I'm afraid Luke doesn't always tell the truth,' he said gently. 'It's time you went back to bed now. Tomorrow you can play with Luke at our house for a change. Would you like that?'

'My daddy *is* coming back,' she repeated confidently, but she decided to check with Luke in the morning. It would be terrible to have killed her grandmother in vain.

Chapter 9

Kathryn stumbled through the next few days in a fog of confusion. She knew that she ought to be more alert but her mind was continually dulled by exhaustion. No matter how much she slept she still longed to be back in her bed again and nothing registered properly no matter how hard she tried to concentrate.

'Shock,' explained Dr Potter when she asked him what was wrong with her.

'Reaction,' stated Owen firmly. 'Nature has its own way of helping people cope. It will pass.'

She hoped that he was right, but still tried to force herself on, worried that she wasn't doing everything necessary. But very quickly she'd run out of energy again and collapse back in bed leaving everything to Owen and his mother.

Two days before the funeral she remembered Victoria, realising that her aunt still didn't know that her own sister was dead. 'I must go and see her,' she told Owen frantically. 'I can't ring up and tell her. Will you take me today?'

Reluctantly he drove her into Grantham and together they broke the news to a surprisingly calm Victoria. While Owen went off to get some petrol, Kathryn began apologising for not calling earlier. 'I feel dreadful about it,' she gabbled nervously. 'I don't know what's wrong but I haven't been able to think clearly since it happened. Nothing's real any more. I can't seem to concentrate.'

'Kathryn, listen to me,' urged her aunt. 'You're in danger. I know you are, just as I already knew that Nancy was dead. Call it second sight or a sixth sense, it doesn't matter. Whatever the reason, I do know things and I can tell that you're in danger. You must go home as soon as your mother's been buried.'

'You *knew* Mother was dead?'

'It's hard to explain but I suppose it was rather like realising there was a picture missing from a wall. She left a space in my mind.'

'Why do you think I'm in danger? Is it still because of Luke?'

'My dear Kathryn, I don't want to alarm you but I suspect it's more dangerous than that and far more complicated than I'd expected. I'm waiting to hear from some old colleagues of mine, but I don't want you to wait for them. I want you to leave the minute you can.'

Kathryn's head hurt and she was only half listening. 'Of course.' she agreed vaguely. 'Is that Owen's car outside? He's been wonderful,' she enthused as they walked to the door. 'I couldn't have managed without his help.'

'Would you like a lift to the funeral on Monday?' asked Owen as they left.

Victoria studied him closely and then shook her head. 'Thank you, young man, but there's no need. I'll do my mourning here, in private.'

'I quite understand.' He smiled. 'Kathryn, are you ready?'

She embraced the old woman, feeling a sudden urge to clasp her arms round her neck and beg to be allowed to stay here. Just being with her aunt made her feel safer, less confused and isolated, although she knew that she was being illogical.

'You were too tired for this,' said Owen on the journey back. 'But she's a very nice woman. I can see that you had to come.'

'She's worried about me,' said Kathryn quietly.

'We're all worried about you.'

Kathryn didn't have the energy to explain about her aunt's warning, and in any case she knew that what she'd been told was for her ears alone.

'In sure and certain hope of the resurrection and the life to come,' intoned the relief vicar who was officiating at the funeral.

If only I could be sure, thought Kathryn to herself, but she wasn't. She didn't know whether she believed in life after death or not any more. All she knew was that she was missing her mother.

In an attempt to keep control she glanced round the tiny pews. Mrs Cook was there, having closed the shop for an hour, and so too was old Mr Bentley. Even Dr Potter was there, dressed in a dark suit, and she saw other people that she knew as well, including Douglas, Owen's senior partner. In the end Kathryn hadn't felt up to insisting that the service should be held in Sussex. As Owen's mother had pointed out, Nancy Laing had been happy in South Willoughby and Kathryn's own feelings shouldn't let her lose sight of that.

'Please accept my deepest sympathy,' said the vicar, shaking her hand after the coffin had been lowered into the ground.

'She'll be missed by us all,' said Mrs Cook, addressing her remark to Owen. 'You should go back home,' she added in an undertone as she walked away past Kathryn.

'I'm very sorry; a fine woman,' said Mr Bentley, moving a mint humbug around in his mouth. 'No doubt you and your lovely little daughter will soon be leaving us?'

'As soon as possible,' agreed Kathryn through clenched teeth, but she lingered by the grave after everyone else had gone. 'I don't want to leave her,' she admitted to Owen.

'She won't be dead if you don't allow her to fade from your mind. You must have a lot of happy memories.'

'I can't talk to her any more. She can't advise me or even complain. If that's not dead, tell me what is.'

Owen sighed, wishing that the children were there to distract her. She'd scarcely eaten since the night it happened and the dark smudges beneath her eyes suggested she still wasn't getting enough sleep.

'I shouldn't have let them bury her here,' she continued. 'I never meant – '

'Kathryn, I'm so very sorry!' exclaimed a light voice and they both turned to find themselves face to face with Clive's wife, Emily. 'I missed the service,' she explained breathlessly. 'I've been away, you see, and Clive only told me last night. I rushed back but the trains missed their connection. I thought you'd need all the friends you could get in this horrible place.'

'It's lovely to see you!' Kathryn felt better immediately. She badly needed another woman to talk to and took hold of the girl's hand. 'You must come back to the cottage with me, Emily. I'm feeling so dreadful and I don't know where to turn for advice.'

'I think you've already got a pretty good adviser!' Emily said with a smile at Owen. He turned Kathryn in the direction of the cottage, relieved that something had got her moving away from the graveside.

'I'm back at work tomorrow, Emily,' he told her across Kathryn's head. 'It will be a relief to know she still has some company.'

'What will you do? asked Emily while Owen was busy in the kitchen. 'I suppose it will take time to sort out her affairs?'

'Ages, particularly as she didn't make a will. Owen's going to try and get a solicitor friend to speed it up but there's bound to be a delay.'

'What exactly happened? Clive was rather vague over the phone.'

'We were out at the time,' confessed Kathryn, sipping gratefully at the tea Owen put beside her. 'That's made it all the more difficult to accept. I feel so guilty. I'd left her alone with Jasmine for the evening.'

'Where is Jasmine?' queried Emily, glancing round the room.

'She's with Luke,' said Owen. 'It seemed like the best idea. She's far too young for funerals.'

'She isn't a bit upset,' said Kathryn in bewilderment. 'It isn't that I want her crying all the time, Emily, but she doesn't care at all.'

'That isn't true,' protested Owen. 'Just because she hasn't shown anything it doesn't mean – '

'Why don't you go home?' suggested Kathryn abruptly. 'You've practically lived in the cottage since Mother died. I'm sure Luke would like to have you home with him.'

Emily glanced at Owen nervously but he didn't seem put out. 'She's very tired,' he told Emily as he left. 'Try and persuade her to rest later.'

121

'That wasn't very kind of me, was it?' asked Kathryn once they were alone. 'The trouble is, I'm beginning to feel suffocated by his attention. I hope he understood,' she finished anxiously.

'He seemed quite happy. Kathryn, have you considered what you'll do once everything's been sorted out?'

'I'll go home, of course. What else?'

'I thought you might stay here. You could always live in the cottage.'

'Why on earth would I stay here?'

Emily smiled. 'Come on, Kathryn! Everyone knows that you and Owen are having an affair. He seems very keen on you. Clive thought you'd probably be getting married.'

Kathryn looked out of the window, noticing that Mrs Cook had reopened the corner shop. 'It's just a holiday romance,' she said slowly.

'Does Owen feel like that about it?'

'No, but he knows I have to leave. Jasmine needs her own home again, she's been badly affected by all this.'

'If you loved him you'd find a way round that. It would be nice for me to have you living here,' she added.

'I'll keep in touch,' Kathryn promised.

'I wanted a friend here, in the village! Don't you love him at all?' she persisted.

A wave of tiredness swept over Kathryn. 'I'm not sure. When I'm with him I think I do; but when I'm on my own I have doubts. I always feel that he's holding back.'

'About what?'

'Everything! His life, his marriage to Tara; I only get surface details.'

'Men are never any good at intimate discussions; besides, he's probably holding back because of the way Tara used him. According to his mother, she was an absolute bitch.'

'Maybe, but I think there's more to it than that.'

'And I think you're imagining things. Owen's always seemed totally open to me. Look, I can see you're tired. You'd better go and rest. Clive sent his good wishes and hoped you'd come and see us before you go. You will, won't you? We never have any visitors because I don't like any of Clive's friends.'

122

'I'll try,' agreed Kathryn, but she didn't really intend to do any socialising before she left. With every day that passed she felt a more and more urgent need to leave South Willoughby. She stumbled up the stairs and into bed, falling asleep within seconds.

When she opened her eyes her head felt heavy and there was a dull ache across her forehead. Sitting up, she was attempting to put her feet to the ground when she became aware that there was someone else in the room; someone who was watching her. She seemed to be alone but when she sat quite still she could even hear the faint sound of breathing and her scalp prickled with fear.

'Who is it?' she asked nervously. It was still a warm day but a clammy chill seemed to fill the room and she rubbed the tops of her arms for warmth. Then she heard a familiar sound; the smallest of creaks, the noise made whenever someone sat on the wicker seat by her door. Peering anxiously across the room she saw the faint, grey shape of a woman materialising. A woman with a child in her arms. The outline slowly strengthened, gaining in substance with Kathryn's gradual recognition. 'Is it you, Miranda?' she whispered in amazement.

The girl from the churchyard was becoming clear now and her round dark eyes stared at Kathryn, their expression pleading for something beyond her understanding, but she sensed that the girl in front of her was suffering and longed to help. 'What do you want?' she whispered.

Miranda's lips moved silently while her hands clutched her child to her breast. He was a lovely boy, soft-featured and round-limbed. A strong, healthy child whose head turned from side to side as he examined his surroundings. Kathryn wanted to touch him, wanted to feel his baby softness close to her skin. Drawn by the child, she moved towards the apparition.

'You must leave now.' Miranda's voice was low and sad.

'Why are you here?' asked Kathryn. 'What happened to you both?'

The girl didn't answer, instead she held her child out to

123

Kathryn. 'Take my son,' she urged. 'He gets so little love.'

The child turned his gaze full on Kathryn and the mute appeal tore at her heart. Impulsively she stretched out her hands and took the small body in her arms. His hands fastened tightly round her neck and he pressed his plump body against hers, making tiny noises of pleasure that made her smile as she bent her face down to his, letting her chin brush against the soft hair on the top of his head.

She'd forgotten how delightful tiny children were to hold, and lifted him up in the air, remembering that Jasmine used to squeal with delight as she was swung down again; but as she held him above her head his bright-blue eyes looked straight into hers and for the first time she felt a chill of disquiet. There was something wrong with his eyes. They were too aware, and there was no childlike innocence in them. They were the eyes of an adult. With a sense of dismay she clasped him tightly and tried to hand him back to Miranda, but immediately his grip on her arm increased.

She tugged fiercely at his tiny hands, only to hear him suck in his breath and feel his sharp little nails digging into her neck. He pushed forward, apparently trying to burrow right through her clothes. She felt ridiculously threatened by the movement and tried to wrench him off but he clung on like a limpet. She suddenly realised that Miranda had vanished, leaving her alone with the ghost of this long-dead child. Her heart pounded as she wrestled silently with the small creature, and when he finally succeeded in sinking his tiny teeth into her throat she gave a squeal of pain.

'Stop it!' she shouted, and with a final effort wrenched him off, holding him at arm's length away from her. He stared at her, his eyes glowing furiously as he wriggled around trying to make contact with her body again. She couldn't think how she'd ever thought him attractive because there was nothing appealing about his expression now and his breath whistled angrily between his teeth.

'Don't!' she exclaimed. 'You have to go back to your mother. You don't belong here.' While she was speaking he extended his fingers towards her and the nails looked like the claws of a small animal. He was forcing himself towards her again, and she suddenly lost control, shaking him furiously as he turned into a twisting, crazed creature intent on fastening himself on her body. Desperate to get rid of him, Kathryn began shouting for help, screaming for her mother, Owen and even Jasmine in her terror.

Then, abruptly, the child uttered one sharp cry and went limp in her arms. Almost as frightened by his silence as she had been by his attack, Kathryn stared down at the boy in her arms. He was now totally inert, his head lolling limply to one side. With trembling hands she laid him on the bed and then sprang away with a scream as the small head twisted to one side and dark-red blood gushed all over her bedspread.

Whimpering, she forced herself to move closer to him and saw that the blood came from his throat, which was torn wide open, exposing the sinews and tissue beneath the skin. But even worse than that was the look in the lifeless blue eyes staring up at the ceiling. A look of such utter malevolence that she threw up her arm to cover her face and protect herself from the evil that so clearly possessed the tiny child.

Sobbing and gasping for breath she stumbled across the room to the door. There was still no sign of Miranda and she didn't know what to do with the terrible mutilated corpse that was lying on her bed. Aware that if she stayed in the room a moment longer she'd go mad, she tugged at the handle and ran screaming on to the landing only to find it blocked by a large dark figure that loomed over her. She gave one final scream as the floor tilted beneath her and she collapsed in a heap at the figure's feet.

When she awoke she was back in her bed and Dr Potter was bending over her. She pushed herself upright, eyes darting nervously round the room. 'Keep still, young lady. Just checking your blood pressure,' he said brusquely.

'Have they gone?' asked Kathryn, her voice tight with fear.

'Who do you mean?' asked Owen, his face concerned.

'Miranda and her baby son. They were here. I held her baby. He was so sweet at first and then he . . .' She choked back a sob, unable to continue.

'Who's Miranda?' asked Dr Potter.

'She's in the churchyard. She was married to the rector, Octavius, and . . .'

'You mean she's dead!' exclaimed Owen, ignoring the doctor's warning frown.

'I know it sounds ridiculous but I've seen her before. When I was in the graveyard.'

'Quite,' soothed the doctor, taking out a syringe. 'I think you'll feel much better after a long sleep. There we go, that should do the trick.'

'She was warning me,' Kathryn explained, struggling to get out of bed. 'I have to go home. She told me to leave now.'

'After your rest,' said the doctor, and watched as she slowly fell back on the pillows and closed her eyes. 'Where did you find her?' he asked Owen as they left the room.

'On the landing. She passed out at my feet.'

'She's certainly disturbed. Her mother's death has affected her very badly.'

'She was still getting over her husband leaving her.'

'I see. Well, we'll have to see what tomorrow brings. I'll call in about twelve, after morning surgery. Can someone stay with her tonight?'

'My mother's already offered.'

'Excellent. Until tomorrow then.'

As soon as Jasmine closed her eyes she found herself flying through space and laughed with excitement at the feel of the night air and the exhilaration that night-walking always gave her. Now that she belonged she was allowed to travel alone. Although proud of this, she missed Luke's company.

Very soon she found herself approaching an old crumbling building set back from the road and for a moment thought that she was going to crash into the thick stone walls, but then she dropped sharply to the ground, landing outside the heavy wooden door.

Usually there were lots of people waiting at the end of night-travel, but not tonight. Tonight she was alone and with increasing nervousness she pushed on the door. After a moment's resistance it swung slowly open with a protesting squeak of its hinges. Inside it was dark and gloomy. Jasmine wished that she'd brought a torch with her. She also wished that Luke was there. When Luke was with her she was never afraid.

126

As her eyes adjusted to the darkness she saw a broken table by one of the windows. On the table was a strange ornament and she reached out to examine it but it began to crumble beneath her fingers.

'Leave that alone!' shouted Luke, suddenly appearing in front of her. 'That was my mummy's hand. She burnt to death in here and her bones were found in a heap by the door. They left it behind when they buried her. If they hadn't been so careless she couldn't have come back.'

'Is she looking for her hand then?' asked Jasmine, hoping that there weren't any other pieces of Tara's body lying around.

'No, but it gave her a link. You have to have a link to make the crossing.'

'What's Penelope's link?'

'Because she died so suddenly she didn't manage to cross over properly. She uses her rage as a kind of energy to try to get back. In the end she'll make the journey the other way, but not until she stops being so angry.'

'Why didn't you burn to death as well?' queried Jasmine. 'You were here, weren't you?'

'The magic saved me,' he said shortly. 'I can hear her coming. Quickly, let's go outside. She doesn't like it in here.'

They were just in time. Tara was already gliding over the grass. She smiled at the children, putting her arms round them both and letting her hands ruffle their hair. 'Come along!' She laughed. 'We're going on a special journey and we have to hurry. You don't want to find a stranger in your bed when you get back, do you?'

'Where are we going?' Jasmine looked excited.

'To Italy, just for you, Jasmine! Luke, hold her tightly. Remember, you mustn't touch anything we see on our travels.'

As they raced through the night sky, Jasmine didn't feel tempted to touch any of the white-faced creatures they passed. There was nothing appealing about them as they stretched out their arms, despair and envy etched on their faces. 'How long will they wait for a body?' she whispered to Luke.

'Forever. They were cheated; they all died before their time.'

127

'Do some of them get back?'

'Quiet!' ordered Tara, pinching Jasmine's wrist with her fingers. 'Concentrate on what you're doing.'

Eventually the sky lightened and suddenly they looked down on a large bedroom. It had shuttered windows and a large statue of the Madonna and Child was set in a small niche in the wall above the oval bed. Jasmine stared hard at the adults lying there, watching them embracing each other, murmuring words that she knew instinctively were words of love. Then the man propped himself up on one elbow and she recognised her father. Amazed, she opened her mouth to call to him but Luke put his hand across her lips and shook his head. Jasmine desperately wanted to tell him she was there and her love for him filled her throat until she thought that she'd choke.

She watched silently as he continued embracing his wife but when he moved on top of her, Jasmine's feelings started to change. A jealous anger washed over her and she no longer wanted him to know that she was there. Then, from another room, there came the sound of a child crying. As Philip left his bed and walked out of the bedroom, Jasmine floated through the wall until she was looking down on a single bed and a cot standing side by side near the window, and now her anger made her clench her fists.

Philip picked up his dark-haired son, who was very like the daughter watching from the darkness. He crooned to him and kissed him, whispering baby words, his pride in the child obvious. Finally the boy's eyes began to close and Philip laid him back in his bed. He then bent over the cot and adjusted the covers on the baby before returning to his wife.

Jasmine had never experienced such hatred. Her body felt swollen with it and she was so tense with rage she could hardly breathe. She'd thought about him every day, remembering the tender way he used to hold her, but now she realised that it had all been meaningless. Happy with his boys, Philip had forgotten her. She hated him and wished that he was dead.

'That's right!' Tara whispered in her ear. 'He deserves to die. Now that you have the power, you can kill him.'

'Take me away!' cried Jasmine in a shrill voice. 'I don't want to see him any more.' Tara and Luke took her hands and their touch helped to soothe her as they journeyed back to the village that was their home.

In his bedroom, Philip finished making love to Pia and suddenly remembered his daughter, far away in England. He remembered the way she used to giggle and how she'd followed him around adoringly. For a moment he felt a pang of remorse for his neglect but it quickly passed. He was basically a shallow man who lived for the moment and lacked much imagination.

When Tara, Luke and Jasmine arrived outside the village church, Tara glanced at the sky. 'It's getting late, we must hurry!' Luke said anxiously.

'All men are like your father,' Tara told the white-faced Jasmine. 'You can't trust any of them. It's better to learn that now than later on, when you get married. If it weren't for Owen I'd still be alive.'

'What did he do?' asked Jasmine in astonishment.

'Never you mind,' snapped Tara. 'But he'll pay. You're going to help me punish him, Jasmine. That's why you're here.'

Jasmine was still feeling terrible, unable to cope with so much hatred. 'Why should I?' she asked sulkily. 'I asked for my daddy back when I joined your club but I'm not going to get him. Why should I help you get what you want?'

Luke sighed. 'You didn't ask for your daddy back. You asked to have *a* daddy again.'

'It's the same thing!' cried Jasmine.

'I'm afraid not,' said Tara, keeping a restraining hand round Jasmine's wrist. 'You will get a daddy again, Jasmine. A different one this time. How would you like to have the same father as Luke?'

Jasmine swallowed hard. 'I didn't mean that I wanted *any* daddy! I wanted my own daddy back.'

'Then you should have said so,' remarked Tara indifferently. 'It's no good complaining when you made the mistake yourself.'

'That's not fair! Why didn't you tell me, Luke? I don't want your stupid daddy!'

'It's too late now!' Tara laughed, her eyes glittering.

'I don't like you!' exclaimed Jasmine. 'You make me feel horrid. I wish I hadn't joined your stupid club.'

Luke looked apprehensively at the gradually lightening sky. 'I told you to be careful,' he muttered.

Jasmine's anger exploded and she sprang towards him, knocking him to the ground and banging his head on one of the tombstones. 'You tricked me!' she shouted. 'I won't ever be your friend again.'

Luke twisted beneath her and cried out as his forehead caught the edge of Tara's tombstone. 'Let go, Jas! We have to get back. It will soon be morning.'

Tara lifted the struggling girl off her son. Jasmine turned away from the feel of the cold hands on her skin and blinked away tears of temper.

'Stay a little longer,' urged the dead woman. 'How would you like Luke to make you a Daddy doll?'

Jasmine could feel Luke tugging at her to come away, but she looked eagerly at Tara. 'Do you promise? No tricks? A proper doll that I can use?'

Tara glanced furtively at the sky. 'Of course,' she murmured absent-mindedly.

A wonderful sense of power coursed through Jasmine. She could wipe out all the pain and humiliation of tonight if she had a doll. Wipe out the pain and wipe out her father at the same time. No one would have him, she thought with joy. Not his rotten second wife nor his stupid little boys. He'd leave them just as he'd left her. Her eyes danced.

At the sound of the church clock Tara gave a sigh of relief, then stumbled and almost fell. Luke looked at her as she struggled to stay upright and realised that they'd nearly left it too late. He snatched Jasmine's hand away from his mother's grasp.

'Come with me,' he called. Hand in hand they rushed above the trees towards their houses, travelling faster than they'd ever done before. Behind them, Tara slid smoothly and swiftly down through a crack in her headstone with a final sigh of relief.

'Hurry!' urged Luke, reluctantly releasing Jasmine's hand. 'I must go back too. See you tomorrow.'

Jasmine waved and felt herself beginning to fall. She closed her eyes, anticipating the moment when she would be back in her bed again, but then she felt a jolt and opened them in surprise. She was floating above her own bed and she could see her body beneath her, but her body was beginning to wake, the eyes to open, and in a heart-stopping moment of agonised comprehension she realised that someone else was inside her. Her empty body had been taken over by one of the lost souls she'd seen that night.

Jasmine didn't know what to do. Nothing had prepared her for this and she screamed hysterically to Luke for help, but he didn't reply. As she continued floating above her body she grasped the finality of what was happening and gave an anguished cry of disbelief.

On the bed, Jasmine's eyes opened wide and her body sat up. The hands moved slowly over the duvet and the head turned from side to side. Above the bed, Jasmine was galvanised into furious action and with all her psychic energy threw herself onto the moving body, determined to force the intruder out. For several minutes they struggled, but the lost one was gaining in strength all the time while Jasmine grew weaker and weaker, battering against her human shell.

The intruder knew that Jasmine was tiring and seemed to enjoy the frantic cries emanating from her fading spirit. 'I have to get back!' shouted Jasmine. 'I want to do another killing spell.'

'That was just a trick,' laughed the intruder. 'She wanted to keep you there. Now go away. You don't belong here any more.'

'Where will I go?' asked Jasmine.

Already she could feel herself being sucked away from her house and out into the blackness beyond the early morning sky. She began to travel faster and the air was heavy, full of terrible sounds. She tried to think about heaven and Jesus, tried to remember all she'd learnt about God, but for some reason her thoughts were jumbled and then in a moment of clarity she remembered that she'd traded her soul in order to join Tara's club. Immediately she knew exactly where she was going, and knew that there was no hope.

Chapter 10

'I must see Jasmine,' said Luke as soon as his grandmother opened the cottage door to him.

'She overslept and hasn't finished breakfast yet. Her mother's still asleep, make sure you keep your voice down. What happened to your head?' she added, seeing a large bruise over his left eye.

'I fell.' Moving swiftly past his grandmother he sat down on the chair next to Jasmine, staring into her eyes intently.

'Have I grown two heads or something?' she demanded pertly.

Luke tightened his grip on his bear. 'Who are you?' he hissed furiously. 'My bear says you're not Jasmine.'

'I am.'

'I like Jasmine. I don't like you.'

'Tough titty!' she sneered rudely.

Luke stared. 'You're one of the lost ones, aren't you? Poor Jasmine! How old are you really?'

'Ten and a half. I feel a bit silly in this body but I'll get used to it.'

'How long have you been waiting?'

'Only a year. I was lucky. Some people have been waiting hundreds of years.'

'How did you die?' he asked, putting his hand over the same small fingers that had held his so trustingly last night.

'My mummy was sad so she sat us all in our car in the garage and poisoned us with fumes. It was disgusting!' Her mouth twisted at the memory.

'Why was she sad?'

'Because my daddy had left us.'

Luke nodded; she was typical of the lost ones. His mother was happy that Jasmine had gone but he felt very sad. He wished that he'd taken her away earlier last night, when he'd first become worried, but his mother hadn't let him. Tara had got what she wanted, while Luke had lost his very first friend.

'We're going out to play,' called Jasmine, swallowing her last piece of toast.

'Make sure you're back here by lunchtime. Keep an eye on the village clock.'

'We will. Come on,' she urged Luke. 'I need to know everything that's happening here.'

His explanation took a very long time.

When Owen came to call that evening, Kathryn was sitting in a chair while Jasmine sat on the floor at her feet, playing with a pack of cards. He ruffled her hair. 'All right, beautiful?'

Her dark eyes looked up at him. They were cool and assessing, with none of Jasmine's normal warmth in them.

'Learnt a new card game?' he queried, putting his arm round Kathryn's shoulders as he spoke.

'I'm playing patience.'

Kathryn looked at her in surprise. 'Who taught you that?'

'I taught her,' said Luke quickly, coming down from the bathroom. 'My bear's good at patience.'

Later, when both children were in their beds, Kathryn took a deep breath. 'Owen I'm very worried about Jasmine.'

'She looks fine to me. It's you I'm worried about. How have you felt today?'

'I'm not ill. I was just frightened. That baby was absolutely terrifying. One minute he was – '

'It was only a dream, darling.'

'It wasn't a dream!' she exclaimed angrily. 'Miranda was in the room with me and she said that I have to leave here now. She was adamant about it.'

'You want to leave anyway! This dream was only an extension of your conscious thoughts. Because you're not a hundred per cent sure about going, your subconscious is trying to put the responsibility on to someone else.'

133

'It wasn't like that at all! Why won't you believe what I say?'

'Frankly, it's downright impossible to believe a story like yours. I mean, why would a girl who's been lying quietly in her grave for nearly a hundred years suddenly decide to start haunting this cottage?'

'She wants to help me.'

'But you don't need any help!'

'I do! Miranda and my aunt both know that I'm in danger.'

'If you ask me, your aunt's totally out of her tree. I hold her responsible for all this nonsense about ghosts and dead children. Look at it from my point of view. Would you believe me if I started talking about visitors from beyond the grave?'

'Yes, I would now.'

'That wasn't what I meant.' He looked at her worried expression and knew that she wasn't well enough to argue. 'Let's forget it, shall we? Dr Potter said you needed rest and quiet.'

'I don't care what Dr Potter says. I'm going back home tomorrow. I'm quite well enough to do the drive and I won't relax until I'm away from here.'

'What about us?' asked Owen quietly. 'I love you, Kathryn. I don't want you to vanish from my life. Would you like me to come back with you for a week?'

She twisted her fingers in her lap. 'I'm beginning to think that I should make a clean break from this place.'

'You mean stop seeing me altogether?'

She nodded.

'You're mad!' he shouted furiously. 'Why give up what we've got because of some stupid dream? When we're together we're happy. We get on well, never argue or fight. And we suit each other in bed and out of it. At least, I think we do. Perhaps you don't feel the same?'

'I do!' she protested. 'If I'd met you anywhere else then it would have been perfect, but I didn't. I met you in South Willoughby and there's no future for us here. I have to get Jasmine home, back to normality again.'

'You can't turn back the clock,' he said wearily. 'Jasmine's grown up since she's been here, that's all. Obviously your mother's death has upset you but going home won't bring her back.'

134

'I've changed too,' she admitted softly. 'You've helped me a lot.'

'But not enough to make you want to stay with me?'

He looked utterly dejected and Kathryn felt wretchedly guilty, wishing that she could explain her feelings to him. Since her mother's death there was something about South Willoughby that repelled her. It wasn't just that the people were unfriendly, she'd got used to that. The whole atmosphere had begun to frighten her. The inhabitants didn't seem to remember that there was a world outside their village and their faces suddenly seemed more furtive and cunning than unfriendly. She was frightened and she believed that her fear was intended; that it was Miranda reinforcing the warning.

'It isn't your fault, Owen. It's mine. If anyone had told me that one day I'd run away from a place because a ghost said I was in danger, I'd have laughed in their face, but that's exactly what's happened and I have to go. Miranda was real, and so is the danger. Can't you see that there's something wrong in this village?'

'I wish you'd be more specific,' he said angrily.

'The birds don't sing.'

He looked at her in disbelief. 'You're telling me that you're leaving here because you haven't heard any birds singing?'

'Think about it!' she urged him. 'When did you last hear a bird?'

'There are loads of birds around, that's why there are scarecrows in the fields.'

'But they don't sing! It's so quiet here that I sometimes forget any other place exists. There's no through traffic. People don't drive *through* South Willoughby. No one stops at the corner shop. Even the ambulancemen who brought Mother home wouldn't stay five minutes. Outsiders all know better than to come here, and I should never have tried. If I stay, something dreadful will happen to me, I know it. I could have loved you, Owen, but not here.'

'I'll move! It won't be difficult. I'll move nearer my office. Luke will just have to accept it. We'll get married and buy a house in – '

'No! Owen, how can I make you understand this? No matter where we go, South Willoughby will always intrude.

135

You were born here; you belong. I don't think it would let you go.'

'That does it!' exclaimed Owen, getting to his feet. 'Why didn't you just say that you wanted us to finish? It would have been kinder than spinning a yarn about dead women and antagonistic villagers. Surely you didn't really think I'd believe you? I suppose you hoped I'd take the hint and give in gracefully?'

'No! I've told you the truth!' she protested.

'If that's what you believe then you're sick in the head. Anyway I've had enough. We probably won't see each other again so I'll just say thank you and have a safe journey home. Goodbye, Kathryn.'

As he slammed the front door behind him, Kathryn burst into tears, but even if Owen had heard he wouldn't have come back. At that moment he was wishing that the second sex had never been invented.

'Where's Owen gone?' asked Jasmine sleepily, standing at the top of the stairs.

'He's gone home and I'm going to bed now, so hurry up and use the bathroom if that's why you got up.'

'The shouting woke me!' she said petulantly.

Looking at her daughter's downturned mouth, Kathryn remembered what she'd started to tell Owen – before their quarrel – about Jasmine and how strange she'd become. Today she'd seemed like a different child, even rejecting all her favourite foods in favour of tinned peas and chips, neither of which had interested her before.

She'd also puzzled Kathryn by a new fluency with numbers and money. She'd checked the change from the milkman when he was paid and added up the money she'd spent at the corner shop. It was all done with an ease that stunned Kathryn. Only three days earlier she'd tried, without success, to make Jasmine understand why two fifty-pence pieces made a pound.

Luke had been a silent observer to these new skills and he'd glanced constantly at his ever-present bear while Jasmine showed off her abilities. It was very peculiar and she'd wanted to talk to Owen about it, but now it was too late.

'I'm sorry if we woke you, Jasmine.'

'Has he gone forever?'

'For some time. We're leaving tomorrow and going home.'

'I don't want to go home. This is my home now.'

'Don't you want to see all your old friends again? I'm sure Keely's been missing you.'

'I don't remember Keely.'

'Of course you do! Jasmine, what's wrong? Is there anything worrying you, darling?'

The familiar brown eyes stared at her and there was no hint of the softness that was normally so appealing, no trace of the animation that always illuminated her features. It was as though a light had gone out, leaving her face the same but dull, all vivacity gone.

'Stare-cat!' she jeered, sticking out her tongue and squinting.

'Don't be so rude!' said Kathryn, badly shocked. 'I expect to see a better-behaved Jasmine tomorrow. Is that understood?'

'Yes, Mummy.'

Kathryn lay awake for hours thinking about her daughter. Although she'd become slightly difficult soon after they'd arrived, she'd remained basically the same girl until today. Today she'd behaved like a totally different child, and a distinctly unlovable one. She was still trying to think of an explanation when she finally drifted off into a light doze.

She was woken by the sound of Jasmine crying. The deep, heart-rending sobs had grown familiar to Kathryn after Philip left and she immediately assumed that he was behind this sudden change of character. Obviously Jasmine had started thinking about her father again, and with a sudden rush of understanding Kathryn pulled on her cotton robe and hurried to the attic bedroom.

When she opened the door, the light from the landing shone straight in on the bed and she realised that Jasmine was sleeping peacefully. She had one hand beneath her cheek and the other wrapped round a stuffed monkey that she loved, but her face was calm and there were no traces of tears on her cheeks.

Bewildered, Kathryn remained standing by the bed, aware that the noise had temporarily stopped. Then it started up

137

again and the sobs were unmistakeable. She knew that it was Jasmine and yet the figure on the bed was still tranquil.

Totally disorientated, she tried to pinpoint the source of the crying, which seemed to be coming from somewhere above her head. After a moment she turned her attention back to the heavily sleeping child beneath the duvet.

'Mummy!' Kathryn drew in her breath with shock. The hoarse whisper came from Jasmine but the mouth of the sleeping child hadn't moved.

'What's happening?' she asked incredulously.

'Help me, Mummy. I'm afraid,' whimpered her daughter.

'Where are you?' Kathryn's eyes scanned every corner of the room. 'I don't understand. Is this a trick, Jasmine? Are you playing some sort of game?'

'It's cold and dark here, Mummy.' The voice was growing fainter. 'Please help me. I won't go to the club ever again if you can get me back, and I'm very sorry about . . .' The voice tailed off into silence.

'*Jasmine!*' Kathryn's scream made the figure on the bed turn uneasily and mutter in her sleep. She began to shake the little girl until she reluctantly opened her eyes. 'Who are you?' she screamed hysterically. 'Tell me your name.'

The girl's eyes were blurred with sleep and she looked puzzled by Kathryn's anger. 'Mummy?'

'No, I'm not!' exclaimed Kathryn though clenched teeth. 'I don't know what's happening or where my daughter is but you're not Jasmine. Now tell me who you are.'

'I don't want to go out to the car,' grizzled the girl. 'I want to sleep. Leave me alone, Mummy.'

'I'll leave you alone when you tell me your name. What is it?' Grabbing the child by her shoulders, she dragged her up into a sitting position.

'I'm Claire, of course!' muttered the stranger, staring at her through eyes that were Jasmine's and yet not Jasmine's. 'Can I go back to sleep now?'

With a cry of anguish, Kathryn relaxed her grip and the child fell back on her pillows. Kathryn ran from the bedroom and rushed downstairs, racing mindlessly from room to room in a desperate search for her daughter.

Jasmine's voice was no longer audible but her fear and

desolation were all too tangible to her mother, who continued the frenzied search until the cottage looked as though it had been ransacked by burglars. Only when there was nowhere else for her to search did Kathryn sit down and start to weep. Once she'd started she was unable to stop and she was still sitting there, red-eyed and exhausted, when Jasmine came down to breakfast the next morning.

'May I have some breakfast?' she asked apprehensively. Kathryn stared furiously at her. 'What is it? Aren't you feeling well?' she continued, giving her mother a wide berth as she went towards the kitchen table.

'If you want breakfast, Claire, then I suggest you get it yourself.'

'Who's Claire?' asked the child, putting two slices of bread in the toaster.

'You are. You admitted it last night.'

'I was frightened last night. Why did you keep shaking me?'

'*Where's my daughter*?' screamed Kathryn, leaping to her feet. 'I want to know what's happened to Jasmine.'

'I'm Jasmine. Look, there's my picture on the sideboard.'

'Yes, you look the same but inside you're different. I know that you're not my daughter and I want to hear what's happened to her.'

Jasmine bit on her bottom lip in a familiar gesture, but Kathryn knew the truth. This impostor might make the same gestures and talk in the same voice but that didn't alter the situation. She continued staring accusingly at the little girl. 'Why don't you think I'm Jasmine?' she asked at last.

'Because I heard her crying last night and yet it wasn't you. When I looked in the bedroom you were quite peaceful, but Jasmine kept crying. And then she spoke to me.'

'What did she say?'

'She said she was frightened and lonely!' sobbed Kathryn. 'She asked me to help her get back. So who are you and how did you get rid of her?'

'I don't know what you're talking about.' There was the suggestion of a smile about her mouth, as though she'd enjoyed hearing of Jasmine's distress.

Kathryn shivered. 'I don't care what I have to do,' she said slowly. 'I'll get her back even if it means killing you first.' And

139

she was certain that she could hear Jasmine faintly urging her on.

The girl moved behind her chair and watched Kathryn pick up a vegetable knife from the worktop before advancing across the room towards her. Realising the danger, the little girl ran to the front door, scrabbling with the heavy bolt. It was stiff and at first she couldn't move it. Immediately, Kathryn knew that she had the impostor trapped and her hand flashed out, but the child moved like lightning, dodging to one side at the last minute. Then, while Kathryn struggled to pull the blade out of the door, she finally worked the bolt free and wrenched at the door, banging it against Kathryn's hand as hard as she could before racing down the front path.

The girl ran frantically through the village until she reached the safety of Luke's house, where she fell into a panting heap on the front porch. Only after she'd regained her breath did she bang with the brass knocker. It was important that she got her story right and an exhausted person can very easily make mistakes.

'I'm going to the cottage,' said Owen as soon as Jasmine had finished sobbing out her story. 'Kathryn shouldn't be left on her own; there's no knowing what she'll do.'

His mother nodded. 'I'll ring the doctor and ask him to join you there.'

Owen frowned. 'Let's see how she is before we get the doctor involved.'

'She's mad! She should be locked up,' cried Jamine.

Owen turned a speculative glance on her and she began to blush. She had a nasty suspicion that Owen didn't entirely believe her story, but knew that once he'd spoken to Kathryn he'd have to accept it. 'Stay here with my mother,' he ordered. 'Luke's upstairs. You can play together until I get back.'

Mary Hughes stood anxiously by the phone. 'I still think I should let Dr Potter know, Owen. Suppose she's violent?'

'If you really want to help, why not put the kettle on? It sounds as though she'll need a cup of tea once I've brought her back.' His mother shook her head but did as he asked.

At the cottage he tapped lightly on the door. It swung open beneath his hand and he walked cautiously into the room. Kathryn was sitting by the table with her head in her arms. She was crying quietly and didn't look up at him.

Checking the inside of the door, he saw the mark where she'd tried to knife Jasmine and frowned. Obviously Jasmine hadn't exaggerated the incident. Crossing the room he put a hand on her shaking shoulders. 'What's the matter?' he asked gently.

'Jasmine's gone,' she murmured brokenly. 'She's gone and I don't know how to get her back.'

'Jasmine's at my house. She's perfectly safe and probably playing happily with Luke right now.'

Kathryn swallowed hard and rubbed at her eyes with the sleeve of her dressing gown. 'That isn't Jasmine: that's Claire. I don't know where Claire's come from or how she did it, but she's living in Jasmine's body and poor Jasmine can't get back.' She moaned to herself in anguish.

Owen felt a chill of fear touch him. 'How do you know?' he asked softly.

'Jasmine was talking to me last night. She pleaded with me to help get her back. I kept asking where she was but she didn't say. She was frightened, Owen, and so am I. What should I do?'

'Come back with me,' he urged. 'You can't stay here alone like this.'

Kathryn's eyes blazed and she sat upright in her chair. 'I'm not going anywhere. Jasmine's here and she needs my help. I have to get rid of Claire.' Her gaze wandered towards the kitchen and he wondered if she was remembering the knife.

'Kathryn, this has to stop. Everyone can see that Jasmine's just the same as usual. If you try telling people this fantastic story about – '

'It's the truth!' she interrupted. 'I know it sounds crazy but I heard Jasmine crying. I know that girl isn't my daughter and I have to get rid of her.'

'Is there anything different about her?' he asked reasonably. 'I mean, if you hadn't heard Jasmine's voice, would you still have known?'

'Of course I would. For one thing she's wonderful at maths,

more like a ten-year-old than a pre-school child, and her likes and dislikes have changed. She's suddenly keen on chips and tinned peas.'

'Lots of children like chips and tinned peas!'

'But Jasmine always liked what she called "real" potatoes. She didn't enjoy chips.'

'Perhaps she's changed her mind. People do, you know.'

'But she even looks different. Her eyes aren't the same and her mouth turns down all the time. Jasmine was never sulky. I'm not mad, Owen. Please, please say you believe me.'

'Even if I do, no one else will,' he said at last.

'Then you think I'm telling the truth?' she said tenatively.

'I believe that you think it's the truth.'

'You're just humouring me!' She could have wept with disappointment. 'You're hoping that if you pretend to believe me I'll keep quiet.'

'Be reasonable, Kathryn. You say that Jasmine's different and I'm willing to keep an open mind for the moment, but for goodness' sake don't tell anyone else about this.'

'Tell them what?' asked Dr Potter, coming breezily into the room.

'What are you doing here?' asked Owen shortly.

'Your mother asked me to call.'

'I can't imagine why. Kathryn's just upset, she doesn't need a doctor.'

'Let's see how your pulse is doing, shall we, young lady?'

Kathryn snatched her hand away. 'There's nothing wrong with me. If you want to check anyone you should try Jasmine.'

Owen shook his head warningly.

'Is Jasmine sick?' the doctor asked, his eyes assessing Kathryn professionally.

'Why don't you look at her and see what you think? You might get quite a shock.'

'In what way?'

'Because she isn't Jasmine any more, she's Claire and she – . Owen squeezed her hand savagely and she bit back the rest of her sentence.

'What do you mean, she's Claire?' asked Dr Potter casually.

142

Kathryn kept silent.

After he'd taken her pulse and checked her reflexes, the doctor took Owen to one side. 'She should go to hospital, she needs total rest. The only place for that is in hospital under supervision.'

'Which hospital?'

'I thought Rauceby.'

'She is not going into a mental hospital and that's final. If she needs a rest then she can come and stay with us. Mother will take care of her.'

'Your mother's too frightened by Jasmine's story to take kindly to that idea. You have to admit it's rather bizarre behaviour. Be sensible, Owen. There's no disgrace in a mental collapse these days.'

'She's not going into hospital,' persisted Owen stubbornly.

'Very well. I'll give you some tranquillisers and get her an appointment with Dr Yarwood. He's new in Lincolnshire and having great success.'

'All right,' he conceded grudgingly. 'But only if she wants to go.'

Both men glanced to where Kathryn was sitting, rocking backwards and forwards. 'She's past knowing what she wants,' said the doctor frostily. 'I can't force you to agree but hospital really would be in her best interests.'

After he'd gone, Owen sat down next to Kathryn and put his arm round her. 'Will you come home with me?' he asked quietly. 'You can't stay here like this.'

'I have to. Jasmine needs me.'

'Just come for a few hours.'

She'd heard the conversation with the doctor and knew how close she'd come to being put in a psychiatric ward. This was an acceptable compromise. It meant that she could come back to the cottage each day and talk to her daughter.

At the Manor house, Jasmine and Luke pressed themselves against the hall panelling as Owen guided Kathryn into the house. Their hands were clasped and their eyes wary. She went past them without even a glance, holding tightly to Owen's arm.

'My bear thought she'd go into hospital,' said Luke in surprise.

'Well, your bear was wrong. Stupid old bear!'

In the front room, Kathryn sat down on the sofa with a small sigh. 'I know I'm right,' she said fiercely. 'When I walked past the girl in the hall I could tell that it wasn't Jasmine.'

'That girl is your daughter, Kathryn.'

'She is not!'

'In the eyes of the world she is. You'll have to pretend to believe that if you want to stay out of hospital.'

Kathryn bit the inside of her cheek to prevent herself from screaming. 'Do you think I'm mad?' she asked quietly. 'I want to know the truth, Owen.'

He walked across to the window and stared down at the front garden. She noticed how broad his shoulders were and had a sudden desire to feel his arms around her again, but she stayed where she was and waited for his answer. At the moment she needed emotional support even more than physical comfort. She wanted him to be on her side.

'I've read books about this sort of thing,' he conceded. 'Tara had some strange reading material and one of her books dealt with possession of a living person's body but I can't remember any of the details. I could try and find it,' he offered hesitantly.

'Please do!' she begged. 'I get the feeling that time is terribly important. Perhaps after a while it becomes impossible for Jasmine to get back. Or maybe this Claire gets spiritually stronger the longer she's inside Jasmine's body. I don't know, but I'm sure we have to act quickly. I just wish I knew how it had happened. Miranda was right, wasn't she? I should have left when she said.'

Just then Jasmine came into the room. She went straight over to Kathryn and put a small hand gently on her arm. 'Are you feeling better, Mummy?'

Kathryn fought down a desire to strike out at the child, screaming for Jasmine. 'Yes, thank you,' she said slowly.

'Is there anything I can get you, Mummy?'

Owen noticed the unnecessary repetition of the word 'Mummy', and his eyes narrowed thoughtfully.

'Would you like a cup of tea? Luke's grandma's made a fresh pot.'

'That would be lovely,' she said stiffly, and Jasmine gave her a sweet smile before returning to the kitchen.

'Kathryn, I do have to go to work this morning,' said Owen reluctantly. 'Will you be all right without me? The doctor left some tablets. You ought to take one now and another after lunch. I think they're a mild sedative.'

'I'm not taking anything. I need to stay alert. Jasmine might need me.'

'If you don't take a tablet I can't leave you here with the children. It isn't fair on them.'

'What do you think I'm going to do?' she asked angrily.

'Judging by the way you looked at Jasmine just now it won't be anything pleasant.'

'She *isn't* Jasmine!' Kathryn shouted, jumping to her feet. 'I thought you understood that.'

'Tea, Mummy,' said Jasmine, carrying a small tray carefully into the room. 'I hope it's sweet enough,' she added with a glance at Kathryn's set face.

'I don't take sugar!' said Kathryn triumphantly, looking to Owen for some reaction.

'I know that.' Jasmine smiled. 'The sugar's for shock.'

'I'm not in shock now. I'm just going out of my mind trying to help my daughter!' screamed Kathryn.

Jasmine frowned. 'I'm your daughter.'

'You're not! You're Claire. You told me that yourself. Oh, God! Why can't I have Jasmine back again?' and she started to sob.

Owen signalled for Jasmine to leave and then took Kathryn in his arms. 'It will all come right,' he promised, stroking her hair off her forehead. 'Give it time.'

'I haven't got much time. Owen, you really do believe it's possible, don't you?'

'Of course,' he assured her, but his eyes were troubled and before he left he made sure that she took one of the yellow capsules prescribed by Dr Potter.

'She should sleep a lot,' he told his mother as he climbed into the car. 'If she gets hysterical again, give her another tablet. They're in the bottle by the clock.'

145

'What about the children?'

'Keep them well away from her. I'm sorry to leave you like this but I've got two important meetings today. I'll try and get some time off so that I can help her through the worst of this, whatever it is.'

'That poor little girl!' murmured his mother, but Owen wasn't sure that he agreed with her.

Chapter 11

'Are you sure that you don't mind having the children, Andrew?' asked Owen anxiously.

'Of course not, we wouldn't have suggested it if we'd minded. Where's Kathryn?' he added, glancing towards the parked car.

'Still packing. She must think the climate's very variable in York!'

'We haven't seen much of you two lately. Everything all right?'

Owen nodded. 'Fine, thanks. Naturally it's taken Kathryn quite a time to come to terms with her mother's death.'

'Is that right? I heard she'd been – '

'Right, I'll be off,' said Owen quickly.

'No engagement yet?'

'Mother sent her good wishes,' said Owen, retreating down the path.

'Thanks. She doesn't live with you any more, I gather?'

'No, all in all it seemed better if Luke and I started coping on our own.'

'With Kathryn's help!' Andrew smiled.

'That's right. See you on Sunday night.' With a final wave to the children, Owen made his escape.

He knew that people were talking about Kathryn. In a small village like South Willoughby it was difficult to keep anything secret for long, but as far as he knew no one had heard that she believed her daughter to be possessed by a dead ten-year-old called Claire. He hoped that this short break might help her. It had taken him days to talk her into leaving the village at all, and only the threat of Rauceby hospital had persuaded her. He also hoped that the children enjoyed the weekend with Andrew and Maggie. Andrew had certainly been surprisingly keen to have them.

'This is a very big house,' commented Jasmine, settling herself in one of the twin beds in the top-floor bedroom that night.

'I don't like it. I want to go home.'

'What does your bear think of it?'

'Nothing,' said Luke nervously. 'My bear hasn't said a thing all day.'

'That makes a change! Good night, Luke.'

She quickly fell asleep, but Luke was still awake at midnight and he sat up anxiously when their door opened and Andrew entered. 'What do you want?' he whispered.

'Get dressed and come downstairs,' said Andrew curtly. 'Be sure not to wake the girl.'

Luke wriggled further down his bed. 'I don't want to come.'

'Do you want us to send something for you?' asked Andrew softly.

He didn't. Quickly he pulled on his clothes, then went down to the large living-room where they stood waiting for him. He knew them all.

Without a word they began filing out of the house and Luke went with them. They walked down the slope, past the village green, and then turned the corner to the back of Dayton village church, finishing up in a small, bush-lined clearing. Luke's teeth began to chatter and he was glad that he was still holding the bear.

The coven formed their circle round him. He sat on the grass, taking little notice of the chants and incantations that opened the meeting, although he was rather surprised to discover that he understood all the words they said and knew what words were still to come.

His interest aroused, he looked at the adults more closely and as he studied each face he realised that he suddenly knew things about all of them. He knew that Chrissie liked his father and had hoped to marry him after Tara died; he knew that Douglas Randolph had put a spell on his wife and that his 'overlooking' was slowly killing her. When he came to Dr

148

Potter he even knew that Dr Potter was aware of the spell and had agreed to let Mrs Randolph die.

Luke was still puzzling over his new knowledge when the chanting stopped and the thirteen adults looked expectantly at him. 'Tell us what we should do,' said old Mr Bentley, his voice quavery with age.

'Should she go or stay?' asked Maggie.

'Live, or die?' demanded Mrs Cook.

'Will she marry him or not?' Chrissie's voice was sharp with jealousy.

Luke stared blankly at them. All he wanted to do was go back to bed.

'Tell us!' chanted the coven, leaning forward in their excitement. 'Tell us what we should do.'

He studied their hard, inquisitive faces and his bottom lip trembled. He didn't like any of them and he didn't understand why he was there. He hoped that he was ill and this was a nightmare, but when he pinched the back of his hand it hurt too much to be a dream. As they reached out towards him he whimpered and clutched his bear round the waist. 'Go away!' he cried. 'I don't like you. I want my mummy.'

'Concentrate,' said Douglas Randolph sternly. 'Let your mind go free. You have the knowledge now. Tell us what to do.'

He wanted to say that he didn't have any knowledge, he didn't even know his tables yet. He opened his mouth to tell them, but suddenly there was a flash of light in his head and his mind cleared. Now he could hear his mother's voice speaking, reciting spells and equations. He was full of knowledge, knowledge that had been handed down by word of mouth for centuries, and all at once he was confident, and a great calm descended on him.

Suddenly he understood that this was why he'd been saved. He had lived because his mother had given him all her knowledge and that knowledge had protected him. For a moment he wondered why it hadn't protected her. The touch of Douglas' hand brought him back to the present.

'What does she say?' asked Douglas.

Luke listened. 'I can't hear anything.' Douglas' mouth twisted with annoyance. 'She isn't here,' apologised Luke. 'It isn't night-travel time.'

149

The coven stared at him, still waiting, but Andrew's wife understood his confusion. 'What does your bear say?' she asked kindly.

That was easy. 'He wants Kathryn to stay. He says Kathryn *has* to stay.'

A murmur of disapproval ran round the circle. 'Are you sure?' demanded Andrew.

'Of course I am! He says she's needed.'

There was a short silence. Dr Potter was visibly annoyed. 'What about us? Isn't she a threat to the coven, to the entire village? The rule's always been no unbelievers under the age of sixty.'

'My bear says she isn't a threat to your stupid little meetings.'

Their immediate anger frightened him but that was what the bear had said and he didn't dare tell them lies. 'He says revenge is what matters and you must get her to stay. If you don't, Mummy will be very angry.'

Visibly annoyed, Andrew reached out for Luke but the boy turned sharply towards him and began to chant. The circle moved back a little, remembering Tara's power and the scope of her knowledge, so far ahead of theirs. With a cry of pain, Andrew withdrew his hand and looked at the huge blisters forming on the palm. 'Bitch!' he muttered furiously, but he didn't try to touch the boy again.

'We'll make sure Kathryn stays,' promised Chrissie, tossing back her long blonde hair.

The bear suddenly jerked in Luke's hand and she staggered backwards, her hands across her breasts. 'The bear doesn't like you,' explained Luke.

'Shut up!' cried Chrissie angrily.

Luke glared at her. 'It's not my fault!' he shouted. 'I didn't want the knowledge. I hate you all. I just want to be left alone.'

'Leave him,' said Douglas casually. 'He's told us what we needed to know. We'll do as Tara says because we daren't do anything else, but he isn't important. He's just a mouthpiece, a breathing telephone. He can't be our new leader.'

'He has the knowledge,' Andrew reminded him.

'But not, I think, the desire to use it,' replied Douglas.

150

With murmurs of agreement they all went into the bushes in a group, leaving Luke alone with his bear. He followed slowly behind them and then stood at the edge of the shrubbery and watched. He studied who was with whom and how they took their pleasure.

'That's what it's all about for them,' said his bear contemptuously. 'They're amateurs. They don't know anything about the true path to Lucifer. If they did they wouldn't need sex. Power is far more exciting than what they're doing.'

Luke turned away from the writhing bodies and returned to Andrew's house. He felt tired and confused, his mind still occupied with some of the images that had flashed through his brain when he released the knowledge. 'Why didn't she just appear in front of them?' he muttered angrily. 'Why did she have to do it through me?'

'She can show herself to you because you have the knowledge too. The coven hasn't got it and she needs to talk to them another way. That's why I'm here. I'm your link to the other side.'

'If I threw you away she couldn't,' said Luke thoughtfully.

'I'd come back. I'd keep coming back until it was all over.'

'I thought you would,' muttered Luke as he climbed back into bed. 'Fancy old Mr Bentley kissing Chrissie like he did. I bet she hated it.' The bear shared his thoughts and was pleased.

'Everything OK?' asked Owen when he collected the children after lunch the following day.

'Hardly knew we'd got them!'

'What do you say, Luke?'

Luke bent his head and muttered a half-hearted thank you. Jasmine put out a hand and smiled up at Andrew, thanking him very sincerely, but Andrew still wasn't comfortable with her.

Kathryn sat in the front passenger seat and watched as the children approached. She couldn't understand why everyone didn't realise that Jasmine was different. If they had to listen to the quiet weeping that haunted her every night, they might look at the girl with fresh eyes, she thought bitterly.

Owen glanced at her and smiled encouragingly. She wondered what she'd have done without him over the past few weeks. There were times when she thought that he believed her and times when she was certain that he didn't, but his kindness had helped her keep a hold on her sanity.

'Did you have a nice time?' she asked Luke, ignoring her daughter.

'Not really,' said Luke irritably. 'I couldn't sleep.'

They all went back to the Manor House. Kathryn and her daughter had stayed there ever since the night Jasmine vanished. They would have gone back to the cottage sooner if Jasmine hadn't been able to reach her mother in Owen's house; as she could, Kathryn was glad of Owen's company and Luke kept Claire out of her sight for most of the time.

Once the children were asleep, Owen poured them two brandies. 'At least you've had a short break,' he said with a sigh. 'I take it you couldn't hear Jasmine in York?'

'I couldn't hear her, but I knew that she was calling me. I shouldn't have gone. It was selfish.'

'I can't go on like this, Kathryn. It's got to come to an end.'

'I'm going to see my aunt,' said Kathryn firmly. 'I've been putting it off for too long. I'm frightened of what I'll hear but unless I can talk to someone soon I shall end up in a locked ward.'

'I wish I knew what the truth was!' said Owen despairingly.

'What about those books you said Tara had?'

'They've vanished. Perhaps they were in the pile that Maggie kept.'

Kathryn rested her head against his shoulder. 'I wish I could pretend it wasn't happening,' she said quietly, 'but I can't. I have to help her, whatever the cost.'

'I don't know what to do any more,' said Owen miserably.

'Take me to bed,' she whispered, and he did. He was such a skilled and passionate lover that it was impossible for Kathryn to think of anything but him when they were together. It was the only time she had a respite from Jasmine's distraught pleas for help and sometimes she wished that they could stay in bed forever.

As soon as Owen left for work the next morning she rang her aunt.

'Kathryn! How nice!' exclaimed Victoria. 'I was beginning to wonder if you'd gone back south without letting me know.'

'I should have gone by now but something terrible's happening here,' she explained. 'Can I come and see you this afternoon? It really is very important.'

'That will be lovely, my dear. I've got a lot to tell you too. Some of my old friends have been very helpful about Owen's first wife. It's really quite extraordinary.'

'I'll see you around two,' said Kathryn gratefully and waited impatiently for the morning to pass.

The curtains were all drawn in Victoria's flat and Kathryn had difficulty adjusting her eyes to the gloom. She stubbed her foot against a chair in the kitchen and stumbled.

'I'm sorry about the light, dear. I don't want anyone to see us together.'

'Why not?'

'It could put me in considerable danger.'

'You?' said Kathryn in surprise.

'Yes. They're relying on your ignorance, and certainly won't want anyone to enlighten you at this point in time.'

'Who are "they"?' she asked incredulously.

'Those who belong to the dark side,' said her aunt softly.

Kathryn was confused. 'I've come here about Jasmine. What do you mean, the dark side? Is that where Jasmine is?'

'Kathryn, South Willoughby has been a centre for witchcraft for more than a hundred years, and the villagers have always made a point of keeping to themselves. In recent times their covens have caused very little trouble, but it wasn't always like that. The village used to be home to a group of satanists, people dedicated to evil for evil's sake. They ruled the whole village by fear and weren't averse to the ritual of human sacrifice. The worst leader ever recorded was actually rector of the church at that time. The story is that he allowed his own baby son to have his throat cut while his young wife looked on. Her ghost is said to haunt South Willoughby.'

'Then I did see her!' said Kathryn triumphantly. 'Her name was Miranda.'

The old lady looked troubled. 'Previous sightings have always been linked to disasters. Did she speak to you?'

'She begged me to leave the village.'

'Why didn't you listen to her?' said Victoria despairingly.

'Because of Jasmine. Did you find out anything else?'

'Tara Hughes – Beswick, as she was born – brought true evil back into the village with her. Her mother was a witch, trained by the infamous Gerald Gardner, and she'd educated her daughter well. When she married Owen and moved to South Willoughby, satanism came back to the village. Not long ago, a young girl died in the churchyard. Her throat had been cut in the same way as the rector's son's nearly a century earlier. The church should have been destroyed at that time, of course, but the rector prevented it. Now it's a focal point for all the evil in the area.

'Tara appears to have been a skilled witch and a highly unpleasant person. She slept with any man who took her fancy and flaunted her affairs in her husband's face. It was too much for some of the older villagers, but if they protested they were quickly removed. Deaths among the older inhabitants of South Willoughby rose alarmingly last year. It was as though she was clearing away all opposition.'

'What about Owen?' asked Kathryn anxiously. 'Was he involved?'

'Some people say that he was never a member of the actual coven and that his marriage to Tara was an unfortunate accident. Others think that he was sent to Cornwall to find her because the coven had heard of her power. There's also a rumour that after a time he tried to divorce her but the coven stopped him. The truth is probably a mixture of all three. He must have known there was black magic in the village, he'd lived there all his life, and it does seem unlikely that he could marry an advanced priestess of satanism by chance. However, he's never been seen at any sabbats.'

'He must have known something,' murmured Kathryn.

'I would imagine so. By the time she died, Tara Hughes held all the village in the palm of her hand. She'd begun travelling round the area, training young people in the art of satanism, and in time she would doubtless have travelled the whole countryside, just as Aleister Crowley and Gerald Gar-

154

dner did before her. But she died, and the village has probably returned to its old ways with sabbats held once a month on a Sunday night. Hopefully when Tara died she took the true evil with her.'

'How did she die? I'd have thought she could have saved herself.'

'She was murdered,' said Victoria softly. 'A priestess of Tara's ability would have expected to live out her three score years and ten without interruption.'

'Who was powerful enough to murder her?'

'In the village? No one. An outsider may have been brought in; someone even more advanced than Tara, whose magic was stronger than hers.'

'Do you believe that's what happened?'

'It's the only logical solution, but it leaves two questions unanswered. Who brought the killer in? And did the rest of the coven know what was happening?'

'Where does Luke fit in?' asked Kathryn. 'You thought that he was dangerous, didn't you? Could he have killed his mother?'

'That would be impossible,' said her aunt firmly. 'She had years of experience behind her. Even if she'd brought her son up as a satanist he couldn't have overtaken her. No, I think that Luke is dangerous now because he's been given some of his mother's power.'

'No one knows why he survived the fire that killed Tara. I suspect that she saved him by giving him her knowledge as she died. That would have kept him safe.'

'But if her knowledge saved Luke, why couldn't it save her?'

'Someone must have put a spell on her. A specific killing spell naming Tara Hughes. If a skilled satanist had decided that she must die, then nothing she did would save her. Naturally her son wouldn't have been included in the spell and would therefore be protected by the knowledge.'

'Does that make him the new head of the coven?'

'That was probably Tara's intention, but I believe there's a weakness in the boy that she may not have noticed. He has the power but not the desire to use it. The coven must have hoped that he would take over but have probably already realised

155

their mistake. They're almost certainly searching for a new leader.'

'If Luke doesn't want to use his powers, why is he a danger to me?'

Victoria rubbed a hand wearily over her face. 'I wish I knew. I suppose it's possible that what I sensed was the normal hostility of a young child for anyone who threatens to take his mother's place, but I don't think so. It's a more powerful emotion than that. I wonder if it's all part of the knowledge from his mother.'

'You mean it's Tara who's making him hostile towards me?'

'Luke could conceivably be transmitting his mother's emotions. His own feelings towards you may be quite amicable but a personality as strong as hers in life would undoubtedly be equally powerful in death.'

'Why should she hate me?'

'Owen was her husband; perhaps she resents you being close to him.'

'I don't believe it,' said Kathryn. 'I know there's something wrong with Luke – the way he talks through his bear gives me the creeps – but I can't believe that it's Tara influencing him. If she could contact Luke, surely she'd be more interested in taking revenge on her murderer?'

'I don't pretend to understand it, Kathryn, but I do know that you should leave South Willoughby immediately.'

'I wish I could, but I have to stay here now because of Jasmine.'

'What's happened to Jasmine?' asked her aunt.

Nervously at first, but with increasing confidence, Kathryn told her story.

When she'd finished, Victoria looked out uneasily from behind her net curtains. The forecourt was deserted, not even a car was parked there, but she still felt as though she was being watched.

After listening to her niece she wished that she was younger and stronger, acutely aware that her powers were no longer at their height. She wondered what Kathryn expected her to do.

'Kathryn', she said softly. 'If what you say is true then Jasmine is beyond your reach now.'

156

'*No!* That can't be true. There must be a way of getting her back.'

'I wish there were.'

'How did it happen? I don't understand how Claire ever got the chance to take over from Jasmine. Where was Jasmine at the time? Asleep? Unconscious?'

'Did Jasmine ever talk to you about her dreams?'

'Yes, she did! She'd had terribly vivid ones over the past weeks. In fact, she sometimes had difficulty in understanding that they were dreams. It was very strange. Just before we came to South Willoughby she kept talking about a boy called Luke that she met in her dreams. Then we arrived and the first person we met was Luke Hughes.'

'Undoubtedly the same child,' said Victoria sadly. 'Jasmine wasn't dreaming. She was leaving her body and going on night-journeys. It's called astral projection and it's very dangerous.'

'How did she ever learn to do such a thing?'

'Some of us have a more developed astral body than others. Possibly someone encouraged Jasmine. They could have been trying to forge a link with you, using your child.'

'Where did she go on these night-journeys?'

'She could have gone anywhere. Once she'd abandoned her body, time and distance as we know them ceased to exist. Unfortunately the danger to night-walkers is that their astral body may become detached from their physical body when the body's resources are depleted. The early hours of the morning are always a dangerous time.

'It's probable that Jasmine – either through her own carelessness or someone else's determination – arrived back late and found that her body was already waking, inhabited by someone else.'

'But where did Claire come from?'

'There are always lost souls; souls unable to make the transition from life to death due to shock or anger. They wait in limbo until something helps them across, and while they're waiting they're constantly searching for an empty body that offers them a chance of returning to life. No doubt the child Claire died abruptly and rather shockingly. Another girl's body would provide her with a wonderful opportunity to live again.'

157

'Are you saying that I've got to accept Claire as my daughter or be locked up as insane?'

Victoria nodded.

'Well, I won't. I'd rather kill her.'

'That wouldn't bring Jasmine back.'

'If she can't live, why should Claire? Surely someone can help me, Aunt. You must see that I have to do something.'

'If Jasmine's death was deliberate,' said Victoria reluctantly, 'you could try and find out who was behind it.'

'By doing what? I don't know who she met on her night-journeys. Except Luke, of course,' she added thoughtfully. 'Suppose I do find out, what then?'

'I'm sorry,' said her aunt sadly. 'There are some things you really shouldn't know. I've said too much already. Perhaps you should go; I'm feeling rather tired.'

'*You have to tell me!*' shouted Kathryn. 'I'm her mother. I'd do anything to get her back.'

'Would you be willing to get involved in black magic? Would you consider making a bargain with satanists? Because that's the only way you'll ever get rid of Claire and bring Jasmine back. They have the power to do all this, but it will be on their own terms.'

'What would they want in return?' asked Kathryn hesitantly.

'Don't even contemplate it, Kathryn. Contact with these people would be dangerous for you and everyone around you. Somehow you must come to terms with what's happened and pick up your life again.'

'Is Claire part of this new life? Am I expected to take her with me? How could I? No, I'm going to do anything that's necessary to get Jasmine back. I know you mean well but you simply don't understand. How could you? You've never had a child of your own.'

Victoria began moving slowly towards the front door. 'She may not be the same if you do get her back,' she said gently. 'Might it not be better to leave things as they are?'

'I can't! I shall go mad if I can't put things right again. It's like living in a nightmare all the time, only I know I'm never going to wake up. I have to do anything I can. At least you've given me a little hope.'

158

'I didn't mean to,' said her aunt sadly. She sagged against the doorframe as her niece drove away. She knew South Willoughby was tightening its grip on Kathryn and she was totally helpless. She couldn't think of anyone who could help Kathryn now.

Once they'd killed her, as she knew they would, Kathryn would be entirely alone.

Chapter 12

As dusk started to fall, Victoria checked her flat carefully. The doors were locked, the windows closed, yet she knew that these were childish measures. She was helpless if the coven had determined she should die. At eight o'clock she went to rest on her bed. The tension of the day had exhausted her, drained her strength. She was too old to try and fight them, too old to do anything that would be effective. They would come for her and she would die. She hoped to die well; it was the waiting that was difficult.

Her eyelids drooped and she dozed a little, her wrinkled hands folded neatly on her chest as though in prayer. She knew that she should try and pray but doubted if it would be effective. Only a priest could fight them now and these days she didn't know any priests. She had known some once, men of insight and breadth of vision, but they'd left their church, shaken by its refusal to accept the truth. These days Victoria had no contact with organised religion.

A slight sigh alerted her and she opened her eyes. She had expected to see the boy but she'd been wrong. A woman stood by her dressing table. She was tall and thin with long dark hair and her piercing green eyes were fixed on Victoria. Cold, assessing eyes that were full of the knowledge. The room felt cool and the old woman shivered.

'You had no right to talk about night-travel,' said the woman savagely. 'Now she's prepared. She was meant to stay an innocent.'

Victoria stared back at her visitor, refusing to be cowed by her. 'I wanted to warn her,' she said defiantly. 'She needs protecting.'

160

'Luke is all the protection she needs.'

'I meant protection against you,' retorted Victoria.

'Aren't you afraid?' asked Tara and her lips curved in a smile.

Victoria's fear was so great that her teeth were chattering together and she could feel her stomach tightening. Abject terror swept over her until she thought that it might kill her before the coven could, but she shook her head in an angry denial. Tara ignored her. She could see the truth for herself.

As the dead woman moved closer to the bed, Victoria felt a light, tingling sensation creeping insidiously over her body, followed by a constriction round her chest as though the skin was too tight. One look at Tara's gloating expression made her realise that this was the beginning. Anxiously she tried to work out what they intended to do, but she could make no sense of it. Then she glanced at her hands and saw that her thin shrunken fingers were suddenly puffy and the loose skin on her wrists seemed fleshier.

The blood coursed loudly through her veins, her ears reverberated with the sound of her heartbeats, and with petrified eyes she watched her skirt and blouse balloon up from her body as though a breeze was trapped beneath them. When Victoria put a hand on her skirt to flatten it she met with unexpected resistance.

She struggled to sit up but felt heavy and awkward. Then she caught sight of herself in the wardrobe mirror and stared at her image in disbelief. Her entire body was swollen; her ankles and feet nothing more than shapeless blobs of flesh, the bones beneath the skin entirely hidden by the increasing mass of tissue. Her ears rang with the pressure and she felt the button on her waistband break loose, allowing the material to cope with her increasing bulk.

Her outline had become grotesque and she could see the veins of her now bulbous hands throbbing beneath the skin. Slowly the pressure in her ears increased and a strange rippling sensation coursed up her arm. Peering through swollen eyes she saw that the skin was splitting to reveal the flesh beneath and in one dreadful moment she realised what was going to happen. She was going to burst.

Her eyeballs bulged as she struggled for sanity, until her

161

heart, pushed beyond its limits, gave out a few blessed seconds before her entire body exploded, covering the walls and ceilings with bone and tissue.

Tara's work was finished. Her outline blurred and her features dissolved as her energy drained away, exhausted by what she'd accomplished. Within seconds of her disappearance the entire room burst into flames. Five minutes later the occupants of neighbouring flats were being evacuated by the panic-stricken warden and his wife, but they searched in vain for Victoria.

It was a very quiet funeral, and would have been even quieter if the disaster hadn't caused some of the more ghoulish people in the area to attend out of curiosity. Kathryn read a fireman's account of what they'd found – a flat so devastated by heat that it looked as though a fireball had swept through it – and knew that Victoria had been murdered. She didn't confide in Owen. From now on she was going to handle things alone. One death was enough.

'Why won't you marry me?' asked Owen yet again as she lay in his arms that night. 'You never use the cottage now. We're behaving as though we're man and wife. What's holding you back?'

'I've no emotional energy left for marriage,' explained Kathryn evasively. 'Perhaps when this is over it will be different.'

'When what's over?' he asked irritably.

'We'll talk about it again if I get Jasmine back.'

'What makes you think you can get her back – always assuming she's actually missing, of course?'

'Aunt Victoria said there was a way.'

'I still love you, Kathryn.'

'Even if I'm mad?'

'I've never said you're mad.'

Kathryn looked speculatively at him. 'I know, and I keep wondering why. Most men would have got shot of me as soon as I started talking about possession. I sometimes think you know more than you're telling me, Owen.'

'I don't know anything at all. I just want to marry you and take you away from all this.'

'You know I can't leave.'

'Not long ago you wouldn't marry me because you had to leave here. Now you won't marry me because you've got to stay!'

'I'm sorry,' she murmured, and she really was, but these days all she could think about was Jasmine, and contacting the people who knew how to get her back.

The next morning the children were in the front garden when they saw a young woman drive up in a smart Fiat sports car. She gave them both a friendly wink as she passed and they turned to stare after her.

'Emily!' exclaimed Kathryn, opening the door. 'What a surprise! I wondered if I'd upset you. It's been ages since we met up.'

Luke watched her go indoors and raised his eyebrows. 'My bear says she spells trouble,' he told a scowling Claire. 'We have to go to the churchyard. Come on, race you there.' He set off as fast as he could but knew that he wouldn't win. Claire had the advantage of better physical co-ordination and once more he wished that Jasmine would come back.

They sat on Tara's headstone, swinging their legs so that their heels scuffed against her name. 'Why did your dad put such a funny inscription on this?' asked Claire. 'What does it mean?'

'It's a secret,' said Luke shortly.

'What do we have to do now we're here?'

'Tell the coven, of course. They need to know about Emily.' He shut his eyes, slowed his breathing and thought hard about her. He conjured up a picture of her as she'd looked when she got out of the car, recalling in minute detail her black cotton shirt, full red skirt and black court shoes. Then he concentrated on her face, the smiling mouth and bright eyes. He had a good visual memory and the picture was perfect.

Behind his large leather desk, Douglas Randolph suddenly lost track of what the bespectacled client opposite him was saying as a vision of a young girl in a bright-red skirt flashed across his brain. For a moment he was puzzled, then he recognised Clive's southern wife and his mouth tightened. She'd never fitted in, but they'd been prepared to accept that. Interference was another matter altogether and must be punished.

Clive too lost his concentration in mid-sentence, as he saw his wife walking into Owen's house. His heart sank as he realised what this meant. She was interfering, and at the most inappropriate time. With a muttered excuse he stumbled out of the building and back into his car. He was heartbroken. Emily meant so much to him, but there was no choice. The coven and its work had to come first.

Andrew and Maggie were both out in their garden at Dayton, attempting to make sense of the rockery, when they received the message. They glanced at one another and gave the slightest of nods as recognition of what it meant. They didn't mind. Neither of them cared for Emily.

Within the space of twenty minutes, all thirteen adults involved knew that Tara's plan was under threat. They all made their way home to unite their powers and make sure Kathryn stayed in South Willoughby.

Back in the house, Kathryn and Emily were still talking. 'You have to believe me!' Emily insisted, pink in the face. 'I couldn't credit it either. I followed Clive because I thought he had another woman. I didn't believe South Willoughby was the sort of village to have a residents' association and I was right. But it wasn't another woman.'

'No,' agreed Kathryn, 'obviously not. But how can you be sure it was a coven?'

'They'd left the library window open because it was so warm and I heard them swearing loyalty to Satan. How much more proof do you need?'

'My aunt warned me about a black-magic circle but I didn't know who made up the group. Now that I do, I can make contact with them.'

'Are you out of your tiny mind? The last thing you should do is talk to them. I came to warn you so that you could get the hell out of this place. The coven were talking about you. They're using you for their own ends, waiting for you to contact them so that they can finish off their plan, whatever that may be. You mustn't do it, Kathryn. You must get out of here *now*.'

164

'If I let them make a bargain with me they won't hurt me. My soul in exchange for Jasmine, or something weird like that!' She tried to laugh.

'Kathryn, your soul isn't something to be tossed away lightly. It's *you*. The real you, the essence of your being. Without your soul you're nothing. Just an empty shell, not much better than Jasmine.'

'But if it brought Jasmine back . . . ?'

'Why should it? People like that never keep their word. They don't belong to a Boy Scout troop. This is black magic, not a bit of crystal-ball gazing. These people are dangerous.'

'Your husband's one of them,' pointed out Kathryn.

'Which is why I'm leaving him.'

'When?'

'Today; I plan to be gone when he gets home from work. I can't stay here. He's a satanist, a man who worships evil and uses it for his own purposes. He isn't the Clive that I thought I knew, he's someone entirely different. I'm going, Kathryn, and I'll take you with me if you like.'

She was very tempted. The thought of leaving the village now, forgetting everything and going back to Sussex was wonderful, but it would mean taking Claire with her and leaving Jasmine behind. She couldn't do that. Regretfully she shook her head. 'I can't.'

'You can! Listen, suppose you take Claire to a spiritualist when you get back? Surely they can contact lost souls? Who's to say that you can only help Jasmine by staying here? I'd have thought you could get this Claire exorcised or something by one of these ministers who specialise in that sort of thing. The church is far more open-minded about possession these days. Come on, Kathryn. We'll leave this afternoon. Don't pack, don't do anything that might warn people. We'll say we're going shopping in Leicester and once we're out of the village we won't look back.'

Kathryn hadn't considered an exorcism, but what Emily said made sense and now she too wanted to get away. Even hearing that Owen wasn't a member of the circle hadn't changed her feelings about marriage. She didn't want to be his wife. The idea of following in the dead Tara's footsteps was decidedly unappealing. 'All right,' she said decisively. 'Claire and I will be ready by two.'

165

Emily sighed thankfully. 'Good! Just think, Kathryn, in a few hours we'll be out in the real world again. I can hardly wait!'

After she'd gone, Kathryn went to find the children. As she'd expected they were in the churchyard. Luke was sitting on his mother's grave while Claire was skipping on the footpath. Remembering how Jasmine had never learnt to skip, Kathryn felt a surge of the familiar hatred for this imposter. With a great effort she put a smile on her face.

'Jasmine, Emily has asked us both to Leicester this afternoon. We'll have a nice girls' afternoon going round the shops.'

'What about Luke?'

'I can always go next door,' said Luke. 'I hate shopping.'

'Lunch will be at twelve. Come back promptly please.'

'Yes, Mummy,' said Claire politely, smiling at the expression that crossed Kathryn's face.

As she left, Kathryn crossed the grass to look at Miranda's headstone. 'I'm going,' she whispered softly. 'I've decided to take your advice. Thank you for warning me.'

She had half expected to see Miranda again, but she didn't materialise and Kathryn turned to go. Then she noticed something strange about the tombstone. The inscription looked different. It was in modern lettering and far more clearly etched in the stone. Assuming that someone had cleaned it up, Kathryn bent down. Then everything started spinning crazily round her and she gave a low moan as she found herself staring at an entirely different name.

Emily Parsons
Beloved wife of Clive.
Born 8th March 1966 and
departed this life 12th September 1982.
In the midst of life
we are in death.

She felt terribly sick, and it was difficult to breathe. The words blurred in front of her eyes, jumping about in chaotic disorder only to return to their devastating message. No

166

matter how many times she looked away, the inscription remained the same.

Eventually she got unsteadily to her feet and stumbled out of the churchyard, unaware of the children's scrutiny. She had to call Emily straight away, tell her what she'd seen and beg her to remain indoors for the rest of the day. They could always leave South Willoughby tomorrow. Tomorrow was the 13th September, the danger would have passed by then. It was today that was dangerous.

She was feeling so shocked that at first it didn't register that a crowd of people were gathered on the pavement by the bend in the road, but finally the size of the gathering alerted her to the fact that something was wrong and with a sinking feeling in the pit of her stomach she walked slowly towards them.

She saw the lorry first. A large, continental juggernaut had jack-knifed across the road and the driver was standing by his cab, white-faced and trembling as he talked to a policeman. Letting her gaze move on, Kathryn finally found the courage to look at the twisted wreckage beneath the huge vehicle, and saw the crushed remains of a bright-red Fiat sports car. The top half had been sliced off and there was no sign of the driver.

'What happened?' she asked the nearest woman.

For once a villager didn't seem to resent her presence. The woman's face was as shocked as Kathryn's and she shook her head sadly. 'He lost control on the bend. The other driver didn't stand a chance. A dreadful thing; totally decapitated, they say. A woman, too. Seems worse somehow when it's a woman.'

Kathryn turned and ran for home. She was gasping for breath and her legs felt like jelly but she forced herself on until she fell into the hallway, sinking down on the wool carpet with her head between her knees.

'What are you doing?' asked Luke, who had followed right behind her.

Kathryn didn't answer.

'Have you hurt yourself?' he enquired politely.

'No, I . . . I . . . I've had a shock,' she gasped, trying to stop her teeth from chattering.

'What a shame,' he remarked and then stepped over her. 'We're going to get a drink if that's all right.'

167

Claire didn't speak to Kathryn, but as soon as she was indoors she began reciting a rhyme and the words made Luke crease up with laughter. It took a moment or two for them to sink in, but when they did, Kathryn was stunned by their calculated cruelty.

'Oh, dear Mama, what is that thing,
Spread out like strawberry jam?
Hush, hush, my dear, it's poor Papa,
Run over by a tram.'

It was too much. With a cry, Kathryn jumped to her feet and grabbed hold of the child, shaking her furiously and accidentally banging her head against the wall.

'Don't you dare come in here with your revolting rhymes!' she shouted. 'Emily's dead. There's nothing funny about that, and you're a horrible, horrible child. Jasmine would never have been so vile. She was a kind girl and I loved her. I hate you!' she finished with a sob. 'I wish you'd die and let me have my daughter back.'

Claire's eyes were terrified and she struggled to get free, twisting and turning until Kathryn finally released her. 'You're mad!' she shouted, running for the front door again. 'I didn't say anything about Emily. I was just telling Luke a funny rhyme and I'm going to tell on you. I'll tell Dr Potter and he'll have you locked up. And serve you jolly well right too.'

Kathryn stared after her, her heart pounding in her chest, until with a whimper she sank back to the floor. After a moment she forced herself to think carefully. Obviously Claire was going to fetch help and she had to decide what to do before Dr Potter arrived. At least she was better prepared to face him than she would have been if Emily hadn't managed to talk to her.

Dr Potter came cautiously into the house. He knew how important this moment was and hoped that he'd handle it correctly. If he failed, retailiation would be swift and terrible, but if he succeeded then he would gain in status and power.

168

Kathryn had gone into the drawing-room and was sitting in the bow window on the cushioned seat that ran the length of the wall. 'Emily's dead,' she said in a flat voice.

'I know, I was called to the accident.'

'It was you, wasn't it?'

'It was a lorry that killed her. That bend is very dangerous.'

'I saw her name on a tombstone in the churchyard. I knew then what you were going to do but I was too late too warn her.'

'It was an accident, Mrs Talkes.'

'I mean the coven, not you personally.'

He moved a little nearer to her motionless figure. 'What kind of nonsense is that?'

'Emily saw you, Dr Potter. She followed Clive to a meeting and listened through the open window. She named you all.'

'Emily is dead now. This could well be a recurrence of your previous illness. First your daughter isn't your daughter, now there's a coven in the village!'

'Both facts are true. I'm not asking you to confirm anything. I want you to set up a meeting for me.'

'A meeting with whom?'

'The person who's in charge, I suppose. Anyone who can tell me what I have to do to get my daughter back.'

'And what am I meant to do about Jasmine's story? You did attack her.'

'I did not. It's just her word against mine. Surely you should believe the adult?'

'Luke was a witness.'

'And will the coven let him talk?'

'Probably not.'

'Precisely. I'm moving back to my cottage this afternoon. Will you contact me as soon as you can?'

With a murmur of assent the doctor turned and left her.

For a long time Kathryn continued looking out at the garden. The leaves were falling from the large oak tree by the gate. Soon the weather would turn, she thought to herself. The summer had been dry and warm, ideal country weather, but once the evenings began to draw in the thought of being cut off from civilisation wasn't so appealing. She must get her life straightened out and then move on.

169

Eventually she returned to the churchyard and Miranda's headstone. It looked perfectly normal, the letters once again difficult to read and worn away by the wind and rain.

She had never liked it there before but this time it seemed more peaceful. She didn't feel as out of place, not so much an outsider. It was as though the church and its surrounding ground were becoming used to her, accepting her as one of their own.

As she began to give herself up to the sudden welcoming warmth she was brought back to reality by the sound of Jasmine's voice. The little girl was crying piteously, calling her mother's name over and over again, pleading with her to help, and the feeling of belonging vanished, to be replaced by the more familiar white-hot rage against the village and what it had done to her child.

When Owen came in from work that evening he was astonished to hear that Kathryn was returning to the cottage. 'What have I done?' he asked in confusion. 'I know you didn't want it to be permanent but last night I thought . . . We get on so well. Why move out now, Kathryn?'

'I need more privacy,' she said shortly, hardening herself against the look of hurt in his eyes. She had to be cruel to be kind. If he was involved then he, like Emily, might die. She didn't want more deaths on her conscience. Alone was best.

Claire made no objections. She ran happily round the cottage and went up to her room early, expressing great pleasure in sleeping in her own bed again. 'I like it here, Mummy!' she said with an ingenuous smile as Kathryn tucked her up. 'Let's have a big cuddle now we're back.'

Kathryn pulled away, unable to put her arms round the imposter. For one fleeting moment the dark eyes narrowed and an expression of pure rage crossed them, but then it was gone and the little girl became a sad, rejected child trying to hide her pain. Looking at the face that had once been Jasmine's, seeing the tears in the soft brown eyes, it was very difficult for Kathryn to remain unmoved, but the memory of Jasmine was too fresh for Claire's subterfuge to work.

'Go to sleep, Claire,' Kathryn said shortly and then left the room.

'Miserable old bitch!' snapped Claire, grabbing one of Jasmine's books. 'I'm glad her stupid little girl's gone away. She's just as horrid as my mummy was.'

Downstairs, Kathryn sat in her mother's old chair and waited. She felt certain that someone would come tonight and wondered which of them it would be. Probably Douglas Randolph, she thought; he seemed a natural leader with his commanding personality.

She waited until midnight before admitting to herself that she'd been wrong. Then, acutely disappointed, she locked the front door and took her dirty cup into the kitchen. She scarcely had time to register the sudden drop in temperature before she realised that she wasn't alone after all.

The woman standing by the sink was at least five foot eight tall and her long hair was jet black, parted in the middle and falling in two dark curtains over her shoulders. Her eyes were a deep green, unlike any other eyes Kathryn had seen. They were slightly slanted, as though somewhere in her ancestry there had been foreign blood. Her mouth was wide but thin-lipped, a dark-red gash in a pale face. She was wearing a navy skirt that reached down to her ankles and a dark-red blouse, with a tie at the neck. Her expression when she looked at Kathryn was unfathomable.

'You asked to see me.' Her voice was tinged with a faint Cornish burr.

'I asked to see a member of the coven,' replied Kathryn, trying to quell her rising panic.

'My knowledge is greater than theirs. They turned to me for advice.'

Kathryn swallowed hard. 'Are you Tara?'

'Of course.'

'My aunt said that you hated me. Why would you be willing to help?'

'Your aunt was wrong.'

Although Tara smiled, Kathryn believed that her aunt had been right. This woman did hate her. It showed in her eyes and in the rigidity of her stance. 'Why did you take my daughter away?' she demanded abruptly.

'Jasmine's accident was her own fault. My son had taught her how to go night-travelling and she chose to see her father.

171

The journey took longer than she'd thought. She was warned. It was a tragic accident.'

Kathryn wanted to believe her. She needed to think that this woman was innocent of any involvement with Jasmine because she had no one else to turn to. 'Can you help me get her back?' she whispered.

'Eventually.'

'I want her back now. She's been lost for weeks and her cries are getting fainter.'

'Jasmine won't vanish. She's trapped for eternity. You'll get her back, after you've kept your side of the bargain.'

'What bargain?'

Tara moved slowly across the room until she was standing directly in front of Kathryn. 'We can't send poor Claire away without a very good reason. After all, she's one of us. Her hatred for her mother and the manner of her death made it easy for us to take her. We don't like betraying our own people unless there's a very good reason.'

'What have I got that you want?' demanded Kathryn.

'You've got it all wrong. We want to give you something.' Tara smiled.

'I don't understand,' said Kathryn nervously.

'We want you to have a child.'

There was a long silence. Kathryn stared at Tara in astonishment. 'A child? But why?'

'We want a child of our own.'

'You mean I'm to marry Owen?'

'Surely you won't mind that? You seem to enjoy sharing his bed. That's one thing I did manage: I turned Owen into a remarkably good lover. It's a pity that I didn't live to take greater advantage of it.'

'Why do you want us to have a child?'

'Whoever said anything about the child belonging to Owen? He'd give it his name, stand proxy for the father, as it were, but it wouldn't be his. Not biologically.'

'Then whose?'

'It would belong to the great one, the Fallen Angel. My master, Lucifer.'

Kathryn shook her head. 'No! No, I couldn't!' Her voice was shrill with panic.

172

'You said you'd do anything to get Jasmine back.'

'Yes, and I would, but not . . . I just couldn't! It would be like blasphemy. I . . .'

'Are you religious?'

'No, but . . .'

'Then surely it's easy. One brief moment of discomfort, and after that your daughter would return.'

'How would it happen?' she whispered.

'He would come to you. It has happened before. There have been other children.'

'What became of them?'

'They did well. Wars, anarchy, assassinations; they all did something to further the cause.'

'No,' she repeated. 'It's unthinkable. A child like that would be – '

'It would be destined for greatness. A child born with a truly malevolent soul. It would achieve so much. It's time we tried again.'

'*Not through me!*' shouted Kathryn, backing away from Tara. 'I won't help you do this. Not even for Jasmine.'

Tara drew in her breath sharply and her eyes gleamed like emeralds. 'Then Jasmine must stay in purgatory,' she said softly. 'And so will you. You will go mad listening to her cries day and night, week in, week out, year after terrible year. Can you face that prospect? Do you really think you can live like that?'

'I don't have any choice!' she cried, hearing Jasmine's cries starting up again, louder and more panic-stricken than ever before.

'But you do. Is it really so much to ask?'

'It wouldn't be fair on Owen. I couldn't let him bring up a child like that, thinking it was his own, worrying about its behaviour when all the time it belonged to Satan!'

'He's been chosen too,' said Tara sharply. 'There are good reasons, reasons you wouldn't understand, why he should be the father.'

'He's an honest man!' protested Kathryn.

'He killed me!'

The stark sentence stunned Kathryn. 'Killed you?'

'Owen killed me because he'd fallen out of love. Do you

173

really think he deserves any consideration after that?'

'You're lying. He wasn't even a member of the coven. How could he possibly have killed someone as skilled as you?'

'He used the dark power against me. He studied my books, learnt how to call up demons and then made a pact with them. My life for – But that doesn't concern you. All you need to know is that a bargain was struck and in return for what he promised I forfeited my life.'

'Why did he have you killed? What had you done?'

'He was a fool,' she said contemptuously. 'He wanted to tie me down, keep me at home, belonging only to him. In the coven we give ourselves to one another as a matter of course. It's a sharing, a committal to our belief. He didn't understand. He called me a whore. And then when I refused to give him money for his stupid houses he threatened to divorce me.'

'Didn't either of you think about Luke?'

'Luke is a child of the coven.'

'You mean, Owen isn't his father?'

'Douglas is Luke's father. I'm surprised you haven't noticed the similarity. Owen did.'

'Does Luke know?'

'Luke knows everything I knew. But he's disappointed me; he's a reluctant member.'

'So Owen's a murderer?'

'He laid the spell that destroyed me. He intended that I should die and I did. I think that makes him a murderer.'

'Is that your revenge? Making him the father of Satan's child?'

'It's part of my revenge.'

'Well, I won't do it. He's suffered enough because of you.'

'Look!' exclaimed Tara. 'Watch carefully.' She walked to the window and blew gently on the surface. Immediately it clouded over and through the mist Kathryn saw figures struggling. Shapes and bodies, creatures from nightmares with misshapen faces and hideous, deformed bodies all in a writhing, heaving pile, and in the midst of them, struggling for air, mouth agape with terror, she saw Jasmine. Jasmine as she'd looked when very young, dark curls plastered to her forehead, rosebud mouth trembling and hands stretched out in a desperate appeal.

Around her daughter the creatures of darkness slithered and writhed, their hands clinging to her, their lower limbs entwined with hers, and she saw how Jasmine tried to draw away from their fetid breath and lecherous touch.

'You can save her from that,' said Tara softly. 'You have only to agree and she will be free. How can it be wrong? You're her mother. You are all she has. Can you let her stay there and live with yourself again? Say yes, Kathryn. Say yes and she will be free.'

Jasmine gave a moan of despair. Her eyes looked straight into Kathryn's as she called for help. It was the first time that Kathryn had seen her since Claire took possession of her body and the shock was dreadful. Suddenly she remembered exactly how sweet and wholesome her daughter had been and she gave a scream of anguish.

'*Yes!*' she shouted, her hands reaching to the window in an effort to help her lost child. 'I agree. I agree to anything, only let my daughter go.'

The window went blank. The picture faded and the mist cleared. There was nothing there any more. 'Where is she?' asked Kathryn, but even as she spoke she realised that Tara too had vanished. She was alone in the kitchen of the cottage and it could all have been a dream.

By the time Kathryn was in bed she'd convinced herself that she'd imagined it all. Hoping that she would hear from the coven the next day, she fell asleep.

Chapter 13

She woke in the early hours of the morning needing to visit the bathroom. Still half asleep she put on the bedside lamp and swung her legs out of bed, but a sudden blast of freezing air made her draw them quickly under the duvet again. She looked at the window. It was firmly closed and the curtains were still.

When nothing further happened she again got out of bed and was walking towards the door when a thin spiral of black smoke appeared in front of her. It rose up to the ceiling, filling her nostrils with an unpleasant sickly-sweet smell. Remembering the fire that had killed her aunt, Kathryn dashed for the window and flung it open, but one glance over her shoulder showed her an ordinary bedroom again. The smoke had gone.

Slowly she retraced her steps over the carpet. When she reached the spot where the smoke had been, a dazzling shaft of silver light illuminated the room and she shut her eyes against the glare. When she opened them again the pillar of light was still there and inside it, smiling warmly at her, stood Emily.

There was a radiance about her that made Kathryn feel very happy for her friend. She looked calm, loving and happy and Kathryn moved closer, hoping to be touched by the security of her affection. It was an extraordinary feeling, as though this was the meaning of love, this inner radiance of the spirit that was beyond sexuality, and with her hands outstretched she walked into Emily's welcoming embrace.

As soon as she was close enough to touch her friend the

expression in Emily's eyes changed. Tears filled her eyes and her mouth twisted in anguish. Before Kathryn could speak to her and ask what was wrong, she vanished, leaving Kathryn alone in the beam of light.

The colour was constantly changing. It went from a shining silver to light grey, then on through shades of purple and red until it finally settled into total blackness.

The beam was neither hot nor cold but tepid, like bathwater left too long to cool. Kathryn took a step backwards, anxious to seek the safety of her bed, but the edges of the beam solidified, trapping her inside.

She was alone and yet not alone because suddenly her skin began to prickle as strange sensations shot along her nerves; small darts of pain that were almost enjoyable, intense sensations that jolted her nerve ends. Her nightdress vanished from her body and then she felt alien hands on her flesh. Harsh, cold hands that touched her everywhere, intruding into all her secret places and causing ice-cold burns that left her flesh trembling, but whether from agony or ecstasy she didn't know.

The hands became harsher, pinching her body in all its most tender areas, while long, sharp nails scratched at her, scrabbling painfully across the surface of her skin. She couldn't see anything but, after a time, she felt a body press against hers and to her horror her abused flesh responded to the invisible presence.

Only when the presence began to invade her did Kathryn actually try to draw herself away, but her feet refused to obey and her arms were suddenly pinned to her sides by what felt like tight strands of cord. She screamed hysterically as an ice-cold erection slammed into her body, and then gasped with shock, twisting frantically to avoid the dreadful pain as it pierced her from head to foot. Her body trembled as it endured a terrible battering that bore no relation to anything she had ever encountered in her life before.

As she continued to be violated, the air around her grew close and fetid. Her nostrils were filled with a stench of putrefying meat and decay and she gagged against it, feeling the bile scalding her throat. She would never have imagined that such agony could continue for so long without her losing consciousness, yet for what seemed like hours the entity continued to possess her, using her body in ways unimaginable to normal men, leaving her stripped of all dignity and all pride. Then, at last, hands plucked her away from the creature that was possessing her and she was thrown clear of the beam.

She seemed to fly through the air, floating above the ground out through the door, then spinning around until her vision blurred and she felt herself falling through an endless gaping hole into unconsciousness.

When Kathryn awoke, she was in her own bed and the room was light. She glanced nervously down at her body and was relieved to find that she was still wearing her nightdress. Surprised, she climbed shakily to the floor and pulled it over her head, scrutinising herself for scratches and bruises. There was no suggestion of violence anywhere on her body. 'I must have dreamt it!' she whispered incredulously to herself, shocked by her own imagination.

'Mummy!' called Claire from outside the door. 'It's late. I'm hungry.'

'Wait a moment,' she replied, picking up her watch and staring in astonishment at the hands that showed eleven-thirty. 'I'll get dressed,' she called back. 'You could always put on some toast.'

'I don't know how.'

'Yes you do!' she retorted angrily. It was Jasmine who hadn't been able to switch the toaster on; Claire had no trouble at all.

'I don't! Mummy, please hurry up. I'm really, really hungry.'

'All right!' Irritated by the whine, Kathryn flung open her bedroom door and glared at Claire. 'If you're really that hungry then . . .' Her voice tailed off as she looked into the eyes of her daughter.

'Jasmine! Is it really you? But how . . . ? What happened? When did you get back?' She wrapped her arms tightly round her daughter, almost suffocating her with her affection.

'I haven't been anywhere!' said Jasmine in surprise.

'You have! You've been missing for weeks. I could hear you crying but I didn't know what to do. Oh, poor Jasmine, you must have had a terrible time. How did it happen? What made you go away?' All the time she was asking the questions, Kathryn was kissing her daughter's face and neck as tears rolled down her cheeks.

'Why are you crying, Mummy?'

'It's because I'm so happy. I was trying to get you back myself but you've managed it on your own. Now we can go home again, darling. Home to Sussex.'

Jasmine pulled away from her mother. 'You are funny!' She giggled. 'I haven't been anywhere. Is Luke coming to play today?' she continued. 'I can't remember what he said. Yesterday seems a very long time ago!'

Kathryn felt light-headed with joy as she put the eggs on to boil. While plugging in the toaster she noticed a smudge on the kitchen window. It looked as though someone had drawn on it when it was steamed up. Reaching over to wipe it clean, her hand stopped in mid-air as she realised the significance of the smear. There *had* been a drawing on the window, a drawing showing Jasmine surrounded by hideous creatures of another dimension; and now Jasmine was back. She was back because Kathryn had done as she'd promised. She'd given her body to Satan.

'Is my egg ready?' asked Jasmine cheerfully. Kathryn turned to look at her, studying her closely, eyes searching for any trace of Claire but there was none. Jasmine was herself again, and last night definitely hadn't been a dream.

As she moved about the cottage, Kathryn's aching body confirmed her worst fears. Last night had happened, and the pact was already under way. Her joy at having Jasmine back was now muted by the realisation that this was the beginning and not the end of the bargain. From that hideous coupling would come a child destined to destroy the world.

She reminded herself that her daughter's soul had been freed, but as the hours went by the knowledge of how she'd achieved this weighed more and more heavily on her. By agreeing to the terms Tara had offered, Kathryn had ruined the thing she most wanted. From now on, every time she

179

looked at Jasmine she would remember what she'd done to save her and the price would always be too high.

Her long silences didn't seem to trouble Jasmine, who kept herself occupied all day playing with her doll and some Lego. 'I missed my doll, Mummy,' she confided over lunch.

'What do you mean?'

'I don't know! I thought for a minute I'd been away, but I haven't, have I? Silly me!'

'Where did you think you'd been?'

'Nowhere! I went to nowhere and now I've come back!' She laughed and Kathryn relaxed. It was the closest Jasmine had come to remembering anything at all.

After tea, Luke came calling. Kathryn let him in and watched with interest as he ran over to where Jasmine was sitting on the floor. He knelt beside her and stared directly into her face. For several minutes neither child spoke.

'Where have you been?' Luke finally asked.

'Today? I've been playing.'

'My bear said that you'd come back.'

'Back from where?' asked Jasmine. Kathryn stayed absolutely silent, hoping that they'd forget her.

'From nowhere, of course!' They looked at each other solemnly for a moment and then began rolling round on the floor in a mock fight. Their delight in being together again was unmistakeable.

'Can we go out?' asked Luke eventually.

'Not for long. The evenings are drawing in.'

'My daddy's coming soon. We'll come back with him.'

As they slammed the front door behind them, Kathryn sat down in her mother's chair and wondered what she was going to say to Owen. She had to marry him, that had been part of the bargain, but she couldn't think how she could deliberately trick him when she knew what their future held.

As the evening was so mild, she went down the path to watch for him. Across the road, Mrs Cook was just closing her shop. She stayed open most nights until eight and normally she studiously avoided looking across at the cottage if Kathryn was outside. Tonight was different.

Tonight she waved as though she and Kathryn were the best of friends, her smile warm and unforced.

180

'A lovely evening, my dear.'

'Yes, it is,' replied Kathryn feebly.

'Your little girl's looking well today. I though she'd been off-colour lately. Really not at all like herself.'

Kathryn stared at the woman. 'That's right,' she agreed at last. 'She hasn't been herself for ages, but I think she's back to normal now.'

'I'm very glad. Such a cheerful child. Good night, Mrs Talkes.'

'Good night.'

Kathryn realised that the coven knew what had happened to Jasmine. She only hoped they didn't know what had happened to her last night.

Lost in her confusion she didn't see Owen until he was nearly at the gate. He glanced at her anxiously, apparently unsure of his welcome. 'I wasn't sure if you'd want to see me, Kathryn.'

'Why ever not?'

'Well, you made it pretty clear you wanted to get back to your own cottage last night.'

'I just wanted some time alone to think,' she said quickly, and slipped her arm through his. Across the road, Mrs Cook watched from her upstairs window and nodded approvingly. It was all going well.

'What did you think about?' Owen asked when Kathryn had given him a lager from the fridge.

'About us.'

'Did you reach any conclusion?'

This was the difficult part, she thought. She had to make herself sound convincing without overdoing it, and above all she had to conceal her guilt. 'I think I've been rather stupid lately,' she said slowly. 'I've been so obsessed with what I thought was wrong with Jasmine that I haven't been thinking straight.'

'What you *thought* was wrong with Jasmine? Does that mean that you think she's all right now?'

'I think I've been over-dramatising what's happened to her. You were right; she's growing up, that's all. Perhaps deep down I didn't want to accept it. Once she starts school that's another step away from me. It was all too much to handle and I tried to turn the clock back.'

181

Owen frowned. 'You told me that her entire character had changed. You said that she could now do maths and understood money.'

'I was wrong. She's as hopeless as ever.'

'So you believe that Jasmine is still the same girl?'

'Yes.'

'What about Claire?'

Kathryn shrugged her shoulders apologetically. 'What can I say? I suppose I must have invented Claire. It all seems incredible now, but it was real at the time.'

'It certainly was. I've never seen anyone as convinced as you. I even started believing it myself.'

'I'm sorry, Owen. I promise it won't happen again. Whatever the cause, I'm better now. I realise that I've got to let Jasmine go a little more every year and I don't want to live my life through her. I want a life of my own, Owen. With you, if you'll still have me.'

'We're back!' called Jasmine, running into the room 'We saw Luke's daddy and came straight home.'

Kathryn felt a glow of happiness at the sight of her. 'Good girl!'

'Jasmine, how much pocket money do you get?' asked Owen with a smile.

'Twenty pence every Saturday.'

'Luke gets fifty pence.'

Her eyes widened. 'That's a lot.'

'I suppose it is. Can you tell me how much more than you he gets?'

'Fifty pence.'

'That's not what Daddy meant!' exclaimed Luke. 'It's a sum, Jasmine. Fifty pence take away twenty pence.'

Jasmine chewed thoughtfully on her bottom lip. 'A pound?' she said hopefully. 'Ten pence?'

'Never mind!' Owen ruffled her dark curls. 'Once you're at school you'll understand money better.'

'I can read,' she said indignantly. 'I'm not stupid.'

'No one said you were,' Kathryn assured her, aware that Owen had been testing out the truth of what she'd said, and aware too that he hadn't accepted her story.

The children got out a model park and started playing with

182

the figures. Realising that the adults were busy, Jasmine bent her head close to Luke's. 'Do I still belong to your club?' she whispered.

'I haven't got a club.'

'The one your mummy comes to. You know, the dream club. I can't remember if I still belong. I must have had too much sleep last night, my brain's gone all fuzzy!'

'It was only a pretend club,' he said vaguely. 'My mummy's dead. She couldn't come to any meetings.'

'Last night I dreamt that I was lost in space,' said Jasmine quietly. 'I was spinning round in the darkness and there were lots of horrible creepy-crawly creatures there who pulled at my clothes. I was very glad to wake up.'

'My bear says that your mummy and my daddy are going to get married,' Luke murmured. 'Do you think that will be nice?'

'I suppose so. My daddy won't ever come back now, will he?'

'No, but my bear says that Mummy hopes to come back one day.' They looked thoughtfully at one another.

'Look at those two!' Kathryn smiled. 'They natter away together like a couple of old-age pensioners.'

'Or two children who haven't seen each other for a long time.'

Kathryn decided to ignore this. 'I meant what I said, Owen,' she reminded him. 'I would like to spend the rest of my life with you.' Owen didn't reply.

When he and Luke had gone and Jasmine was asleep, Kathryn remained downstairs trying to work out what she should do. She'd agreed to marry Owen, that had been part of the bargain, but she hadn't anticipated that he might not want to marry her. She wondered what she was meant to do if he continued avoiding the issue.

For the next three days she had time to worry even more as Owen went to Manchester to see a client. She tried to keep busy by giving the cottage a thorough cleaning and tidying up the garden, but all the time it niggled away at her.

Owen returned at ten on the third evening and came

straight to the cottage. When she saw him standing stern-faced on the step she immediately thought that he'd come to say he no longer wanted her, but his warm kiss of greeting pushed the idea away.

He opened the bottle of Beaujolais that he'd brought and they sat down on the cramped sofa together. Owen raised his glass. 'To us, Kathryn, and our life together.'

'To us,' she replied and smiled with relief.

He took only a sip before putting the glass carefully on the floor. 'Before you actually commit yourself, Kathryn, there's something I think you ought to know.'

Her heart pounded rapidly and she wished that she could tell him what he should know as well. 'What's that?' she asked nervously.

'I'd wished that Tara would die.'

'Why was that?'

'Because she no longer loved me. In fact, I doubt if she ever loved me. She'd had an affair with Douglas, you see.'

'Your boss?'

'Yes! Somehow that made it worse; he was my boss and a friend. They both let me down, rather like your husband and your girlfriend. She didn't care for Luke properly either. He was badly neglected. She was always off on her nature studies and things like that. He was a tie to her.'

'I'm sure a lot of men wish their wives were dead at some stage or other in their marriages. The only difference is that Tara did die.'

'But it made me feel responsible, as though my wishing made it so.'

'Did it?' she asked quietly.

'Of course not! How could it?'

Kathryn smiled, but she knew very well how. He'd taken terrible steps to make his dream come true and now he was trying to push the memory away. She was disappointed that he didn't trust her enough to tell her the whole truth.

'It doesn't matter, Owen.'

'I didn't want to go into this marriage with the myth of my regret hanging over us.'

'You never pretended to be very sorry.'

'It was my pride,' he explained quickly. 'I didn't want you

184

to know quite how much she despised me. She used to taunt me with it. "Call yourself a man?" she'd say and laugh. "You'll never be half the man Douglas is." And I don't think I was. She wanted a domineering husband and that isn't my style.'

'It doesn't matter,' she repeated.

'It will be a fresh start.' He smiled. 'We'll put Tara and Philip right out of our minds.'

Now that his so-called confession was out of the way, Owen seemed to relax completely, and by the time he left they'd decided to marry before Christmas so that they could start the New Year as a proper family.

After he'd gone, Kathryn went upstairs and cried. They were both trying to hide secrets, but hers was easily the worst. Or so she believed.

Chapter 14

They were married at Grantham registry office and spent their honeymoon quietly at home with the children. They both enjoyed their first Christmas as a family and Kathryn took particular delight in watching Jasmine. Whenever she remembered the baby within her, she would hurry to her daughter's side, reminding herself of the reason for the terrible pact.

Both the children started at the village school at the beginning of January and Kathryn was quickly involved in their activities. The other women were friendly now; they all chatted to her as she waited outside the school gates, but although she was polite she didn't allow herself to become over-friendly. She understood why they were trying to be her friends and refused to allow them to get close to her. She had no intention of becoming involved in their secret life. At the end of January, Dr Potter arrived on her doorstep. 'I thought I should pay you a call, my dear,' he said benignly. 'We must take good care of you and the child.'

Kathryn regarded him levelly. 'What child?'

'The child you're carrying for us.'

'For you?'

'For those of us who follow the dark path.'

She shivered. 'It's too soon,' she said swiftly. 'I'm not positive I am expecting a baby and I haven't mentioned the possibility to Owen yet.'

'Very wise; far better to wait until it becomes obvious.'

'A lot can go wrong in the beginning,' she reminded him.

Dr Potter shook his head. 'Nothing will go wrong, Kathryn. That's why I'm here.'

'I suppose you want a urine sample,' she said sulkily.

'Not at all. It could well be negative and that would confuse people.'

'Why negative?'

'This is no ordinary child. Why should you expect the pregnancy to be normal?'

For the first time a new fear entered Kathryn's mind. 'Do you mean that it won't look normal?'

'Normal by whose standards? I'm sure its father will recognise it at once.'

'I've worked out it will be born at the end of August,' she said in a tight voice.

'Early July.'

'I should know, I was there,' she said indignantly.

'We were all there, Kathryn. We all saw what happened.' He smiled as hot colour flooded her face and neck. 'Just the same it will be early July. The child will grow more quickly than most.'

Kathryn looked anxious. 'When I agreed to this I thought it would be an ordinary child. What will Owen think if it's abnormal?'

'You mustn't worry, my dear. Worry is bad for you both. I'm going to leave you some pills. They're essential for the health of you and the child.'

'What are they?' she asked suspiciously.

'They're prepared from a secret formula known only to a few. You needn't worry, no one would harm you now. Take one tablet every morning before your first meal. If you forget, then take it as soon after the meal as possible. Do you get very tired?'

'Not really; I sometimes feel a bit queasy, that's all.'

'These will help. I'll call again in a week; in the meantime, take good care of yourself. You're very precious to us all.'

When he'd gone, Kathryn took one of the tablets and then went upstairs, stripped off her clothes and stood in front of the full-length mirror in their bedroom. She studied herself closely, turning to each side and peering at her reflection. Her breasts were already fuller and there was an unmistakeable roundness to her previously flat stomach. She wondered what size she'd be by the time the child was born.

When she'd dressed again she started to pull up the bed but suddenly a wave of anger swept over her. It was all Owen's fault, she thought furiously. If it hadn't been for him, she would never have been trapped in this nightmare. Jasmine would have been left alone and by now she and her daughter would be safely home in Sussex, getting on with their quiet lives.

At first the hatred felt like a tiny pinpoint of pain in her solar plexus, but the more she thought about what he'd done, the more she reflected on the lies he'd told her, the greater the pain grew until it felt like a giant fist flexing its fingers beneath her ribs.

Everything was his fault, she thought furiously. He was the one who'd made all the running in their relationship. He had pestered her until she'd gone out with him. He'd introduced her to his so-called friends so that they could see her and work out how to use her in their plans, and he was the one who had lied about Tara's death.

Tara's desire for revenge suddenly seemed understandable. She'd been deprived of over half her life, snatched away because her husband had lost interest in her. It was monstrous, totally unfair, and he should be punished.

The mirror showed Kathryn's hands clenching and unclenching with fury and she began to breathe more heavily as the rage welled up inside her. Abruptly she whirled around and ran to the kitchen. There she grabbed a sharp knife before rushing back to the bedroom, making small sounds of rage as she ran. With a muffled shout she flung open Owen's wardrobe door and stared at the row of crisp cotton shirts, the only kind he'd wear, and his selection of suits all hanging tidily in order. Her hand lunged forward and with a gloriously satisfying ripping sound his favourite pale-blue shirt split from collar to hem. With a smile of satisfaction she pulled back her arm for a second blow.

The village clock striking three brought Kathryn abruptly awake. Blinking sleepily, she wondered how long she'd been sleeping. In a hurry now, she pulled on a skirt and jersey, boots and her new suede coat – a present from Owen – and then hurried out of the house. She didn't even notice that the wardrobe door was slightly open.

Luke and Jasmine chattered non-stop about their day and it wasn't until after tea that Kathryn went to the bedroom again. This time the door did catch her eye. She went to close it, then stopped at the sight of the torn material lying on the carpet. She quickly opened the door and then gave a cry at the sight of the mutilated clothes within.

When Owen came home at seven he found the children watching a highly unsuitable television programme while his wife sat sobbing in the bedroom.

'Whatever's the matter, darling?' he asked anxiously.

Unable to speak she pointed at the wardrobe with a trembling finger. At the sight of his ruined clothes, Owen gave an involuntary exclamation that was a mixture of shock and fear. His face turned very white and he glanced nervously at his wife.

'What happened, Kathryn?'

She continued sobbing and although she tried to speak he couldn't make sense of the words.

'Did you do this?' he asked at last.

Kathryn lifted her head and stared at him in desolation. 'Yes,' she sobbed. 'I did, but I don't know why. I can remember doing it, but . . . I don't understand!' she finished despairingly.

Owen's eyes fell on the small bottle beside their bed. 'What are these?' he demanded, picking up the tablets and scrutinising the label.

'Give them to me!' she shouted, jumping to her feet. 'They're mine.'

He held them out of her reach. 'Tell me what they are,' he said sternly.

Once again the rage swept over her. She bunched her right hand and drove it straight into his stomach. Owen doubled up in pain and she grabbed the bottle back from him. 'They're vitamin pills,' she screamed. 'Keep your frigging hands off!'

Appalled, he simply stood and stared at her. Her face was ugly with temper and she clutched the bottle in one shaking hand. After a moment's silence she went downstairs, leaving Owen trembling with shock and the dreadful realisation that something was going horribly wrong.

They didn't speak to each other for the rest of the evening. As soon as the children were in bed, Owen put all his ruined clothes in a plastic bag which he then put in the boot of his car. He would take them to the council rubbish tip. He didn't want the refuse collectors talking about them. They'd seen it all once before.

In bed, Kathryn tried to go straight to sleep but Owen put his bedside lamp on and turned her to face him. 'Kathryn, I have to know where you got those tablets.'

'From the chemist,' she lied.

'There's no label on them. Chemists don't sell unlabelled bottles.'

'I can't imagine why you're so interested. They're only vitamin pills.'

'Then why the secrecy?'

She sighed heavily. 'Dr Potter gave them to me. Satisfied?'

'Why should he start giving you pills? Are you ill?'

'They're for my nerves. I had such a terrible time when Jasmine vanished that – '

'You said that was all a mistake, that you'd distorted things.'

'What is this?' she shouted, sitting up in a temper. 'Yes, I did get it wrong but it was real to me at the time and my nerves are still bad. Does that satisfy you?'

'Are they vitamins or tranquillisers?'

'How the hell should I know? He gave them to me and I swallow them. If you're so interested, ask him yourself.'

'What's the matter, Kathryn? I've never heard you like this before. You sound so angry.'

'Someone's got to have some character round here,' she snapped. 'Sometimes I don't know if you're a man or a mouse.'

'That's what Tara used to say,' he said in horror.

'I can see why. I'm beginning to feel quite sorry for your first wife.'

'You're beginning to sound like my first wife!' retorted Owen disbelievingly.

The white hot rage was building up in Kathryn again. It seemed to take her over, almost choking her with its intensity. 'In that case, I'd better hope you don't decide to murder me!'

she yelled. As soon as the words were said, all the rage and pain drained away and for the first time since she'd mutilated Owen's clothes, Kathryn felt like herself again.

Shocked by what she'd said she put out an involuntary hand towards her husband but he moved away towards his side of the bed. His body began to tremble. 'How did you know?'

She was puzzled. 'Know what?'

'That I murdered Tara.'

'She told me,' she said softly.

Owen shook his head. 'You're lying. Tara's dead. How could she possibly tell you anything?'

Kathryn didn't know how to answer him.

For a long time they stayed staring at each other in silence and then she moistened her lips. 'I haven't been honest with you, Owen. I wanted to be, but they wouldn't let me. We had to get married, you see, and they probably thought that if you knew, you wouldn't want me as your wife any more.'

'I've wanted to marry you ever since we met.'

I'm pregnant,' she said abruptly. 'I'm pregnant by someone else. That's why I married you.'

'Who's the father?' His face was suddenly blotched with rage and he put his hands on her shoulders. 'Tell me who he is or . . .'

'I can't.'

'It's Clive, isn't it? That's why your friend Emily was driving her car so fast when she got killed. She was trying to get away from you after she'd found out.'

'Of course it wasn't Clive. It wasn't anyone you know.'

'But why? Our sex life's always been good.'

'It had nothing to do with sex,' she said wearily. 'It was all part of the bargain.'

Owen sat down on the end of the bed and studied his wife carefully. 'What did you mean when you said that Tara told you I'd killed her?'

'It was because of Jasmine. When I told you that I'd imagined what happened to Jasmine, it wasn't true. The last time I saw my aunt, I told her about Claire, and she explained how it had probably happened. She also told me that the only people who could help were the coven.'

'What coven?'

'The satanists here, in South Willoughby. Apparently they've been here for hundreds of years but Victoria said that Tara was in a different league from the rest of them and that when she died she held most of the power here. Was she right?'

Owen nodded.

'Although she told me that Tara's followers might be able to get Jasmine back, she warned me against contacting them because the price would be so high. I didn't listen. I wanted Jasmine back whatever the cost and so I did make contact.'

'And then?'

'I expected someone from the coven to visit me the first night I went back to the cottage. Instead Tara appeared. She told me how you'd used her own power against her and said that she wanted revenge. Then she showed me Jasmine.' Kathryn's voice shook. 'It was dreadful, Owen. Once I'd seen her surrounded by all those terrible creatures I had to get her back. I'd refused before, said that I couldn't do it, that I'd rather leave Jasmine where she was, but once I saw her I couldn't hold out. I'd have done anything at all at that moment, and so I said yes.'

'To what?'

'I agreed to give them a child,' she sobbed.

'The coven?'

Kathryn nodded.

'Why do they want another child? Isn't Luke enough for them? I'm sure Tara's told you that he's Douglas' son?'

'Yes, but that doesn't make him the coven's child.'

'He was the result of some frantic midnight coupling after one of their meetings. Oh yes, she enjoyed telling me all about how she conceived Luke. That was the final straw, hearing that the child I'd thought was mine belonged to them. That was when I decided to get rid of her.'

'Using demons to cast out demons,' said Kathryn slowly. 'That explains the inscription you chose for her headstone.'

'It seemed rather apt. I suppose Tara hadn't told you any of this?'

'It wouldn't have made any difference. I didn't agree because I thought you were wrong or because I wanted to help Tara. I thought she got what she deserved. I did it to save

192

Jasmine and, whatever happens to me, I succeeded. She came back.'

'But who's the father?' he persisted. 'Will this child be any more special to them than Luke?'

'I'm afraid he will,' she whispered, hanging her head in shame.

'Tell me who he is!' shouted Owen.

And then she did.

For a long time Kathryn couldn't stop crying but Owen was very kind. He kept his arms round her and dried her tears with his handkerchief, and never once did he show any revulsion over what he'd heard.

When she finally quietened he pulled her closer to him. 'This is all my fault, Kathryn,' he confessed awkwardly. 'They've been very clever. You see, I tried to double-cross them. In return for Tara's death, I promised them the soul of my first-born child. It was the only thing they'd accept and I was so desperate to have Tara killed that, like you, I agreed to their terms. Later I realised that I'd never be able to hand a child over to them and so I made sure that the problem couldn't arise. I had a vasectomy.

'It seemed the ideal solution. If there never was a child then that was their bad luck. I really believed that I'd got away with it, too. I should have known better. Since I won't give them a child myself it appears they're going to give me one of theirs. And I thought I'd been so clever.'

'What can we do?' she whispered. 'I'm afraid of what it will look like. And how can we let it live when we know the harm it's going to do? We can't let that happen.'

'We don't seem to have any choice.'

'If it's deformed the hospital might take it away and let it die without telling us.'

'I can't see Dr Potter letting that happen, can you?'

'It isn't fair!' she cried angrily. 'None of this is my fault. I didn't even know Tara. I only came here because my mother was ill. Why me?'

'Tara probably knew I'd be attracted to you. I wanted to fall in love again, I needed to prove to myself that not all women despised me, and you're the complete opposite of Tara, which was an added attraction.'

'But Tara couldn't have known that I was coming here!'

'I found that photograph of you and Jasmine that you said your mother used to keep on display. It was hidden underneath Luke's mattress. Tara probably used it to get you here. She'd have heard enough about you from your mother to know you might be suitable.'

'You mean that Tara caused my mother's illness?'

'Yes,' he said reluctantly. 'I'm beginning to think that Tara's been planning her revenge for a very long time.'

During the following week, Owen and Kathryn spent hours discussing Tara, the coven and the child, but no matter how much they talked it was impossible to find any solution. They were both trapped; Owen by his earlier involvement with the occult and Kathryn by her previous determination to save Jasmine.

They considered ways of bringing about a miscarriage, but deep down they both understood that in order to kill this child, Kathryn would have to kill herself as well. On bad days she thought this would be preferable to giving birth and then it was only Owen who could lift her from the black despair that so frequently engulfed her.

Finally they faced up to the fact that there was no solution. Not yet; not while the child was still in the womb. But after it was born, once it was susceptible to the normal hazards of everyday life, then it would be different. They both felt that as a small, vulnerable baby the child would be far easier to destroy.

It seemed to Kathryn that the long dark weeks from January to the end of March were never-ending. Her whole world had shrunk to the house and the few hundred yards to the village school. Apart from collecting the children, she never went anywhere. The people were too friendly; their smiles made her clench her teeth as she forced back the words she would have liked to say. Once their dislike had distressed her; now their friendship was unbearable.

At the end of the spring term the children persuaded her to attend their Easter parade. She sat at the back of the hall, ignoring the other parents, and as soon as it was over she went

194

to collect Luke and Jasmine from the cloakroom. Suddenly she found herself surrounded by school children. They ranged in age from four to seven and gathered round her in awed silence. Then one of the bigger girls pushed her way to the front and, reaching out, she let her hand brush against Kathryn's stomach.

A collective gasp went up from the other children and they stared solemnly at Kathryn's bulge. The girl who had touched her gave a sigh of pleasure and her eyes shone. 'You are lucky,' she told the rigid Kathryn. 'I wish my mummy had been chosen.'

'Chosen for what?' asked Kathryn sharply.

'It's because we've been loyal,' continued the girl excitedly. 'This village has been loyal for over a hundred years. That's why he will be born here.'

'We've made a kind of calendar,' a little boy told her eagerly. 'Like an advent calendar. We open doors each day and learn something new about your baby.'

Kathryn began to shake. 'Luke, Jasmine, hurry up. I want to get home,' she called, but they were standing in the middle of the crowd and didn't move.

'We know his name,' said another child.

'And his weight!' called another.

'And the day of his birth!'

'And the colour of his hair!'

'It will be a special day, like Christmas, when he's born.'

'We'll all get presents!'

'And have a feast!'

Their excited words seemed to get louder and louder and Kathryn clapped her hands over her ears.

'We'll worship him!'

'Bow down to him!'

'Protect him!'

'I want to go home!' screamed Kathryn.

At once they fell silent. The girl who had touched her turned away and started to put on her outdoor shoes. The small boy who'd mentioned the calendar looked upset, but his mother came and cuddled him, whispering in his ear until his face brightened again. Quickly and silently they filed out of the cloakroom until only Luke and Jasmine were left.

195

'Do you have a morning assembly here?' asked Kathryn.

'Yes,' replied Luke hesitantly.

'Do you have prayers, Bible stories, that kind of thing?'

'We say prayers,' confirmed Jasmine.

'The Lord's Prayer?'

'We say it backwards. It's all part of the club.'

Kathryn stared at her daughter. 'What club?'

'The club that I joined when I killed Grandma.'

'When you what?' demanded Kathryn in astonishment.

Jasmine went pale and looked to Luke for assistance, but he ignored her.

'Did you say you killed your grandmother?' repeated Kathryn, taking hold of Jasmine's shoulders.

'I had to!' she explained. 'I wanted to join so that I could do all the things Luke did. They suggested killing Grandma for my evil deed. You know, like Brownies have to do good deeds, only this was an evil one.'

'Grandma had a heart attack!'

'We used a killing spell; a pin in a doll.' There was no shame on Jasmine's face. She looked at her mother as though what she was saying was the most normal thing in the world. Kathryn buried her head in her hands.

'She was old,' said Luke kindly. 'It was time for her to die.'

'I did it all for nothing,' said Kathryn quietly. 'Victoria died because of you. I went to her to try and save you. I thought that you . . . I didn't know! I wanted things to be the same again. I wanted my daughter back, but you're not the same at all. I was too late.'

'I'm still Jasmine.'

Kathryn shook her head. 'I should have remembered,' she said sadly. 'I knew you'd changed but once Claire came I put it out of my mind. I told myself that I'd imagined it, that if I could get you back things would be normal again.'

The children stayed silent. After a moment, Kathryn turned and began to walk slowly out of the school. She'd been tricked, just as Owen had been tricked. Only she hadn't done anything to deserve it. Owen had double-crossed them, but she had only tried to save her child. Now she knew that everything she'd done had been in vain. She'd lost Jasmine long before Claire took possession of her body. She'd lost

Jasmine almost as soon as they'd come to South Willoughby, but it had taken her all this time to admit the truth. She had made a totally unjustified bargain with evil and now she had to live with that knowledge.

'Kathryn won't go anywhere or do anything!' a worried Owen told Dr Potter. 'She's stayed in bed for over a week now. She scarcely eats and all she'll say is that she killed her aunt and Emily.'

'She's tired,' replied the doctor. 'Most pregnant women need a rest.'

'Rest! She's totally bedridden. That can't be healthy for herself or the baby.'

'The baby's fine. She does take her pills, I hope?'

'Yes. What's happening to her?'

'She's perfectly well, Owen. A little pale but some anaemia's to be expected.'

'*Listen to me*! My wife's killing herself and you stand there talking about rest and anaemia. I want a second opinion. I want – '

'A second opinion on the fire that killed your first wife might be equally useful,' said the doctor icily. 'Kathryn is not ill. There is nothing physically wrong with her. She wants to die, it's as simple as that.'

'Are you willing to stand by and let that happen?'

'She will live until the child is born. After that it's of no importance to us at all. Perhaps, in your moments of despair, you should give a thought to the old saying, "He who sups with the devil needs a long spoon." A fact that I fear both you and Kathryn forgot.'

'Bastard!' Owen slammed the door behind the doctor and hurried upstairs to see Kathryn. She was propped up against a pile of pillows, her hair limp and her face drawn.

'He says you'll be all right,' said Owen reassuringly.

'I did it for Jasmine,' she explained.

'I know that. No one's blaming you. When I killed Tara I didn't have any excuse; what you did was different.'

'I did it for Jasmine but Jasmine was already dead.'

'Kathryn, that's nonsense.'

197

'You don't understand,' she said flatly.

'You mustn't give up!' begged Owen. 'Once the baby's born we'll . . .'

'I don't want to talk about it any more, Owen. I never want to talk about any of it again.'

'But we must. I thought that . . .'

'When did you ever have an intelligent thought!' she sneered, her face suddenly flushed. 'You've never been any good at anything.'

Owen blinked in surprise. Before he could defend himself the colour faded from Kathryn's cheeks and tears filled her eyes. 'It's Tara,' she whispered. 'I can feel her trying to take over, Owen. She's waiting there all the time, waiting for me to let her in.'

'That's impossible!'

'Nothing's impossible for Tara; I'd have thought you'd have realised that by now. Can't you hear her in the things I say?' She knew by the look on his face that she was right. 'That's another reason why the baby must die,' she said urgently. 'Tara wants to come back and look after it, I know she does. Well, I won't let her.'

'Neither will I,' promised Owen. 'Don't worry, you won't have to do it alone.'

'Why don't we go night-walking any more?' Jasmine asked Luke one warm evening in June. 'Last year we had lots of fun on summer nights.'

'There's no need for night-walking now. My mummy's got what she wanted.'

'What was that?'

'Revenge on Daddy.'

'She tricked me!' said Jasmine angrily. 'I killed Grandma so that I could belong to the club and now there isn't a club any more.'

'People who follow the dark path always tell lies.'

'It didn't seem like a lie when she said it.'

'It never does! The baby will be here soon.'

'Will it look horrible?' asked Jasmine.

'I suppose it might.'

198

'I've never seen an evil baby. Is Satan really its father?'

'I think so. She took my power away,' he confessed.

'Who did?'

'Mummy. Once she knew about the baby she took all my magic away from me. I suppose it will go to the baby. I don't mind. It made me feel horrid inside.'

'I'm not looking forward to this baby.'

'Nor am I,' said Luke fervently. 'After the baby's born nothing will ever be the same again.'

'For us?'

'For anyone in the world.'

Kathryn stared at the faces above her and tried to work out who was there, but her vision was blurred and all her energy was being used up by the birth. The pains were terrible, far worse than when she'd had Jasmine, and the violence of the contractions threatened to throw her off the bed, yet she felt quite calm. After the birth would come the death, it was this thought that sustained her.

'Bear down!' exhorted Dr Potter, his forehead covered in sweat. 'Come along, Kathryn. You're doing splendidly. Just one more push and it will be here. Push, my dear. Push hard!'

She did as she was asked and felt the child slip from her in a rush of warm wetness.

'Kathryn, it's a boy!' said Owen urgently. 'Look, darling, it's a beautiful little boy.'

She looked at her husband, the man who had been unwittingly responsible for everything that had happened to her in the last year, and she couldn't believe the look of excitement in his eyes. 'He isn't yours,' she whispered. 'Remember whose child he is.'

'But he's fantastic! There's nothing wrong with him at all. There was nothing to worry about, Kathryn. He's absolutely normal.'

'A wonderful little boy!' agreed the village midwife, holding the baby with great reverence, her eyes fixed adoringly on his face.

'Let me see him,' said Kathryn at last.

199

Dr Potter took the baby from the midwife and put him in Owen's arm. 'Let her see him. She *is* his mother.'

Owen sat beside his wife and tilted the baby so that she could look directly into his eyes. The eyes were open, dark-blue with long lashes, and his face was smooth and unwrinkled. His cheeks were round and pink while in his chin there was a bewitching dimple.

'Isn't he handsome?' said Owen with awe in his voice. 'I'd imagined such dreadful things. Two heads, a tail, a body covered in thick hair, all kinds of horrible things, but he's perfect, a lovely boy. Kathryn, perhaps we were wrong. Perhaps he is mine. Maybe the operation didn't work. We don't know for certain, do we?'

Kathryn's heart sank. If Owen, who knew the truth, could be so affected by the baby's magic, then what hope was there for the rest of the world? She tried to sit up a little and Dr Potter put a steadying arm round her.

'I should have known,' she murmured to Owen. 'This baby has far worse things than the abnormalities we were imagining.'

'What?' he asked in bewilderment.

'Beauty and charm. They're an irresistable combination.'

After a few minutes Dr Potter sent Owen out of the room while he attended to Kathryn. 'You see,' he said, smiling. 'All your fears were groundless. He's a baby any mother would be proud of.'

Kathryn knew that he was studying her carefully, trying to assess her true feelings, and she forced herself to meet his eye. 'He isn't what I expected,' she admitted truthfully.

The midwife placed the newly washed baby tenderly in the crib next to Kathryn. Her face was adoring. She was overwhelmed by the honour of being in attendance for such a birth.

'He should be put to the breast,' said Dr Potter, watching Kathryn's face as he spoke. She gave a nod, not ecstatic but not antagonistic either, and he handed her her son. 'Have you thought of a name?'

'We thought Nicholas would be appropriate.'

'Young Nick! An excellent choice.'

Kathryn felt the baby's small mouth tugging at her nipple

and fought back her instinctive desire to tear him off and throw him across the room. His small sucking sounds brought a wide smile to the midwife's face. After Nicholas had finished, the doctor felt satisfied that a bond was being forged between Kathryn and her son, but to prevent any possible violence he didn't leave until Kathryn had swallowed two sleeping tablets. By morning the baby would be safe.

Alone with Kathryn at last, Owen looked anxiously at his wife. She removed the pills from under her tongue and swung her legs out of bed. 'Where are you going?' he asked anxiously.

'To the church, just as we planned.'

'Perhaps we should wait. He's such a lovely baby and – '

'He's the son of Satan and he has to die. If you won't help me I'll do it alone.'

'Why there? Why not kill him here?'

'That's where they sacrificed all their victims. He must die there too so that Miranda and the others will finally be free.'

'I don't think I can,' said Owen quietly. 'I know you're right, it's just that . . .' His voice tailed off.

Kathryn pulled on a blouse and skirt, wrapped the baby in a cot blanket and opened the bedroom door. 'Stay here then. For someone who's already killed once you're remarkably squeamish.'

'But he's only a baby!'

'He'll grow, Owen, and he'll get more powerful. It has to be now.'

'I can't,' he said flatly, and turned his back on her.

Kathryn moved silently along the landing, down the stairs, past the now dull pistols and swords, through the hall, beneath the gaze of the snarling fox and the petrified rabbit, and out of the front door, and all the time the baby was silent and still.

She stayed beneath the branches of the trees, remaining in shadow all the way to the church, because this was something that needed darkness. The graveyard too was dark and the church door creaked loudly as Kathryn pushed it open. For the first time the baby stirred, making small sucking sounds with its mouth.

Hurrying up the aisle, she laid him on the communion table

201

just as the clouds outside parted, letting a shaft of moonlight in through the high stained-glass window. The baby's dark-blue eyes stared up at Kathryn unblinkingly.

Carefully she folded the cot blanket into a square and then, with shaking hands, she held it over his face, pressing it against his nose and mouth and ignoring the abruptly flailing arms and legs.

After several minutes his limbs ceased to move, but Kathryn still kept his face covered, terrified of removing the blanket and finding him alive. She knew that she would never have the courage to smother him a second time.

When she finally took the blanket away his eyes were closed and there were white indentations round his nose and mouth where her fingers had been pressing, while his lips were tinged with blue. He really was dead, she realised with a surge of triumph. She'd managed to kill Satan's son, and she gave a shout of triumph that rang round the deserted church, shattering the silence.

Suddenly her legs felt weak and her stomach heaved in revulsion against what she'd had to do. Turning away from the dead body she stumbled towards the door, only to freeze in terror as she heard unmistakeable sucking sounds from behind her. With a scream of anguish she ran back to the communion table and as she looked down at her son his eyes snapped open and he stared up at her.

'No!' she whispered. 'You're dead. I know you're dead; I killed you myself.'

His lips moved and he turned his head, searching for food. Kathryn shuddered, then reached determinedly for the blanket again, but her hands stopped in mid-air as the church abruptly filled with the dreadful sound of a woman screaming. The screams were almost inhuman in their intensity, rising and falling in such agony that Kathryn felt cold to her very soul. Suddenly the darkness of the church seemed to lighten, the air stirred and in front of her startled gaze a woman appeared.

She was young, no more than twenty, and would in normal circumstances have been pretty, but now her face was distorted with despair as she stood in a thin cotton nightdress clutching a tiny baby to her chest. She was so close that

Kathryn reached out to touch her, offer assistance, but there was nothing tangible there. Whimpering, Kathryn moved closer and as she saw the baby's face, with the white marks round the nose and mouth and the horribly familiar blue-tinged lips, she realised what she'd done.

She'd killed an innocent child. At the same moment she understood that this was the way it would always be. Nicholas would never die, only other children. Every time anyone tried to kill Nicholas, another child would die. This was how Satan intended to protect his son.

The vision faded, the air was still again, but Kathryn didn't move. She remained in the church for a long time and the darkness pressed down on her, bearing its own, secret message. Finally she got to her feet, picked up her son, wrapped him in the blanket again and walked slowly back home through the silent streets.

As she carried him into the hall his eyes fixed themselves on the glass case containing the petrified rabbit and the corners of his mouth lifted in appreciation. With a tiny glow of pleasure Kathryn realised for the first time what a truly beautiful baby her son was . . .